PRAISE FOR *SUCH GOOD WORK*
by JOHANNES LICHTMAN

"Lichtman [is] a remarkable thinker and social satirist . . . *Such Good Work* introduces a writer who is willing to openly contradict himself, to stand corrected, to honor both men and women, to ask sincere questions and let them ring unanswered . . . Jonas finds a companion in his neighbor Anja, one of the more autonomous, intelligent and unpredictable female characters to grace a male novelist's debut. Lichtman has a terrific ear for the tiny linguistic cues that reveal completely correct English to be nonetheless foreign, and Anja's dialogue is delivered in sometimes heartbreakingly poignant German-English . . . The reader feels the potency of a kind of communication between lovers that is non-national, non-hierarchical and pronounced in peace . . . The novel outgrows its own boundaries, becoming stranger and more robust."

—*THE NEW YORK TIMES BOOK REVIEW*

"*Such Good Work* is, indeed, a bit Jonas-like: it's wary of affectation or grandstanding; it works small, as if from a sense of modesty, a reluctance to presume; it cuts sincerity with the driest of humor . . . *Such Good Work* [is] alive to the contradictions between morality and comfort that exist everywhere under global structures of capitalism and politics. Moving to Sweden is a way for Jonas to reconcile his privilege with his ideals—perhaps it is easier, in the land of subsidized housing and schooling and health care, to live well, to care about injustice, and to not be a hypocrite. The [book contains] both sadness and expectation—leav[ing] the reader grazed by tempered hopes."

—*THE NEW YORKER*

"The international refugee crisis and the struggle to stay sober pre-occupy roughly equal portions of this thoughtful first novel, which follows an American graduate student to Sweden in the fraught years 2014–15 . . . [It] casts a sharp eye over the Swedish social and political landscape . . . Lichtman's low-key treatment of two highly charged subjects is refreshing."

—KIRKUS REVIEWS

"[An] excellent and timely debut . . . Throughout, Lichtman expertly infuses his multicontinental narrative with humor and humanity, suggesting the dangers of intolerance while also poking fun at the white savior trope. Jonas may be helping others to make himself feel whole, yet his heartfelt actions stick with the reader in this winning novel."

—PUBLISHERS WEEKLY

"The novel answers its primary question, 'Is doing good even possible?,' with significant emotional honesty, and Lichtman's clear and accessible writing allows readers to explore its complex topics at many levels. Jonas is a bundle of shifting emotions, needs, and coping mechanisms, and rather than doing good, easing the discomfort of being human is at times all he can manage."

—BOOKLIST

"[Lichtman] has written a likeable, funny and thoughtful book with an endearingly frustrating central character. Without appearing to try too hard, *Such Good Work* gets to the heart of what it means to have a conscience and attempts—however futile that attempt may be—to use it for the greater good. It is gratifying that Mr. Lichtman does not endeavour to offer a satisfying answer to these questions of migration, belonging, alienation and addiction. Rather like the solitary characters in *Go, Went, Gone*, Jenny Erpenbeck's novel about Germany's refugee crisis, and *Leaving the Atocha Station*, Ben Lerner's tale of a disaffected young American living in Madrid around the time of the terrorist attack in 2004, Jonas reflects, regrets and moves on."

—THE ECONOMIST

"[A] wise and funny debut novel . . . Lichtman handles this transition with dexterity and humor as he explores what it means to do the good work of being human."

—NEW YORK JOURNAL OF BOOKS

"With intelligent probing, sinuous prose, and considerable charm, this *bildungsroman* charts his journey, an interior trip to the core of being a compassionate human in the twenty-first century. . . . Scenes read like meticulous journal entries as Jonas both records his urge to help and questions his own motives and capacity, unsparing when his attempts fall short. This artful realism lends his account an appealingly honest intimacy and immediacy as the quotidian is scrupulously examined. Jonas is deeply serious about finding meaning and connection."

—FICTION WRITERS REVIEW

"Jonas, the protagonist, is young, smart, wounded, and desperate to do good, which is as perfect a recipe for disaster as I can think of. The book is better on what it means to engage meaningfully with the world than anything else I've read in recent years: like the good liberal he is, Jonas sees through his own pretensions and is aware of all the ways in which any engagement he can imagine will be problematic. And then, instead of withering into cynicism or inaction, he does the very best he can. *Such Good Work* is one of the best—one of the most beautifully written, one of the most thoughtful—novels I've read in the past several years."

—GARTH GREENWELL, critically acclaimed author of
What Belongs to You and *Cleanness*

"I honestly can't think of a novel I would more want to be reading in the very particular now of our world. Lichtman's narrator is an everyman (albeit a singular one) who just wants to be good—that slipperiest of ambitions—and yet his efforts pretty much always go wrong. But also they don't. Wisely comic and tremendously moving, *Such Good Work* thinks in detail about immigration, addiction, privilege, power and loneliness; but it does so by mining the seemingly inconsequential for its true profundity. Lichtman never falls for the siren song of self-seriousness, and that is part of what makes his novel feel so accurate, and so important. In being open to complexity, and sensitive to absurdity, *Such Good Work* gets at the wholeness and difficulty and beauty of lives both ordinary and extraordinary."

—RIVKA GALCHEN, author of *Atmospheric Disturbances*

"Johannes Lichtman has given us a powerful, unsparingly honest portrayal of a soul in torment, trying to find his way to a decent life. How to love, how to work—how to live, however modestly, with meaning and purpose inside a self that for too long has used booze and drugs to avoid the hard work of being human. Building a genuine self, that's an inside job, and in *Such Good Work* Lichtman delivers a deeply affecting novel of one young man's struggle to be whole."

—BEN FOUNTAIN, National Book Critics Circle Award–winning author of *Billy Lynn's Long Halftime Walk*

"I loved the bleary, almost-but-not-quite-hopeless tenderness of *Such Good Work*. The classroom scenes are marvelous. This book is funny, wise, finely paced, and attentive to its every sound. I can't stop thinking about it."

—SARAH MANGUSO, author of *300 Arguments*

Such Good Work

A NOVEL

Johannes Lichtman

Simon & Schuster Paperbacks

New York   London   Toronto   Sydney   New Delhi

Simon & Schuster Paperbacks
1230 Avenue of the Americas
New York, NY 10020

The first chapter of this novel appeared in earlier form in the *Sun*.

First Simon & Schuster paperback edition March 2020

SIMON & SCHUSTER PAPERBACKS and colophon are registered trademarks of Simon & Schuster, Inc.

For information about special discounts for bulk purchases, please contact Simon & Schuster Special Sales at 1-866-506-1949 or business@simonandschuster.com.

The Simon & Schuster Speakers Bureau can bring authors to your live event. For more information or to book an event, contact the Simon & Schuster Speakers Bureau at 1-866-248-3049 or visit our website at www.simonspeakers.com.

Interior design by Carly Loman

Manufactured in the United States of America

10 9 8 7 6 5 4 3 2 1

The Library of Congress has cataloged the hardcover edition as follows:

Names: Lichtman, Johannes, author.
Title: Such good work: a novel / Johannes Lichtman.
Description: New York: Simon & Schuster, [2019]
Identifiers: LCCN 2018016723 | ISBN 9781501195648 (hardcover) | ISBN 9781501195662 (trade paper)
Classification: LCC PR9145.9.L53 S83 2019 | DDC 813/.6—dc23 LC record available at https://lccn.loc.gov/2018016723

ISBN 978-1-5011-9564-8
ISBN 978-1-5011-9566-2 (pbk)
ISBN 978-1-5011-9565-5 (ebook)

For Stu

Wilmington, North Carolina

2013

My students turned in drawings of animals with extraordinary life spans.

I learned that there were species of tube worm that lived for up to one hundred and seventy years.

Arctic whales more than two hundred years old.

Clams with a life expectancy of four hundred.

Sponges that had been alive for more than a millennium.

A kind of jellyfish—the immortal jellyfish—that, after reaching sexual maturity, could revert to infancy again and again, maybe forever.

"Really?" I said, holding up Lucy's drawing.

Lucy nodded proudly. She was a sophomore psych major. Her jellyfish wore a cape. A dialogue bubble above its head stated: *I am immortal and a jellyfish.*

I hung Lucy's picture on the whiteboard next to Ravi's arctic whale, which had a horn and a side-profile smile. Ricky's tube worm was a bright red plume with the caption *The tube worm is a vagina-like creature that can grow to be up to six feet tall. It is a deep-sea invertebrate whose only predators are accidental ones—mainly large mammals trying to have sex with it.*

Kayla's drawing was not a drawing but rather a full page of double-spaced text explaining why there shouldn't be drawing assignments in a college creative-writing class. (*Drawing animals is not creative writing any more than pottery is accounting.*) She sat in the front row and glared at me. She had the posture of someone who spent her childhood balancing books on her head. She was almost certainly the treasurer of a sorority. I hung her essay next to all the animal pictures.

My department chair, Norman, invited me to his office. Norman was a squirrelly man who always appeared to be bracing for a punch. He was from a leafy college town in the Northeast and looked out of place in Wilmington, a waterfront tourist strip that happened to have a university. He had hired me the previous summer after a string of maternity and rehab leaves of absence had left the department in need of temporary faculty who could be trusted to stay childless and sober. I wasn't sure why, out of the pack of graduating MFA teaching assistants, he had picked me, but maybe one of my professors had gotten the wrong idea about me and put in a good word.

"Look, Jonas, I'm not trying to be the administrator here," Norman said. "But a student complained."

This student had felt uncomfortable with last week's homework assignment: attend a stranger's funeral.

"Frankly," Norman said, "I don't know if I can blame her."

This student was Kayla.

Norman waited for me to say something, but my mind was too foggy to find a good explanation.

"No more funerals," I agreed.

Back in my office, I typed up a more traditional assignment: *Write a story.*

My mind was always foggy lately. At age twenty-seven, it was my first semester sober, and without four doses of oxycodone a day, a couple tramadol in the mornings, a few methadone now and then, and a weekend bump of heroin to take the edge off, I'd been having trouble finding my words. Sometimes when I was standing in front of the class and one of the kids asked a good question, my brain would start firing off ideas, and it was like I was alive again. I'd explain the relationship between dialogue and narration in fiction, do an impromptu performance of how a scene from a popular movie would sound if a narrator were commenting on each piece of dialogue, and feeling my energy rising with the sound of their laughter, I'd circle back to answer the original question by describing the moment in their assigned reading when . . . when . . . when . . . but the words would scurry into the fog again and I'd be left um-ing and uh-ing like an idiot.

Monday morning the students slumped through the door. They'd spent almost every Monday since they were five years old in a room like this. It took its toll—so often being somewhere other than where you wanted to be. When I used to get high, places were interchangeable. Everywhere was the best place ever—and then the worst. But now place mattered very much. There were few places I liked more than this classroom, with the cheap blinds over the windows, the long fluorescent light tubes overhead, and the students who, even though I often told them what to do, didn't seem to hate me.

Except for Kayla. Her dislike troubled me.

I stood at the front of the class. I was wearing jeans and a navy cardigan that had been a gift from my ex. I had been growing my hair long since a methadone nightmare the year before had given me a fear of balding. The hair now reached down past my ears. It was strong and brown and shiny and probably the best thing I had going for me.

I held up a stack of student stories. "This was concerning." I paused. "You killed all your protagonists."

The students laughed nervously. Kayla maintained eye contact from her spot in the front row.

"I'll admit that this may be my fault. I probably shouldn't have sent you to the funeral. That's on me. I was trying something new." I paused. "But here's the thing: Life is long and usually ends in death. Stories are short and usually don't. Characters can have problems without having cancer, and suicide doesn't always have to be the solution." I looked out at the students, hoping to see a reaction, which was a stupid thing to do, since, even when the students were in the middle of life-changing moments—when they realized that all experience was subjective or that they didn't have to major in business administration—they almost never visibly reacted. But today, seeing no reaction, I panicked. I took a sip of water and gathered myself. "Please stop killing your characters. It's bumming me out."

After class, I asked Kayla to stay behind for a second. I was nervous. I knew from student evaluations that one-on-one interaction was not my strong suit. In class, Professor Anderson was *hilarious* and *super sarcastic*, but in office hours he was *random*.

"How's the semester treating you, Kayla?" I said, making casual eye contact.

"It's busy." She clutched her binder to her chest.

"Are you enjoying your other classes?"

"I am."

"You're an econ major, right?"

"Psychology."

"Psychology: the econ of the liberal arts."

"What?"

"I get the feeling that you don't like this class."

She mulled the question over. "I don't *not* like it." A pause. "I had planned on liking it."

"You have an A, you know."

She sighed. "I feel like you're not teaching us what you should be teaching us."

"What do you think I should be teaching you?"

"I don't know."

"What do you want to learn?"

She opened her mouth but stopped.

"It would help if you told me," I said. "Maybe what you want to learn is what other students want to learn, too."

"*You're* the teacher," she finally said.

That evening, I went to an Alcoholics Anonymous meeting. Technically, I should have been going to Narcotics Anonymous. But I found that the average age at AA was much higher, which meant that the sharers had better stories and that I was less likely to meet people who looked and sounded like me. After the meeting, I saw Spanish Richard waiting for me in the parking lot. Spanish Richard was a middle-aged three-hundred-pound recovering alcoholic who wore Hawaiian shirts and cargo shorts and cried every time he shared.

"My man," he said, shaking my hand and pulling me into a half hug. "You out on the streets again?"

"I am not. I just haven't been keeping up on meetings." I didn't tell him that I had never been "out on the streets"—I had used drugs in my apartment. "I have to get better about that."

"How long have you been clean now?"

"About two months." I refused to say, *Seventy days.*

"So you're not an expert yet?"

"You are correct."

"Have you started the steps?"

"I'm getting there." I had no intention of doing the steps. AA was like religion—you could take the parts that worked for you and leave the rest.

"My man, at some point you have to ask yourself: How much more am I willing to lose?"

I nodded.

"You already lost a girlfriend. How about your job? How about your home? How about your car?"

I used to find it strange how the men at these meetings put cars on the same level as wives, jobs, and homes on the list of things they lost to drugs and alcohol. Not until I heard a twelve-stepper describing his two hours on the bus each day as "reflecting time" did it occur to me how much more a car could mean to someone who's at the mercy of public transit and a parole officer. In the parking lot, Spanish Richard told me the story of his fall, again, and I found, again, that hearing about all-night drinking, lying, cheating, and car crashing, told with the same emphasis and pauses as the last five times, wasn't boring at all. Just the opposite—it was comforting, like hearing a favorite bedtime story. Spanish Richard said that he now got more real joy from making his bed every morning than he ever did from alcohol. He talked about God as if God were a hotline I could call. He also mentioned a hotline I could call.

"It's twenty-four hours."

Then he put his hand on my shoulder. "You can handle it."

I swallowed. "How do you know?"

Spanish Richard shrugged. "Because *I* can handle it."

Three weeks after our first meeting, I got another summons from the department chair. Norman didn't want to micromanage my process, but he was concerned.

"Maybe you want to use some course syllabi or exercises from the department file." Norman cleared his throat. "Or maybe you would feel more comfortable handing over the courses to someone else."

"I would love to use some course syllabi and exercises from the department file. I've been struggling for direction and I think that could be just what I need. How can I access them?"

"I'll send you the link."

I could feel that there was a *but* coming, so I preempted it. "I realize that I haven't been on top of my game lately. There have just been a lot of changes." I paused. "It's hard to lose someone you care about. I didn't think it would affect my work so much, but it has."

Norman nodded sympathetically. He didn't ask whom I had lost, which was lucky. The implication of sadness from losing a loved one sounded better than sadness from losing the version of yourself who got to be high all the time.

Back in my office, still employed, I ate a multivitamin and wished it were oxycodone.

That evening, I was walking down Front Street, passing by the bars where I used to drink, on my way to the corner store to buy an unsatisfying soda, when I ran into a group of MFA students two years behind me.

"Jonas! Where have you been?" they said, drunk and happy. "We never see you anymore!"

They didn't know about the drugs or the sobriety, so there was no way to quickly explain why I could no longer be found at Lula's or the Blue Post, where I used to spend five or six nights a week.

"They kept me on for a second semester, if you can believe it," I said. "All it took was for Daniel to realize he's an alcoholic."

"How did he only just realize that now?" said Stephanie. "I realized it when he yelled 'poetry forever!' in the middle of my first-year reading."

"That wasn't part of the poem?" I said. "I like that poem less now."

"Daniel likes epiphanies," said Audrey. "A character can't just *know* that he's an alcoholic at the beginning of the story. He has to *realize* it."

"Come drink with us!" Bobby said. "We are drinking!"

"Christ, Bobby, stop yelling," Audrey said, and yanked him by the shirt.

"I can't," I said. "I'm a real teacher now. If they catch me at a bar, they might ship me off with Daniel."

We shared hugs and they bumbled down the street toward Lula's. By the time they were out of sight I was shaking so badly I could barely stand.

The next day, I biked to work, inspiring two separate pickup-truck drivers to yell their guess at my sexual orientation. In my office I found a story slid under the door. It was from Kayla. A revision. The first draft of her story had been about a young marine whose plane was shot down on his way home from Afghanistan to marry his sweetheart. In this revised version, the marine's plane still crashed into the sea, but this time he was resuscitated by an immortal jelly-fish. The jellyfish gave up his immortality to save the marine, but there was a catch: the marine could never again leave the ocean. So the marine swam across the Atlantic to the coast of North Carolina, where he watched his lost love walking along the beach alone, day after day. Every evening, as she passed, he longed to reach out and pull her into the water. But he loved her too much, so he just floated in the waves, pining. One day he saw a man walking by her side, holding her hand. That night, the marine swam away without anger or bitterness—only sadness that this part of his life had ended.

* * *

On the last day of the semester, I ordered pizzas for the class. Ricky provided a "vegan pizza," which was simply a loaf of sourdough bread. Lucy brought homemade cookies so perfect they looked photoshopped. We ate and laughed and played YouTube videos on the projector.

I gave a short speech that ended with "Now get out of here before I get emotional," a line that I had planned the night before, but which, as I said it in front of the class, inspired actual welling in my throat.

On their way out, the students dropped their final assignments on my desk. Ravi shook my hand and thanked me for the class. Ricky waited for the others to leave, then looked me in the eyes and told me that this was the least boring class she'd had in a long time.

She closed the door after leaving; I was alone.

I looked at the empty desks. I slammed a pizza box over my knee. I hurled it across the room. I picked up another box and raised it over my knee.

"I can take care of that," Kayla said, suddenly appearing in the doorway.

"Oh. I didn't see you there." I put the box down on the desk and made casual eye contact. "How is the end of the semester treating you?"

Kayla took the box from my desk, opened it, threw away the garlic-crumbed wax paper and the little plastic tripod, folded in the sides, and flattened the cardboard. She packed up the other boxes the same way, then tucked the flattened boxes under her arm.

"I'll just run these out to the recycling bins," she said.

I stood there waiting for her to return and wondering what parting words I should leave her with. It was nonsexual affection, but I didn't want to give her the wrong idea. I just wanted her to know that she shouldn't take my failure as indicative of what life would offer.

I waited. The clock read five past. Students from the next class queued up in the hall. One peeked in to see if I'd left yet. I glanced out the window, but of course she wasn't coming back.

At home, I thought about calling my mom, a spiritual coach who was now living at a retreat in Sedona with no internet access. We had, over the years since I left home, settled into a rhythm where I called on her birthday and she called on mine, and we mailed each other handwritten letters on Christmas. It was a fragile stasis, and an unexpected request for comfort might shatter the whole thing. The more we talked, the greater the likelihood that someone would mention the past, and neither of us wanted to feel that kind of anger toward the other.

I opened my laptop and tried to write a story about immortal jellyfish and the longness of life. I had barely written a word since quitting drugs, aside from a journal in which, for the past 116 days, I had recorded thoughts like *The days are really long* and *I miss drugs*. Given that I had written every day since high school, it was strange to be without it.

When I was a grad student, under the tutelage of an eccentric professor who took a liking to me based on an orientation-day conversation we had about basketball and who I came to suspect was the one who had recommended me to Norman, I had written an unpublishable novel—a long book that managed to say little. Today I wanted to write something small that felt big. But already in the first paragraph, I found myself unable to describe the way a jellyfish swam. That was why my novel had been bad—it took me so long to describe anything. By the time I got to the end of an analogy, the reader had forgotten what thing I was describing in the first place. I wanted a half-sentence description of a jellyfish, fleet and deft and hinting at metaphoric meaning—the kind of thing that people would underline when they read it. But it took me five lines to describe the inflating/deflating plastic-bagness of the jellyfish. I opened a browser window and typed *jellyfish swimming* into the search bar. I clicked on a video from a nature program, in which a British voice narrated the jellyfish's swimming perfectly. The voice spoke with such calculated eloquence that no word was wasted. I shut the computer.

I biked out to the beach. It was a twelve-mile ride, but the late-spring heat had not yet turned vindictive, and even if it had, I wouldn't have felt it. My wallet was stuffed with $300 in twenties, money with which I was going to buy pills from Kit when he got off work at the Applebee's he assistant-managed. It was early evening by the time I reached the coast, the sun hanging low in the sky, and the only people still out were crew-cut marines from Camp Lejeune, drinking bottled beer with their young wives. They'd be sent to Afghanistan, or back to Afghanistan, shortly. If the soldiers on the beach survived the war, they might show up in my classroom one day, straight-backed and polite and quietly desperate to make up for lost time. And what could I teach them?

I laid my bike on the sand, rolled up my jeans, and waded shin-deep into the surf. The water that pooled around my ankles had been part of the ocean before I was born and would be part of that same ocean after I was dead. I wasn't sure what to do with this information.

"Professor Anderson?"

I turned and saw Kayla, walking hand in hand with a broad-shouldered and crew-cut man. He had brown forearms and a white chest that looked like parts from two separate action figures. Kayla wore a bathing-suit top and jean shorts and looked like she was trying to reconcile what she was seeing in front of her with what she knew. I couldn't tell whether her surprise came from catching me wading in the ocean by myself or from seeing me outside the classroom.

"It's a little tradition of mine." I trudged out of the water. "After I turn in final grades, I go for a dip. You got an A."

She smiled. "Professor Anderson, this is my fiancé, Hank."

"Nice to meet you, sir," Hank said.

I braced for an alpha-male handshake, but Hank's grip was gentle. Up close, I saw that he had the face of a boy. It dawned on me that I was the adult in the situation.

"Have you two made any plans for after graduation?"

"I have another year left," Kayla said. "But I'm going to be a flight attendant."

"She's going to see the world," Hank said.

"How exciting. Any particular part of the world?"

"All of it, hopefully," Kayla said.

"And when's the wedding?"

"Next month—right before I ship out." Hank looked over at Kayla with his big young eyes. "I can hardly wait."

Kayla ran her fingers over her ring, which looked more like an earring than an engagement ring—a skinny band with a tiny diamond.

I took the $300 from my wallet, folded the fifteen bills over once, and held them out to Hank. "Happy wedding."

Hank froze.

"Please. I insist. You make a lovely couple."

Kayla took the money from my hand. "Thank you, Professor Anderson."

Hank stared at his feet.

"It's our first wedding present, babe," Kayla said, handing him the bills.

Hank lit up as if he had just realized she was going to marry him. He put the twenties in the pocket of his shorts and shook my hand again, harder this time. "Thank you, sir. That's extremely generous of you."

"Maybe you can buy a dog," I said.

Kayla hugged me. I gave her a quick one-handed pat on the back—my hand stuck to her skin for a moment—and wished them both good luck.

They walked along the water's edge, and I watched their footprints disappear in the wet sand until their bodies had disappeared, too. Out past the breakers, a jellyfish bobbed along with the tide, with nothing to do but live forever.

IN THE FALL, ONCE I SETTLED INTO MY SOBRIETY, I LEARNED that I was a far better teacher when I wasn't high. Even if I had been a decent teacher under the influence—prepared and reliable and often funny—I always addressed a general audience rather than unique groups of students. It was the same audience I addressed when I paced around my apartment late at night, giving speeches because I was too wound up to sleep. I would have talked the same no matter who was listening. Back when I was using, I would call Stella, my best friend from college, to just talk talk talk, to the point where she stopped picking up unless she was drunk enough to want to jump in with her own rambles. Now I was the one avoiding her calls. I couldn't pick up without explaining about the drug problem I'd kept from her, and I couldn't imagine any reaction to that news that I'd like to hear.

That summer, when Norman failed to renew my contract and I left Wilmington after three years of grad-student TA-ing and one year of adjuncting, I had taken a temporary position, with the possibility of renewal, at a little state college in Eugene, a green and rainy city where a white guy in a monk's robe stood on Pearl Street yelling Dalai Lama quotes at passersby. I began to imitate the female colleagues I'd watched work so hard to earn the respect that the students offered any half-competent male teacher. I focused on teaching individuals. I made office-hour meetings mandatory before and after every paper. I assigned difficult theoretical texts that I spent every evening rereading, filtering them down until I could distill their ideas into easily understandable examples. I gave low grades with heaps of comments and offered the students opportunities to revise as many times as they wished. I took up smoking in the quad between classes. I had no pedagogical reason for this last decision, but I thought it might be good for the students to see me unprotected by the podium—to see me, at least temporarily, as a person in need of a break, rather than a teacher they wanted to please, punch, or fuck.

Also: I liked to smoke. More than the nicotine itself, there was the joy of looking forward to the cigarette as the break approached. Then there was the joy of standing outside, holding the cigarette, raising it to my mouth, and inhaling—this totally automatized and consuming set of actions that left no question about what you were supposed to do.

I often smoked with Louise, a middle-aged English lit professor. She had such great advice that when I didn't have real problems to ask about, I would make one up. One October afternoon, as the Oregon rain politely tapped on the awning under which Louise and I stood, I told her that my comp courses were going well, but that I was struggling to get my creative writing students to talk.

"Put them in groups." Louise let out a long trail of smoke. "Assign them a scene to interpret and perform. If it's just you standing at the front of the classroom, their tolerance for silence is infinite. But if it's three or four of them looking at each other, with no mediator to blame, silence makes them nervous. They worry that it makes them look weak. Especially the boys."

The following week, I broke my creative writing students into groups and assigned each group a classic short story that they were to adapt into a dramatic scene.

The first group was to perform Hemingway's "Hills Like White Elephants," which anyone who'd dealt with creative writing in the academy would know by heart. The story was essentially already a play—there was minimal exposition and lots of unexplained dialogue. The two characters, a young man and a young woman, sit in a train station café drinking while the man tries to talk the woman into getting an abortion. I didn't enjoy teaching the story. Since the word *abortion* was never mentioned, many students would have no idea what was going on and would assume the couple were discussing an appendectomy or boob job. Even the students who understood the story ended up writing horribly because they did not yet realize the difference between knowing all the details and sharing only a tenth of them, and not knowing any of the details and just writing cryptic sentences.

The "Hills" group came to the front of the class, and Drew, a strong-chinned business major, positioned two desks facing each other. I rolled my chair to the side of the room to watch.

"These desks will serve as the restaurant table," said Jonathan, a boy who was surely bullied in high school. Round-faced and frowning and always wearing a black T-shirt that was at once too big and too small, he had narrowly missed being born in a time when he could've grown up Goth. Instead he was stuck with whatever subculture the bullied used for armor these days. Even though he spoke with a tone of teenage annoyance, I could tell that he'd spend hours on twenty-minute assignments. I wanted to tell him that he was doing well. That it was okay. That people would probably always want to punch him in the face, regardless of whether he acted superior or disinterested, so he might as well be nice. But that seemed like the kind of speech that might lead to another nonrenewal of my contract.

Alyssa sat down at the restaurant table. She was in both my creative writing and composition courses. Her papers were generally on the C+ level, but she was enthusiastic and responded gratefully to criticism. She was also black—which might not have been relevant if it hadn't affected the way I treated her. She was the only black student in my creative writing course, and one of only three students of color in my comp course. When she had explained her difficulty in making it to the mandatory office-hour meetings due to work obligations, I had agreed to correspond via email instead, which I'd refused to do for the two white students who had asked. If she was a day late on a paper, I would sternly tell her that I'd let it slide this time, and she would thank me profusely, knowing that I would let it slide next time, too.

She took a pair of sunglasses from her purse and handed them to Jonathan. They were of the white-framed, bug-eyed variety. I found it hard to imagine why he would need these sunglasses, or any sunglasses, for "Hills Like White Elephants." Jonathan pulled a black trench coat from his backpack and put it on, and with sunglasses on face, he retreated to stage left of the classroom, while Alyssa and Drew sat down at the restaurant table. Alyssa stretched out her neck a few times. She nodded at Drew.

"Action!" Jonathan yelled.

Alyssa and Drew mimed drinking.

"Those hills out there look like white elephants," Alyssa said.

Drew paused. "Those *are* white elephants."

Alyssa squinted at the imaginary hills, then down into her glass. "God, I'm drunk."

Drew looked at Alyssa sadly, convincingly, as if this wasn't the first girl he'd tried to talk into an abortion. "It's a simple procedure, you know."

Alyssa said nothing.

"It won't hurt at all."

"I wish you would shut up," Alyssa said.

"Ahh!" Jonathan kicked in an imaginary door and burst into the restaurant. "Stop what you're doing!"

"What's the meaning of this?" Drew yelled.

"I have been sent from the future. I've come to warn you about your baby."

"My baby?" Alyssa said.

"I'm afraid it's no ordinary baby." Jonathan removed his sunglasses dramatically. "It's . . . *Satan!*"

I leaned forward.

"My God," Alyssa said. "What should we do?"

"What do you mean?" Drew said.

"Can we keep it?"

"Did you hear what he just said?" Drew asked.

"We could have all this"—Alyssa motioned out the window—"and every day we—"

"That man from the future just said that *Satan* is growing in your belly!"

"I'm afraid there's only one thing to do." Jonathan reached into his coat and pulled out a coat hanger.

The class gasped.

I saw whatever was left of my teaching career flash before my eyes.

Then Jonathan took off his coat, hung it on the hanger, and laid it on my desk. "Sorry, I was getting a little hot there."

"Ha ha ha!" I said.

"But as I was saying"—Jonathan's voice rose a little out of control, thriving on the energy of the audience—"there's only one thing to do!" He pulled a ruler out from his waistband and pointed it at Alyssa's stomach like a gun.

"Over my dead body," Drew yelled, and pulled out a ruler from his waistband.

"Those hills *are* white elephants," Alyssa yelled. She took out her own ruler from her jeans and yelled, *"Pow pow pow!"*

All three of them began to shoot. Drew fell quickly. Jonathan's death was more dramatic; he lay out on my desk and expired in a long, stuttering fit. Every time I raised my hands to start the applause, Jonathan's corpse started shaking again. Finally, he settled and died, and Alyssa, the only one still alive, took a bow. I stood up to cheer. It occurred to me, not for the first time, that I spent more time with these students than with my friends and family combined. Which, at the moment, felt just fine.

I was smoking in the quad with Louise. I told her that her exercise had been a success (which was true), but that I was now having trouble with a disruptive student (which wasn't true).

"Before I went back to do my PhD, I taught high school English." Back then, Louise said, she'd had a student who was always disrupting class, correcting her, making jokes, smirking. "You get one of these boys in almost every class, especially if you're a woman. But this one was different from the others."

She said that this boy wasn't just arrogant and resentful—he was malicious. He didn't just want attention or to show that he was smarter than the teacher—he wanted to dominate.

"One day, he was mouthing off as usual, commenting under his breath after everything I said, flicking balled-up papers at this poor girl, and I said that I'd had enough. I wrote a note and told him to take it to the principal. He said, oh, no, that wasn't necessary. He was only kidding and he'd stop. But I told him it was too late for that now. He had made his decision. And now he had to go to the principal's office." Louise took another drag off her cigarette and exhaled. "His face turned red and he got all worked up, saying I had no right and he hadn't done anything wrong and so on. But when he saw that I wasn't going to budge, this calmness spread over him. He smiled, looked me in the eyes, and said, 'You're such a cunt.'"

"He didn't."

"He did. In front of the whole class."

"What did you do?"

"It threw me at first. I'd already been called every name you can think of and probably a few that you can't. But usually the name-callers were boys in the hall who didn't see me coming up behind them. Or someone who'd scribbled that I was a bitch on a note I intercepted. Or someone writing in Sharpie on a bathroom wall. But it had never happened like this before. No one had ever intentionally said it *to my face* like that before. But I gathered myself. My mentor had told me that whenever you're in doubt, you should ask the student a question. Turn it around. Put them in the position of answering. I looked at the boy. I said, 'Do you know what a cunt is?' He smiled that little superior smile of his and said that, yeah, he knew what a cunt was. That smile of his said that not only did he know what it was—he'd seen his fair share, too. So I said, 'Then why don't you draw one on the board?' He stared at me. 'What?' he said. I said, 'Please draw a cunt on the board for the class.'"

"Ha! What did he do?"

She put out her cigarette. "He marched his ass down to the principal's office."

I laughed, long and sincere, not even faking it. "When I grow up, I want to be just like you, Louise."

She shook her head with a smile. "Now, why on earth would you want that?"

My loft was a nice spot with big windows that offered a sedating view of the rain, but it was priced at just $525 a month—cheap enough for me to put away some savings, seeing as I wasn't paying for drugs, nights out, or pretty much any expenses except groceries—because it was directly across from the Amtrak station. The whole unit shook with each passing train.

That weekend, a parade of late-night horn-blowing Union Pacific freight trains kept me up. In the mornings, the NA meetings were obnoxious. In the afternoons, the new novel refused to be written. In the evenings, I longed for pills. By Monday, I had accomplished nothing besides not getting high, and by the time class started, I was feeling irritable. But I was determined to teach a good class anyway.

"What were our first impressions?" I said with as much pep as I could manage.

The students were supposed to have read a story by a black writer that dealt with race. There was a quiet shuffling, as the kids who always talked waited their customary five seconds before they began talking.

Drew turned his perfect chin in my direction. "It was fine, I guess. I'm just so tired of reading about race."

I felt a sudden urge to ask him to draw a cunt on the board. But it seemed tricky to work that into the discussion.

"What have you read lately about race?"

Drew thought about it. "That story about school integration."

"Okay, what else?"

He was quiet.

"It's just that, if you're saying that you're so tired of reading about race, you must have read about it a lot."

Drew rolled his eyes.

"We've hardly read anything about race in this class. And I can't imagine you're overwhelmed with the topic in your other classes. Is it possible that you're not tired of reading about race, but that you simply don't want to read about it at all?"

"I liked the story," Alyssa said.

Everyone turned and waited for the representative for blackness to speak. I wanted to get them not to look at her like that—but I also looked at her like that.

"What did you like about it?"

"There were black characters."

"I'm sorry. We should read more stories with black protagonists."

"No—I didn't mean it like that! I wasn't criticizing. I just meant that in this story, it was nice. I'm sorry."

"Don't be sorry! I'm sorry."

"You don't have to be sorry! I'm sorry."

Once I was convinced that I hadn't offended Alyssa and that she understood that she hadn't offended me, I found that I no longer knew what to ask about the story.

"So," I said. "What did we think of the structure?"

Once, in college in San Luis Obispo, waiting in line to get into a bar, I saw the black guy in front of me turned away because the dress code forbade plain white T's. I was wearing a plain white T, but my shirt was V-necked and fitted, rather than crew-necked and baggy, and the bouncer didn't hesitate before letting me in.

In graduate school, watching an internet stream of the National Book Awards with my classmates (one of our professors had been nominated for an award), during a black writer's acceptance speech on the struggles of her childhood in the South, a white classmate blurted out, "We get it—you're black."

On an airplane back from New Orleans with my girlfriend, we were seated in the middle of a college baseball team returning after a tournament. A drunk baseball player asked a black stewardess if she liked white chocolate. The stewardess had said, "Sweetheart, you couldn't handle this." The baseball player's teammates laughed and she walked away. But then he asked her again. And again. And again. She was the only stewardess on the small plane, so she had to walk up and down the aisle every few minutes, passing him every time. Finally, after his fifth loud advance, she crouched down, pointed a finger in his face, and said, "You need to cool it." When she stood up, he laughed, turned to his friend, and said, loud enough for everyone to hear over the roar of the plane engines, "As if I would fuck that bitch."

Lying on my couch that day after class, I mentally rewrote each of these memories into scenes in which I'd done something.

It was near the end of the semester that Alyssa showed up to my office for the first time. We'd been corresponding via email every week, and she had been making great progress on her final essay for composition. Her paper dealt with contemporary sitcom representations of blackness, and many times throughout the term, I'd worried that I'd somehow pushed her into writing about blackness, or that the uber-white system in which she was stuck made it necessary for her to address the subject of race. But she'd recently started incorporating personal experience through an elegant authorial *I*. This confident personality shining through her prose quieted my fears. It made me think not only that she had picked the topic she wanted, but also that I was a good teacher.

"How is your son doing?" I asked, making the eye contact I was gradually becoming more comfortable with.

"He's getting big! He's turning four next month. I can't believe it." She took out her phone and showed me a picture of a happy plump boy, who smiled like he knew he was and would always be loved.

"Look at that smile. He's going to be a heartbreaker."

"Not yet!" She laughed. "I'm not ready for him to have any girl-friends."

"So," I said, transitioning into teacher mode, "do you want to talk about your essay?"

"That would be great." She took a legal pad out from her back-pack.

I pulled up her latest draft on my computer and spent twenty minutes going through it page by page, diagramming her para-graphs, considering their relation to the thesis, and asking how she thought each point might connect to the previous point. We made a list of the areas that she'd want to develop for the final draft, and I said, "I'm really impressed, Alyssa."

She smiled, looking relieved. "I'm so happy that you like it."

"Do you have any questions moving forward?"

"No. Thank you so much for your help."

"That's what I'm here for. Even if I don't have anything good to say, sometimes it helps to just hear someone else talk about your paper."

"You always have good things to say!"

"Flattery will get you everywhere." I smiled and waited for her to start to leave, but she stayed put. My smile started to hurt. "How are your other classes going?"

She looked down at her notebook. "Two of my classes are with you, as you know, and those are great. But I think I'm going to fail my other class." She paused. "See, I messed up and now the professor wants to fail me."

"What happened?"

Alyssa said that this professor, a Dr. Harrison, had given her a D on her first paper. But she probably deserved that grade, she admitted. She hadn't understood the assignment and she hadn't asked for clarification. But for the second paper, she had buckled down. She made an appointment with the librarian to help her find sources. She took a rough draft to the writing center for help.

"It's okay if I didn't get an A+. But it was a good paper. I think it deserved at least a C."

But the only comment that Harrison had left was that Alyssa hadn't cited a quote correctly.

"He thought it was plagiarism. He didn't even give me a grade."

She'd cited five sources, but she had paraphrased one point from a writer that she forgot to cite. "I offered to rewrite it from scratch! I didn't just want a free pass." But Harrison said you only get one chance with plagiarism. "So now I have a disciplinary hearing scheduled for after finals."

I was furious. Who did this Harrison think he was? Here was a single mother who, unlike most students, actually wanted to learn, and he was going to ruin her academic career over a missed citation?

"These things tend to get blown out of proportion," I said, mustering professional calm. "I can talk to Dr. Harrison, if you like. I'll bet we can straighten things out."

"You would do that?"

"Of course."

"Oh my God, thank you, Professor Anderson! You're a lifesaver."

"Please, it's nothing."

But it wasn't nothing, and I knew it. I left my office that day feeling better than I had in some time. This good feeling, oddly enough, made me want to get high.

I walked from my apartment down Shelton McMurphey Boulevard, parallel to the train tracks. The pine-tree-studded hills of Skinner Butte stood to the right and downtown Eugene to the left. I tried to convince myself to keep walking—to get my ass to the NA meeting in the Whiteaker. Life was going well. I was helping students. I was filling my days. I needed to stay clean. I hated meetings—especially evening meetings, which were always overcrowded with young people needing to fulfill a court sentence. But the meetings at least distracted me until the urges passed. I kept dreaming that I found a glowing orange prescription bottle of oxycodone under a park bench. That I had all these units of guaranteed joy waiting for me. It was the guaranteed part that was so exciting. The knowledge not that joy *might* be coming, but that it *would* be coming in thirty to forty-five minutes. I'd snorted pills, smoked them, and once Kit had shot me up with spoon-melted roxy. But I preferred the delay that came when you just swallowed them. The time after I took the pill but before the high hit was my favorite. It was all there in front of me.

I walked down into the park under the freeway overpass on Washington Street. On the basketball courts, where the backboards hung suspended from the bottom of the overpass, there was a commotion. A tweaker with a shaved head in a green Windbreaker was kneeling on the court by himself, screaming. He was beating his knuckles on the asphalt. I could see the streaks of red flash through the sky every time he raised his fist. If a person at the meetings recited this story, he would say, "When I saw him on the ground, I knew that that could have been me. That I was one of the lucky ones."

But that *couldn't* have been me. I was better than this tweaker, better than the people at the meetings who'd lost their children to Social Services, their freedom to the state, their legs to car crashes. I had barely lost anything. We may have had similar addictions, but we were not the same.

"That's what you want to do?" the tweaker yelled, looking up at me. "That's what you want to do?" He stood up and charged me.

At six-one, I was maybe six inches taller than the tweaker, and his bony limbs couldn't add up to anything close to my 175. On top of that, a barely dormant rage from pre-growth-spurt smallness and bullying had made my older self stupidly prone to fighting. But when that crazy-eyed, bloody-boned tweaker came at me, I didn't fight. I ran. I ran in long hard strides, sucking in air as I flew through the park and back out into the street. I didn't stop running until I got to the meeting.

"It's not weird," Duke said. We were standing in the parking lot after the meeting, looking over at the barbecue smoke pouring out of Papa's Soul Food Kitchen, one of the many establishments in the Whiteaker that was run out of a converted house. Duke was wearing a worn-out Oakland Raiders sweatshirt and had his black hair slicked back with sunglasses resting on top. He had a tattoo of the pound sign on the left side of his neck. He was either thirty or sixty. "You know why doing something good made you want to get high?"

"Why?"

"Because *everything* makes you want to get high."

I lit another cigarette. Duke didn't smoke.

"I was reading the paper the other day," Duke said as he chewed on a Twizzler, "and it said that Suboxone is so popular in prisons, that at one prison in Tennessee, they randomly drug-tested the prisoners, and ninety-eight percent of them tested positive for Suboxone."

"Wow." I knew the number couldn't be right, but sometimes the exact statistics of a statement weren't as important as what the person was trying to communicate with those numbers.

Suboxone was the drug increasingly prescribed to recovering heroin addicts in place of methadone. It came in a strip that you dissolved in your mouth for a twelve-hour synthetic-opium flow. The first time that I had bought it, years earlier, Kit had warned me that I shouldn't take more than a quarter strip at a time, because it was designed for people who shot up several times a day, whereas, at the time, I had never even tried heroin. But thirty minutes after the quarter strip failed to register any effect, I took another quarter strip. A few hours later, I woke up on the floor, wet from sweat, pulsing neon bliss.

"You know how the guys smuggle the Suboxone in?" Duke said. "They get their friends to dissolve it on the page of a Bible. Then the friend gives them the Bible at visiting hours, and they tear off the page back in their cells and eat it. Can you imagine that?"

I thought about it. "Yeah."

Duke pulled his last Twizzler from the bag. "Yeah. Me, too."

I liked Duke, even if I never wanted to see him outside of the meetings.

I walked back home, still sober. I lay down on my bed to write an email to Dr. Harrison, but instead I clicked on *Dagens Nyheter* to read about Zlatan Ibrahimović leading the Swedish national team through World Cup qualifying. My mother was born in Sweden and had, with great foresight, not only arranged for me to receive Swedish citizenship, but had also gone against conventional wisdom at the time, which said that two languages would stunt a child's intellectual development, and made sure I learned both English and Swedish. While I was fluent and could easily read Swedish newspapers, I had pretty much only spoken Swedish with her, which meant that when I spoke Swedish, I sounded like a middle-aged woman. Zlatan Ibrahimović spoke Swedish with Bosnian impatience, first-generation swag. He had come from the roughest housing projects in

Malmö to become the greatest footballer in Swedish history. Today, I read, he had scored again.

I closed the newspaper window and wrote a draft of a respectful, yet strongly worded letter to Dr. Harrison, in which I vouched for Alyssa's integrity. I wondered, in the least confrontational manner possible, if a onetime mistake couldn't be better remedied with a grade reduction rather than a disciplinary hearing. Then I imagined Harrison's reaction. I imagined him complaining to my department chair that I was putting my nose in other people's business. I imagined my contract not being renewed. I imagined having to start over again.

I saved the email without sending it.

When Alyssa turned in her final paper for my course, I read it with a surge of pride. Her sources showed the depth of her research, and her argument was skillfully laid out in four distinct but connected points. I suppressed my shame at not having argued her case yet and wrote, *You've done such good work on this paper, Alyssa. I'm so proud.*

She responded six minutes later with an exclamation-point-laden email full of gratitude. But at the bottom was a PS: *I was wondering if you had had time to talk to Dr. Harrison? I know you must be very busy, but my hearing is coming up soon.*

I took a deep breath, found the email in my drafts folder, and sent it off to Harrison.

Few things gave me more anxiety than waiting for an email to be answered. If I had the money, I'd hire an intern to do all my emailing. But then I'd probably end up fretting over the time it took for my intern to reply to my emails. I sat in my apartment and waited for Harrison's response. In between, I read the Swedish news, the sports news, and the American news. The fascist Sweden Democrats were gaining momentum in the lead-up to the following year's elections. Harrison had not written back. The LA Clippers, my favorite team since I was seven, when my dad had decided that it was absurd to pay $25 for a Lakers ticket when there was another professional team in town practically giving away seats, had beaten Sacramento in overtime for their fourth straight win. Harrison had not written back. The Syrian government was bombing its civilians to end the rebellion. Harrison had written back. Harrison had written back! The first line of his email glowed bold and black in my inbox.

I'm afraid you've been duped, Harrison wrote.

He said that Alyssa's issue had not been a question of a missed citation, but of numerous sentences taken verbatim from a published paper. He estimated that Alyssa had stolen more sentences than she'd written.

It is the most obvious and appalling case of wholesale plagiarism I've seen in thirty-six years of teaching.

I shook my head and tried the breathing techniques that a guy at NA had learned in anger management. I googled Harrison's name and found his picture on the faculty page. He was white—bald on top with a white ponytail. He wore a beard and glasses. He was late middle-aged, smirking. He looked like the brand of "I'm not a racist" racist who had marched for civil rights forty-five years ago in the warm cocoon of Berkeley and now felt justified interrupting black students midspeech to explain to them what civil rights meant.

35

I typed out a draft asking Harrison if I could see Alyssa's paper so I could judge it for myself. I wrote that I had supervised Alyssa's entire writing process in my class, from topic selection to research, outline, rough draft, revision, and final draft. Which was true. I had been with her every step of the way as she built the strongest paper in the class. I wrote that I had run her essay through plagiarism-checking software and found no oddities. I wrote that I thought it strange that she would wholesale plagiarize one paper while doing such thorough work on another paper written in the same term.

I had never actually used the plagiarism-checking software, since the form of my assignments, with students required to turn in work every step of the way, would have made plagiarism near impossible. But to be on the safe side, before sending Harrison the email, I opened the plagiarism checker, copy-pasted Alyssa's essay in, and waited while the checker scanned its databases.

When the software finished its scan, it spat out sixty-seven cases of plagiarism.

"She found a published paper on her topic at the beginning of the term," I told Louise in the quad the next day, trying to control my pacing. "Then she rewrote the paper to make it sound *less* intelligent! She deconstructed it, point by point, to make it look like a latent idea! Then she put back more and more of the original paper every week to make it look like she was improving. Then she sprinkled in a few personal sentences about her childhood to make it hers—but those were plagiarized, too! She plagiarized stories of other people's childhoods!"

"Wow."

"How did she think she'd get away with it?"

Louise shook her head. "With that kind of plagiarism, it's not just cheating—it's an addiction. And there's no logic to addiction."

I appreciated that Louise never mentioned that Alyssa would have gotten away with it if not for the intervention of a professor less naive than I was.

I lay awake listening to the sound of a night train blowing its horn loud enough to knock birds out of the sky. I thought of emailing the eccentric professor from grad school to ask for his advice. But I didn't want to write until I had good news to share. More evidence of my incompetence, about to be let go from another job, another job he'd recommended me for, was not good news. I tried to think of other people I could talk to, but I hadn't been good at keeping up with friends. The more time you spent apart, the harder work it was to just have a conversation. Stella was the one person I used to be able to talk to because I would never have to bring anything up with her—she could just tell when something was off. Sometimes she wouldn't even ask—she'd just put her hand on mine and say something mean about the person she believed to have caused me pain. But if I called Stella now, I couldn't explain the urge to relapse without explaining the initial addiction. I would have to explain that even though I often texted her stories of the creatively dumb things my students did, I really didn't want to lose them. Jonathan's last story had been funny and sad at the same time. Drew's stuff was getting far less misogynistic. With another semester, I might have him displaying genuine empathy.

But even if they let me teach another year, I wouldn't get Drew for another term. Why would a business major take another creative writing class? Even if they kept me on, every four months I would walk into a room of new faces—a roomful of kids who would begin to forget me the second the semester ended.

The following week, I met with my department chair and Alyssa. When I'd explained the situation, the chair had said that these things happened. But I could tell from her tone that she had already heard from Harrison and that she was wondering how she could have hired someone so incompetent.

Alyssa sat down on my side of the desk, dressed in black slacks and a white cardigan, never meeting my eyes. The department chair sat behind her desk and went through the evidence, point by point. Alyssa stared at the clock behind the department chair's head. She wouldn't look at me. After going through all the administrative protocols, the chair asked Alyssa if she had taken the sixty-seven cases of plagiarism from other sources without citation.

"Yes," Alyssa said. Her eyes didn't move.

I pictured her singing her crying baby to sleep at four in the morning.

The chair said that the required action was expulsion. She asked if Alyssa accepted the required action.

"No."

"That will mean a disciplinary hearing."

Alyssa nodded. "Will that be the same one as with Dr. Harrison? Or do I have to go to a second meeting?"

She left without saying a word to me.

As I walked through the park that afternoon, on my way to a meeting, I reviewed what I'd done. I'd caught a cheater. Now she wouldn't be able to get her degree, which would've made her the first member of her family to graduate college. She'd mentioned that in her paper.

Or had she plagiarized that section, too?

I turned around and walked home.

Back at the apartment, I called Kit.

"Let me go outside," Kit said. "I'm at work." I heard the plates and conversations of postlunch Applebee's fading away. "What can I do for you?"

"I was hoping you could mail me some pills."

"Hey—not over the phone!"

"Sorry, sorry. I was wondering if you had any of those supplies my company was looking to purchase."

"Okay, I got you. We got some valley girls right now and some emeralds."

"What are those?"

"Valley girls are Valium and emeralds are E."

"I'm actually just looking for the usual supplies."

"You mean ShamWows?"

"Do I?"

"That's what I call oxycodone."

"Oh, okay. Then, yes—that's what I mean."

"Because OxiClean is that soap from the infomercials, and Sham-Wows are a sponge thing they sell on infomercials."

"That's good. I like that. So can I buy some ShamWows from you?"

"I don't have any."

A chill passed over me. "Do you know when you'll have some in stock?"

"Not sure. My hookup got arrested for shooting a guy in the Harris Teeter parking lot in Leland last month."

"What?"

"Yeah. When the cops came to my guy's trailer with an arrest warrant, he had the gun lying right there on his bed. Not too smart if you ask me."

"Do you have any, like, ShamWow Lites?"

"What?"

"HydroWows?"

Kit was quiet. "What the fuck are you talking about?"

"Hydrocodone. Vicodin. Suboxone. Methadone. Dilaudid. Tramadol. Codeine. Heroin."

"Dude! Not on the phone!"

"Sorry."

"I'll text you later."

He hung up and I stared at the phone for the better part of an hour. I wondered why I'd never learned how to shoot heroin—it would be much easier to buy if I didn't need a snortable powder. Pain pills were hard to find from strangers. If you asked a shady-looking guy in the park, he always had a friend who had some pills, but then you had to take a cab to get to his friend's house, which you had to pay for, and you were more likely to get robbed than get high. I sent myself a text to make sure the phone still worked. It did. I sweated and waited. I went online and searched for overseas pharmacies that would ship painkillers to the US without a prescription. I tried to order a hundred 5 mg hydrocodone from the least fake-looking pharmacy, but right after my order went through, I got a call from a man with an Indian accent saying that they couldn't process my credit card and needed a copy of my bank statement. I hung up and cleared my browser history.

Then the phone rang. Kit's number blazed up the screen.

"You're about to love me, Jonas."

"Yeah?"

"I can get you four strips of Suboxone for one twenty."

"I love you."

I hadn't felt such a violent happiness since I'd quit drugs. I transferred $150 to Kit's account, including $30 for overnight shipping. The future was boundless. It didn't matter that my contract would not be renewed. I could do whatever I wanted. I needed to get out of Eugene, anyway. I could go anywhere—do anything.

But then, unexpectedly, fear hit. Fear that the high would end too quickly. Fear that it wouldn't be as good as it had once been. Fear that the guaranteed warmth I'd always relied on would no longer be guaranteed.

And a new fear: fear that I would take too much and die.

But they were useless, these fears, because once I had drugs, I would take them. There was no question of not taking them.

In college, I'd been sitting in my living room one Sunday afternoon, full of regret. I'd drunk too much and messed things up with a girl. Stella was out of town and I had no one to share the burden of the hangover with. My neighbor showed up, unshowered in flip-flops and basketball shorts, nursing a cup of coffee, and asked if he could watch football on my TV. I didn't like my neighbor, but I let him in.

As we watched the game, I'd told him, vaguely, "I'm hurting today."

He stared at the TV and nodded without speaking. I felt stupid. But at the next commercial, he went to his apartment and returned with a bottle of Vicodin he'd been prescribed for a broken arm. "Have a couple. You'll feel better."

You'll not only feel better, I learned. You'll watch in amazement as all the sadness and anger and self-doubt disappears. You'll suddenly like yourself. Everyone will like you, and because everyone likes you, you won't need any one person. And for the next seven years, every time you're full of regret, you'll get high. And even if you're not feeling that way, you'll manufacture the feeling for an excuse to get high. Your body will simply learn to feel that way when it wants to get high. You'll later read somewhere, *If you're lucky, you never find your perfect drug.* But you'll already have found it.

Tired of sitting with my thoughts and waiting for tomorrow, I changed into sweatpants and a hoodie to guard against the December chill, grabbed a basketball, and walked down the street to the courts underneath the overpass. Spanish Richard had once said that addicts invented problems so that they could justify using—which was astute, considering that I had never told him about any of the many problems I had invented to justify getting high. But this problem was not invented.

By the time I got to the park it was ten thirty, and the only other people out were a couple arguing underneath the opposite hoop. The woman was taller than the man. They both wore hoodies that obscured their faces, but I could see that they were white. I turned my back to them and focused on shooting free throws.

The woman yelled, "It's not your bike, faggot."

The man said, "It is my bike! I paid for it—and don't call me a faggot."

I shot a free throw that landed three feet short of the rim.

Then a crash. I turned. Both man and woman were on the ground, pulling at the bicycle—a beat-up silver BMX bike. They pulled hard, trying to yank it away from each other. The woman punched the man in the head.

The man stood up and stumbled backward. He clenched his fists and charged toward her.

I dropped the ball and took off. Next thing I knew, I was pushing my way between them.

"Hey!" I yelled.

Then someone punched me in the head. My brain rattled. I was instantly nauseous, a feeling that had come over me every time I'd been punched in the head.

"Oh, shit," the man said, coming into focus. He took a step back. "I'm sorry."

"What the hell!"

"I wasn't trying to punch you! I was trying to punch my girlfriend!"

The woman took this opportunity to hop on the bike, bowleggedly pedal away, and yell, "You're both faggots!"

"Damn," the man said.

I rubbed my head. "Fuck."

"I'm really sorry."

I had never been able to not accept an apology. "It was an accident. Accidents happen."

My ex, Alexandra, whom I'd dated for two years, had twice attacked me—once with a fork that failed to pierce my sweatshirt and once with a glass she hurled at my head. The glass had nicked a vein in my forehead, and my first thought when I saw the blood was joy: I finally had incontrovertible evidence that she was in the wrong. I could use this evidence against her once I decided to take her back, which I knew I eventually would. So it was not without ulterior motive that I asked the man in the park, "Why would you stay with someone who treats you like that?"

The man reached around in his pockets nervously. I waited for him to say something simple and profound—something that only a man who'd slept on the streets could know.

"You smoke rock?" the man said.

He dug into his jeans, pulled out a little plastic baggie, a ball of tinfoil, and a straw wrapped in paper that said *Sonic*. He unfurled the foil, made a little pouch for the rock, and unwrapped the straw. "She broke my pipe," he explained.

He lit the underside of the foil, took a pull from the straw, and blew the smoke from his mouth. The crack smelled like burned rubber.

He handed it to me. I followed his lead, and the little yellow-white rock bubbled black over the heat of the lighter. I pulled in through the straw, then watched the stringy smoke dribbling out my mouth. "Wow."

The man laughed. "Right?"

The sounds of passing traffic and a train horn fizzled into a staticky hiss. I slumped down on the concrete and felt the heat of the high, the love of the high. I wanted to say something to the man, to express to him how okay everything was, but I couldn't think of how to say it.

Then this sound started rising, growing like an approaching siren. A police car? No. The train? No. A dial tone. Like it was coming from the biggest phone in the world left off the biggest hook. My heart wasn't beating right. My lungs weren't breathing right. The tone died back down, until it was just coming from a regular-size phone, and I found my way to my feet. I staggered home, scared that the dial tone would grow. Scared of the sidewalk and the sky and every passing car. My skin itched, but not the good kind of itching like when you fell into a nice nod. I hurried up the stairs to my apartment and curled up on my couch.

The walls of my living room looked exactly as they had always looked, except that they hated me. The floor and the ceiling hated me. I told God that I would never get high again if he would just help me get through the night without dying.

I woke to wet sheets and jet lag. I was disoriented and sad without being able to touch the sadness. I opened the curtains to find a gray morning that felt much darker. I took a shower and tried to wash away the shame. I put on sweats and a hoodie and walked outside to the mailbox. An overnight envelope was waiting for me. Back in my apartment, I ripped it open, found a CD case inside, opened the CD case, removed a blank CD, and dumped out the four individually wrapped Suboxone strips that Kit had tucked under the disc. I tore open the wrapper to one of the strips, joylessly, and, instead of cutting it into quarters, stuck the whole thing under my tongue. I waited for thirty, forty minutes. The sweetish taste of the strip reminded me of itself. Then the heat swept in from the sides and pushed down, down, down. I got under the sheets. I wanted to talk to everyone I'd ever met. I should find my dad. I should call my ex. I should write to Alyssa. We could work it out. I could save her. Then I was gone, then back again. The sheets were so wonderful! Dreams kept interrupting. I was flying upward, trying to get out of the dream, but I couldn't. I was banging on the ceiling, but it was concrete. I was screaming to someone, "Hey! Hey!"

And then I woke with a greedy gasp—like I needed all the air in the world and I didn't care who I stole it from.

Lund, Sweden

Fall 2014

THREE THIRTY P.M. AND DARK OUTSIDE. I LAY IN BED AND watched the garbage roll across the courtyard as it did every time the wind blew in from Öresund. Despite my request for a Swedish dorm, I had been housed with the Lunds Universitet exchange students. Since the garbage room was organized into eleven categories of compost and recycling labeled in Swedish, none of the exchange students knew which bins were for food, which were for colored glass, and which were for used batteries, so they threw all their garbage in the "everything else" bin, and the garbage spilled out on all sides. Several fat crows lived on the overflow.

Anja lay next to me. She flinched as one of the crows squawked past my window. "Those are hooded crows," she said. "They build poor nests."

"Well, they're living in garbage."

"Even if they are not living in garbage, their nests are poor." She turned around to face me. "Did you know that there is a type of female oriole that will not mate with the male until he has a nest she approves of? If she doesn't like his nest, he'll rip it up and build a new one until she's happy."

"If we were birds, I don't think you would mate with me."

She looked at my tiny dorm room. "Yes, I do not think so either."

Anja was a German exchange student who lived two doors down from me and studied biology. She was twenty to my twenty-eight, undergraduate to my graduate, almost six feet tall, broad shouldered, broad hipped, and lovely faced, with long blond hair she wore in a thick braid. She was from the eastern part of Germany, near the Polish border, where, according to the internet, everything was cheap and the architecture was bad. I told her that I was from Los Angeles, rather than from a suburb of Los Angeles in the San Fernando Valley, where the sidewalks were decorative and the apartments were carpeted.

We had just had sex for the first time. For the past few weeks Anja had wanted to wait, but this afternoon she had initiated it without warning. It had been terrifying, then lovely, then terrifying, then over. It had also been my first sober sex in almost seven years.

The relapse had culminated with my fainting in a Eugene pizza place in the middle of the day, waking to a bleeding forehead, and staggering away from the cries of the waitstaff and the approaching siren. Then there were weeks of white-knuckling it, as Duke would say, followed by Benadryl and cigarettes and meetings, meetings, meetings, capped by long nights on the couch where everything I watched made me cry—whether it was *Law & Order*, a basketball game, an insurance commercial, or a documentary about the history of public transportation.

The people at the meetings had always lived in so many cities: Portland, Seattle, Spokane, Boise, Denver, San Francisco, Eureka, Redding, Vegas, Medford. They said again and again that there was no such thing as a geographic cure. But they didn't have a passport that granted access to the most drug-free country in the Western world.

When I had first floated to Duke the idea of moving to Sweden to stay clean, he had shaken his head and said, "You could score on Mars."

But Sweden also offered citizens free tuition and student loans at a fixed interest rate of 0.6 percent. Since the plagiarism fiasco, I had been editing novels and memoirs for rich hobbyists, which had me leaving comments like *Probably best not to compare yourself to a Holocaust survivor—but if you feel it's necessary, I would cut the exclamation point.* Even after my drug spending, I had a few thousand saved, and that plus the $300/month Swedish government stipend and $1,000/month student loan was more than enough to live on. I could spend two years working toward something: a master's degree in literature.

I'd flown to Stockholm in August. It was the first time I'd entered the country since a visit at the age of fourteen. I'd stayed at my cousin's apartment while he was away at his summer house in the archipelago and wandered through the sunny nights jealous of anyone who wasn't alone. Then I'd taken the train down to Lund to move into my dorm, which was in the newer part of the city, east of the medieval city center. The dormitory was a four-story glass-and-plaster cube that looked like an ottoman/storage unit that you'd buy at IKEA. My room had a twin bed from IKEA. Also: a small stove, a sink, and a bathroom. The single window looked out into the courtyard.

That afternoon, a cereal box cartwheeled by, chased by an orange cat the exchange students had named Mr. Cat. I wanted to tell Anja all the things I was feeling—how close I felt to her but how I wanted to scream because I wasn't as close to her as I felt—but it was too much for the moment.

Instead I pointed at Mr. Cat. "*Die Katze ist auf dem . . .* court-yard."

"Yes, it's very good, Jonas." She laughed. "But I never get to practice my Swedish."

"Go ahead. Let's hear some Swedish."

She bit her lip, thinking. *"Ett, två, tre."*

"And a one, two, three to you, too."

"Hej! Läget?"

I laughed. "Not much. 'Sup with you?"

"Do not laugh! My Swedish is very good."

"It's the best." I kissed her. "It's because you have the best teacher. But these lessons aren't free. Teach me something."

"Okay." She turned onto her side to face me and leaned on her elbow. "Do you know that a dead whale can explode just from being touched?"

"That's not German."

"It's science. You're very bad at science. When a whale dies, the gases build up inside of it, and then you touch it and it can just *pssssshhh!*"

"That sounds made-up."

"It is not made-up. You are made-up."

I couldn't help but notice the absence of postcoital panic—the need to be alone that I'd always had to sneak pills to quiet. Lying there in bed, I felt happy. But I was also worried that the happiness would at any second disappear, either literally, with Anja leaving, or mentally, with whatever joy was floating around in my brain suddenly vanishing. This weird thing had started happening when Anja was around. These past few months in Sweden, I had been so uncomfortable—in Lund, in Swedish, in my body, my mind, and my sobriety. But when I saw her, I would pretend that I was comfortable so that she wouldn't want to leave me. And then, without thinking about it, I'd realize I was comfortable. It was what had happened today, when she had shown up at my door, just as I was going through a list of reasons not to get high.

"Do you know why we hiccup?" Anja said.

"I do not."

"It's a leftover from when we were amphibians. We used to breathe through gills in hiccuping motions."

"Do you know that there's a jellyfish that lives forever?"

"Nothing lives forever, Jonas."

"It does! It's an immortal jellyfish. One of my students did a report on it when I was teaching."

She scratched her chin. "Hmm. I don't know if I believe in this immortal jellyfish. I'll do some research."

"I don't know if I believe in your hiccuping story. I don't remember ever breathing through gills."

She rolled over and pulled all the blanket with her. "You must have a bad memory."

Lund was a college town in the south of Sweden, with narrow cobblestone streets, a nine-hundred-year-old twin-towered cathedral, and, if you could find a window higher than ten stories to look out, a view of Denmark across the Sound. It was nothing like an American college town, except it was full of forty thousand young people who couldn't go out until they'd drunk enough to start liking themselves.

The exchange students I lived with—mostly German, Dutch, Spanish, French, and Italian twenty-year-olds from the Erasmus program—communicated in broken English. Which meant that my already-bad Swedish stagnated while my English deteriorated. Dutch English was good, but tended to put a rising inflection at the end of sentences, as if everything were a question. German English tended to conflate *fun* and *funny*, and to change the verb *party* to *make party*. Spanish English tended to not be English.

The exchange students in the dormitory could dance for hours. Once a week, I would tag along with them, mainly so that Anja didn't think I was boring. We'd go dancing in the nations—the centuries-old student clubs around Lund, housed in basements full of strobe lights, smoke, and overactive music. I would take part in their circle dancing for five minutes at a time. Then I would go outside and smoke. Sometimes Anja came and talked to me while I smoked, which I found touching. But most of the time I went outside by myself. I smoked twenty, thirty cigarettes a night. I smoked through the nausea, then went back inside, ordered another glass of water with a lime wedge in a cocktail-size plastic cup, and danced for another five minutes. Dancing was a continuous struggle to appear comfortable while tremendously uncomfortable. Sobriety was a continuous struggle to appear comfortable while tremendously uncomfortable.

* * *

My university classes had been a shock, despite the years I'd already spent on a bachelor's in English and a master's in creative writing. In my first lecture, a middle-aged Swedish professor, who was said to be the foremost expert in the world on Tomas Tranströmer, stepped into the classroom wearing tight jeans rolled up two folds to reveal blue dress socks and expensive brown leather loafers. He was white, tall, and stylish in that way that Swedish men often are at the age when American men begin to assert their independence from their wives by wearing the most creatively awful clothes imaginable. He began the class with "We, as intellectuals, must always consider the meaning behind the meaning."

The professor didn't use air quotes around the word *intellectuals*. He didn't qualify the statement or define what he meant by *intellectuals*, nor did he seem to know how ridiculous he sounded. But my classmates exchanged no titters or knowing looks. I was annoyed, then envious. To live outside quotation marks like that—to take yourself seriously and not realize how ridiculous it was to do so.

At break, I would walk out front to smoke with my Swedish classmates, who would dive into long earnest debates that quickly left the texts of the novels behind altogether in favor of politics, economic systems, or postcolonial issues. It was all strange to me. In the US, I had been taught to quote from the texts, to return to the texts, to honor and analyze and never stray too far from the texts.

I started hanging out with a handsome Swedish hipster from my class who was a few years my junior. Bengt was funny and smart. He wrote culture columns and book reviews for a newspaper in the nearby city of Malmö. But he had this annoying tendency to want to find the bourgeois sellout element in every work of art.

Once, we were sitting at Café Ariman, a student hangout near the cathedral, Bengt with a beer and me with a coffee, talking about a recent American movie. Bengt had no thoughts to offer about the film, except to go on and on about the clumsy product placement, as if the ability to spot the product placement were a sign of intelligence—a sign that you weren't being fooled. Whatever the filmmaker was trying to do wasn't as important as Bengt's observations. I saw this approach to criticism among a lot of my classmates: show how smart you are by finding the one problem. It bugged me. But I also admired the Swedish ability to ask the piercing question of art: Is what you're doing worthwhile? I didn't see this question as much in American criticism. The question in American reviews was more how well you did what you were doing.

But my thoughts about what art or literature did or should do were all hypothetical, since I wasn't writing at all. Without self-consciousness-killing drugs, I couldn't get more than a paragraph into writing before I hated what I'd written too much to go on. I tried to start a novel about a *BuzzFeed* writer going off the rails—a novel told in listicles—but I couldn't even manage writing ten-item lists. I longed for that manic expulsion that I'd get when I was pilled-up and lightning brained, going all day until the computer died and I'd have to scribble on shopping lists, paper towels, or the copyright pages of paperbacks.

But now whenever I caught myself wanting to get high, I'd look back on the stories and essays I'd published during my drug years.

Twelve in all, most of them in small journals, some on the websites of larger magazines. They were sometimes interesting. Sometimes insightful. Sometimes clever. But always hollow. How were you supposed to write human emotion when you could get more joy from a pill than you could from another person?

One afternoon, I biked down to the ICA supermarket on Tunavägen, housed in an ugly little concrete strip mall between the dorms. I picked out my groceries, then stacked my bread, my spreadable butter, my packet of ham, and my chocolate bar on the conveyor belt. There was no temptation to buy alcohol in the grocery store because Sweden didn't sell alcohol in grocery stores—you had to visit the state-run Systembolaget, which had prohibitive hours to encourage moderation. Even in Systembolaget, there were no refrigerated shelves. Beer was sold at room temperature. There would be no spontaneous drinking.

At the grocery checkout, a newsstand displayed the three evening papers above the three morning papers. The headlines of all the morning papers were about civil war in Syria and the stream of refugees trying to get to Europe. The evening papers carried headlines of soccer and the drunk-driving arrest of a reality-TV star. One of the evening papers had a picture of hawk-faced Zlatan Ibrahimović, the most famous man in Sweden, in profile, looking dissatisfied in his PSG jersey, with the headline "Zlatan to Blanc: Get It Together or I'm Outta Here!"

I asked the cashier for two packs of Lucky Strikes, in Swedish, but when I said, "Lucky Strikes," the cashier asked for my ID in

English. I had almost no accent, but whenever I said foreign words in Swedish, I pronounced them American and it gave me away.

I bagged my groceries and walked toward the revolving door just as Anja was coming through it. She wore a winter coat and a giant knit scarf.

"Hello, Jonas!" Her smile was like a hug, though we didn't hug in public. I assumed it was a German thing.

"What are you up to?" I said.

"I was buying some things for my costume for the party next week."

"What party?"

"The Noah's Ark party in Malmö. Aren't you going?"

"I hadn't heard about it."

"Everybody dresses like an animal and the ship sails around the harbor all night. It's going to be very fun. You should go!"

"That doesn't sound like my kind of party. But you could come by before?"

"Don't be an old man!"

"I am an old man."

"It will be fun."

"I don't have an animal costume."

"I can make you one. What would you like to be?"

I tried to think of the most unmakeable costume. "An octopus."

"I will make you an octopus."

"How are you going to make an octopus costume?"

"I am a scientist, Jonas. Goodbye." With that, she scampered away.

Since we'd slept together, I had found myself wondering what Anja was thinking, what she wanted, how she saw our relationship—things I had never cared about when I was high. It was maddening to find that I couldn't figure out the answers on my own. One day I asked her if she considered herself my girlfriend. She answered that she considered herself happy with me. It was, I had to admit, a skillful evasion, especially for someone speaking her second language.

I wondered what her life was like in German. I had been trying to learn German through a computer program, but every vocab slide was just a picture of a cat being on top of things.

Die Katze ist auf dem Tisch.

Die Katze ist auf dem Haus.

I wondered what she was saying when she laughed with her German friends, what she was saying when her mother called and her voice turned soft, what she had said to past boyfriends when they were lying in bed.

Die Katze ist auf dem Tisch.

Die Katze ist auf dem Haus.

That night, I startled awake just as I was falling into sleep.

"Did you have a bad dream?" Anja put her hand on my chest.

"I dreamt that I couldn't wake up."

Anja told me that people sometimes startled themselves awake as they were falling asleep due to a genetic leftover from when we were monkeys, when sleep meant the possibility of falling out of a tree. Our brains had to simulate the event before it happened and we hurt ourselves.

"But you do not have to worry. I will catch you if you fall."

"Or if I dream that I'm falling?"

"Yes, I will catch that, too."

Anja went back to sleep and I lay awake trying to think of ways to be less needy. When I'd organized my days around drugs, relationships had been a burden. When I was done talking to someone, I'd often find, to my great annoyance, that the person still wanted to talk to me. Then I'd be stuck there wasting away my high listening to someone else's monologue. Unless I needed an audience or sex, it was usually better to just be high alone. But now whenever I was alone, I found myself longing for Anja, Stella, roommates from college I hadn't talked to in years, teachers from childhood, everyone I'd ever met.

I woke up late for class. Anja had already left. I jumped on my bike and raced through the cold wind. I didn't have time to make my usual morning coffee, and by the time the course let out, it was three in the afternoon and my head was burning with caffeine aches. I jumped on my bike again and darted out of the newly renovated languages-and-literatures building, past the old brick-and-ivy university library, under the arch of the department of gender studies, and onto the gravel paths of Lundagård, the central area of the university. I passed the brick tower that housed the student union, the old pink Versailles-like university building, and the fountain into which champagne-drunk newly graduated students would dive. Finally, I cut out onto the street, toward the city center and the Central Station. I pedaled hard until I got to the Espresso House, a ubiquitous chain that was bringing the Starbucks experience to Sweden. I ordered a coffee, drank it too fast, and scalded my tongue. I drank until I couldn't remember what the headache felt like.

Sitting there in the Espresso House, caffeinated and headache-cured, it hit me: I could still get high.

I could take the train to Copenhagen and score.

I could be there in forty minutes.

I biked from Espresso House to the train station, then back to Espresso House, six times. I didn't board any trains.

I knocked on Anja's door, but no one answered. I sat in my room thinking of someone I could call, but it wasn't even 8:00 a.m. yet on the West Coast. The internet told me that I could find an AA meeting in nearby Malmö that evening. But it had taken me weeks to get myself to an AA meeting conducted in a language where I was fluent in euphemism—I wasn't about to attend one in Swedish. I sat down and made a list of the consequences of using. My brain made a companion list where every point started with *But* . . .

Eventually I took some allergy medicine and passed out.

The next morning, I woke to a knock on the door. I struggled to reenter the world; there was no part of me interested in making the journey. But I pushed my eyes open and got out of bed.

When I opened the door, I found Anja standing there, smiling. She held up an old purple sweatshirt, with the area below the neck cut into eight strips, sewn into arms. "It's an octopus!"

I batted the gangly tentacles, the six nonfunctional limbs stuffed with socks. "This is the best octopus costume I've ever seen." I pulled her inside and kissed her hard and she laughed.

"It's perfect," I said. "You're perfect."

"Yes, this is what I have been trying to explain to you."

After sex, we played gin rummy. Germans, at least the Germans in my dorm, loved playing cards. Given that poker and gin were the only games I knew, and given that Germans, at least the Germans in my dorm, were terrible at explaining card games in English ("When you put down a queen and then he puts down a queen, then two queens have been put down, and then you know, okay, two queens are down, so it's until the next turn, unless it is broken"), Anja and I played gin. This morning I won the first ninety-five points, then Anja won back eleven.

"The groundhog eats slowly," she said, gloating.

"What?"

"It's an expression. The groundhog eats slowly but is warm all winter."

"That sounds made-up."

"You are made-up. *Mühsam ernährt sich das Eichhörnchen.*"

She spelled it out for me. I typed it into my phone. "It says that means 'Troublesome eats the squirrel.'"

"This is a bad translation!"

I laughed. I wondered if Anja made sobriety okay or if she was just a distraction from thinking about drugs. I wondered if I was just a distraction for her until she returned to Germany and her real life. She was young but she had long known the things I was just now learning. I imagined her on the phone with her friends back in Germany: *Americans are so different. They don't know how to live.*

Early one morning later in the week, still awake following a sleepless night, I walked out toward the mail room to get some air. As I was about to pass Anja's room—I wasn't going to knock and wake her, but I liked passing by her room anyway—the door opened and a tall man exited. He whispered something in German. I heard her laugh.

Spanish Richard had once told me about the reminder cards he made for whenever he had a craving. I pulled my own worn set of cards that I'd made months ago from between the covers of a large, unread book on literary theory.

This feeling will not last forever.
One day you will be nostalgic for this day.
God will take away your pain if you let him/her.

I'd never told Anja about the cards. It was less embarrassing to be addicted to drugs than to believe in God. Looking at them today, I wondered what they'd accomplished—or if they had ever accomplished anything.

I biked to the train station; I biked to Espresso House. I drank a coffee; I biked to the train station. I pulled into an alley; I screamed into my sleeve. A group of handsome Swedish college boys in peacoats stopped to stare at me. I yelled, in Swedish, "What are you staring at?" But they walked on, refusing to fight. I didn't board any trains.

* * *

That evening, as I stomped through the door and into the dormitory hallway, Anja peeked out of her room, as if she'd been out to check every time the front door opened. When she saw me, she rushed into the hall.

"Hey," I said, and tried to walk past her.

But she put her hand on my chest and stopped me. "Hey."

"What's up?"

"I want to explain."

"About what?"

"About Uli this morning."

"There's nothing to explain."

She looked down. "It's very complicated."

"It's not complicated at all. We're not together. You can do whatever you want."

"Why would you say that?"

"Because it's true."

"It's not true. It's just . . ." She paused. "Sometimes I don't know how things are with you. You are very difficult to understand."

"At least now I know how things are with you."

"Why would you say that?"

I walked past her, into my room, locked the door, and punched the wall. The wall was made of cheap material. It spiderwebbed around the impact like a windshield hit by a pebble.

It was Friday night and I was in line outside a student nation with some of the Dutch boys from my dorm waiting to get into the party.

In front of us the Swedish students spoke Swedish and the international students spoke sputtering English.

"The queue has not moved for half an hour?" said Edwin, a tall, happy Dutchman who was studying something to do with technology. "We should go back."

I didn't want to go back. I had made up my mind that it would be all right for me to drink, just this once, just tonight. Alcohol couldn't lead to drugs when there were no drugs around. But we had to get inside to get the alcohol.

"Let's give it ten more minutes," I said.

"They are letting one in for one out?" Edwin said.

"We've waited this long."

After fifteen more minutes in which we moved up only one spot, Edwin said, "Jonas, the queue is not moving."

The Dutch boys muttered their agreement. I was too tired to resist. We squeezed our way through the crowd and out of the line.

"Exchange students," a guy said to his friend in Swedish as we passed. "It must be past their bedtime."

"Is it past our bedtime?" I said in Swedish.

The guy looked at his friend and laughed nervously. "We thought you were American."

"I am." I cocked my fist back and punched the boy in the face.

The boy fell back a step and grabbed his face but didn't fall. I waited for him to swing back. But he didn't. There was stunned silence. I could feel everyone staring at me, but when I looked back, they looked away.

"What the hell?" the boy's friend said.

"Tell your friend to stop talking shit," I said.

"He was just talking!"

"It's not pleasant," I said.

The boy was quiet for a second. "It's not pleasant?"

Edwin put his hand on my shoulder and pulled me away.

We returned to the dorm after a silent walk home. Edwin unlocked his room, and the Dutch boys sat down around his table. Edwin wrapped some ice in a paper towel and handed it to me. I put it on my knuckle.

"You have any beers?" I said.

A look of panic spread across Edwin's face.

"On second thought," I said, "I should probably call it an early night. Thank you for the ice."

"No problem," Edwin said.

After I left, I heard the Dutch boys talking in hushed tones, probably about me. I went back to my room to wallow. Back in Eugene, I'd had this fantasy of returning to college armed with the knowledge I'd gained in my twenties. I would be all the things I wasn't the first time around: confident, comfortable, cool. But on the tenth anniversary of my entry into college life, I found myself living in a dorm again, just as clueless and angry as I had been the first time around.

The year after college, I had moved to Austin to live with Stella and her longtime boyfriend, Zach, in a condo his father had bought as an investment. Stella was my favorite person, and I had always liked Zach, a kind and goofy guy with a calming presence and a lack of need to dominate. He was good to Stella—had been good to her even when the rest of us were competing to prove our manhood by being mean to girls. He didn't make fun of her opinions in front of others and never complained about her when she was out of the room. Since they'd started dating, people had stopped asking me why Stella and I weren't going out, and I could stop explaining that she was the perfect friend, and people could stop raising their eyebrows at my explanation, assuming that when a guy is friends with a pretty girl he must be harboring unrequited feelings. When Zach had asked if I wanted to live in their second bedroom, I didn't even have to think about it.

Shortly after moving in, we had met one of our neighbors by the pool, a tanned and muscular twentysomething named Travis who repeated your name at every opportunity. He invited us to a kickback at his condo. I didn't want to go to a party where I had no standing—the roommate of the girl the host really wanted to invite—but Stella said that we should make some friends in town. The upside of going was that I could justify sneaking an extra dose of oxy to prepare for the evening. As far as Stella and Zach knew, I used drugs like everyone else, doing a little coke or molly every month or so—not taking pills once or twice a day, as I was doing at the time. There were friends I'd made over the last few years who had no idea that my high self wasn't just my normal personality.

At Travis's, pleasantly high, I sat down in an overly air-conditioned living room with a leather sectional couch, framed movie posters, and an acoustic guitar hanging from the wall. Travis stood up frequently to refill his drink and announce things, two girls sat on one section of the couch and scrolled through their phones, and three guys sat on another section and talked over each other about the crazy things people had done at their fraternities. I smiled at one of the girls a few times, but she didn't see me. I added in a joke about a football scandal the guys were discussing, but no one heard me.

"Jonas, a hedge fund isn't a fish, because it can fly," Travis said in the longest conversation I had that evening, "but it isn't a bird, because it can swim."

Stella gave me a covert eyebrow-raise to apologize.

As my high waned, Zach, always the perfect guest, left to buy more beers, and Travis, starting to sound a little sloppy, told Stella he had a circular bed in his room. "I'll show it to you."

His friends laughed.

Stella said, "I can picture it fine from here—like a normal bed, but round?"

Travis said he'd had the bed custom-made by his friend's start-up. "They pair you with an engineer to design your ideal bed, and then they make it, deliver it, and set it up in your room. And it's exactly the way you designed it!"

"Cool," Stella said.

"Do you know how much it cost?"

"A hundred dollars."

"Try four thousand." Travis paused. "Come see it, Stella."

"I'm good here, thanks."

I began to zone out, fantasizing about impressing these people I hated: performing a song on the acoustic guitar, heroically fighting off a masked intruder, being wildly famous. There was something in me that needed praise and violence.

But then Stella was saying, "Jesus Christ, let it go!," and Travis was saying, "Quit being such a bitch and just come look at my bed!," and I was throwing a Budweiser bottle at him. It hit him in the forehead not like shattering glass but like a decidedly solid rock.

"Whoa!" his friends yelled, and jumped up.

Travis brought his hand to his forehead in search of blood that wasn't there. "That was a mistake. That was a fucking mistake." He stood up—he was about my height but wider in the shoulders—and pulled one arm across his chest, then the other arm, then tried to crack his neck a few times.

"Are you stretching?" I said.

"You're about to find out." He waited for his friends to hold him back.

I began to laugh. "What are you going to do about it? You're not even a fish."

He took a step toward me.

One of his friends held him back and yelled at me, "You need to go!"

Stella grabbed me by the arm and led me out the door.

In the courtyard, we ran into Zach, carrying a twenty-four-pack. "Where are you going?"

"Come on." Stella led us back home.

"What happened?" Zach put the case down on the counter and opened a beer.

"Travis was being a dick to me so Jonas threw a bottle at his head."

Zach took a sip and nodded. "Good." He reached into the case and handed me a beer.

The next morning, after a sleepless night in which I both regretted throwing the bottle and not throwing more bottles, I went out to breakfast with Zach and Stella.

When Zach went to the register to pay the check, Stella put her hand on mine. "You know I love you. But you're so dumb. Please be more careful."

"I will," I said and felt good and bad at the same time.

I waited up all night and all morning for the Lund police to come around, but they never did. In the afternoon, I watched the garbage blow across the courtyard from the window of my dorm room and thought of how I should call Stella and Zach. But it was 6:00 a.m. in California. I was slow-brained from sleeplessness, and now that I knew that the police weren't going to knock on the door, I wished that Anja would. Then there was a knock on the door.

I opened to find Edwin typing on his phone.

"Hey, I'm sorry about last night—"

"It's Floyd Mayweather!" He looked up as if surprised to see me. "Did you knock anybody out today?"

"Not yet."

"We are pre-partying down the hall!" Then, suddenly somber: "But it's over now because we drank all the beer. But Floyd Mayweather! You must come to the Noah's Ark party tonight and protect us!"

That night I dressed in my octopus costume and took the train to Malmö. It was only a twelve-minute train ride to Malmö Central, but I had never been to the city before, as it had been described to me as a postindustrial ghetto that had given Sweden Zlatan Ibrahimović and nothing else. When I stepped off the train, the downtown looked nothing like what I'd pictured. There were bridges, glowing canals, an elegant hotel with a copper roof, and sleek glass-fronted buildings along the water. It looked old but recently remodeled.

I walked down toward the harbor. The party boat, docked in the canal that let out into the Sound, hadn't opened its doors yet. Students were lined up at the waterfront: a hundred monkeys, reindeer, leopards, alligators, fish, bats, and cats, ready to desecrate the legacy of a central Christian narrative.

I saw Anja up ahead. Before we stopped speaking, she had told me that she was going as a Bambi, which I had told her was a character, not an animal. (To which she had responded, "No.") She wore a fur vest and face paint, with long black lashes glued to her eyelids. Next to her stood Uli, with a Batman mask, black jeans, and a black T-shirt. I looked around for the Dutch boys. Just then, a herd of tall men in horse-head masks ran toward me. I clenched my fists and took a step back.

"Are you ready to party, Mayweather?" Edwin yelled, pulling up his mask, patting me on the chest drunkenly.

"We're boarding up the windows tonight!" I said, unclenching my fists.

The Dutch boys laughed and offered me high fives. They liked it when I used American slang they hadn't heard. But they all watched American television and listened to American music, and I had run out of American slang they hadn't heard after the first week. I had since been making things up.

I lit a cigarette with one of my two working arms.

The boat was a double-decker called *The Dubliner*. I followed the Dutch into the lower level, where a dance floor had opened and a few dozen animals were already dancing terribly.

Edwin told me about Johan's Ark, a life-size replica of Noah's Ark built to biblical specifications by a Dutch creationist.

"That sounds like something an American would build," I said.

"It does!"

The walls of the dance floor flashed Studio 54–like with hundreds of colored lightbulbs. I found myself dancing in a circle with the Dutch. Anja and Uli and a few other Germans from the dorm joined the circle. I wanted Anja to look at me the way she used to look at me from across the room. But if she had looked at me, I would probably just have looked away. The DJ played a nineties rock song mashed up with a dance beat under a loop of a few lines from Obama's inauguration address. Edwin danced in a spastic rhythm that made sense because he appeared totally comfortable in it.

I walked over to Anja and leaned in. "I'm going to go smoke."

She leaned over to my ear, cupped her hand, said, "Okay," and started dancing again.

I had always thought of getting high as taking a vacation from myself—a break that I had earned from all the hours I spent being me. I had considered this a very intellectual way of thinking about it, until I'd started attending meetings and heard heroin addicts and tweakers and homeless pill fiends say that they'd thought of getting high as taking a little vacation from themselves.

"But the vacation always ends, man," Big Ed had said. He'd lost his legs when he fell from the extended ladder of a stolen fire engine that his friend was driving. "You always have to come home to you."

On the top deck of the boat, I saw a boy in a full-body alligator costume, something like a football mascot might wear, holding up a girl in butterfly wings. She straddled his waist, pulled him toward her, and stretched over the railing suicidally. I lit my cigarette and looked out at the verdigris rooftops of downtown Malmö. We hadn't left the dock.

I found a security guard with a shaved head and a red tattoo of an eagle on his left forearm. I asked him in Swedish why the cruise hadn't left the dock.

The security guard said that this wasn't a cruise—it was just a party on a boat.

"You think we want to go out on open water with two hundred drunk college students?"

I wanted to ask him about his tattoo, then about drugs and if he knew someone who sold them. But the small talk that preceded asking for drugs sounded all wrong in my head, and in trying to translate *You getting into anything later tonight?* into Swedish, I remembered that I didn't do drugs anymore.

Back in North Carolina, right before I tried to quit for the first time, I had, hoping to subdue a heroin hangover, taken too much methadone and Valium. The combination had left me struggling to stay awake in a frightening way that was nothing like falling asleep. I walked out of my apartment telling myself, "You're awake, you're awake," focusing hard on every step, every breath. I found a taxi and rode to the emergency room.

At the desk I was met by a young woman in sky-blue scrubs. "How can I help you?"

That's when I woke to the mistake I was making—the control I'd be giving up as soon as I told her what I'd done. They could do whatever they wanted to me in there.

"I don't have insurance. I can't afford this." I turned and hurried to the exit.

Just as I reached the door, I heard the nurse yell, "Wait!"

She came running after me. Her voice sounded so worried that I would've told her whatever she wanted to know.

"You have to sign this form." She handed me a paper. "It says that you're leaving of your own accord and that you accept the risks."

I'd signed the paper and left. I hadn't died, of course—I'd just gotten sick and then slept so deeply that I was surprised when I woke up.

The bass pounded the deck from below. I walked back over to the security guard.

"You know where I can find some *ladd*?" I said in Swedish. *Ladd* was the only slang for drugs that I knew in Swedish. It meant "cocaine," which was not exactly what I wanted—but, communication-wise, it would have to do.

"Why would I know that?"

I shrugged. I offered the security guard a cigarette. The guard accepted. I lit it for him, cupping my hand around the flame, then igniting the sleeve of a dangling octopus arm. "Shit." I swatted at the arm until the fire was out.

The guard laughed. "I don't have any coke. But I might have a friend who has pills."

"What kind?"

"MDMA."

"Does he have the pills that kill pain?"

"What?"

"Strong painkilling medicine?"

"Sometimes he has Dolol."

A rush of warmth shot up through me. I remembered seeing a mention of Dolol in a book by a Palestinian Danish poet. It was the European name for tramadol, which, while not nearly as good as oxycodone, gave you a nice calm ride, like a weekend trip to a nearby city, which would have been nothing special if not for the fact that you lived in a shithole.

"Let me find an ATM. Don't go anywhere."

"Where would I go?"

I stomped out my cigarette and speed-walked back to the door. A voice screamed in my head, but it was distant, like a child being beaten next door. I was already alone in my room with the pills.

"Hey, octopus!"

I turned around.

"I was calling after you many times." Anja walked toward me. She was out of breath and had a little sheen of sweat on her makeup.

"I was lost in thought."

"What were you thinking about?" She stopped in front of me.

I scratched at one of my working arms. I was impatient to get the money. "I hate dancing. That's what I was thinking about."

"I know you do." She laughed. "Every time you dance you look like you're trying to solve a math problem."

"So then why do you dance with me?"

"Because I like dancing with you."

"Okay." I needed to leave. "I have to find a bathroom."

"If you spoke German, I think I could make you understand."

I sighed. "Make me understand what?"

She tilted her head and looked at me, like, *Come on.* Then she leaned in and whispered the softest German. It started with *"Du bist."* At one point she said *"aber ich."* But I didn't understand the rest.

"What did you say?"

She threw up her hands in exasperation. "If I could say it in English, I would say it in English!"

She grabbed an empty sleeve and tugged me close.

We stood there for a while and I felt like I could stay there for a while longer—that I could carry on with both the body and the mind I had been assigned.

ABOUT A MONTH BEFORE THE END OF THE SEMESTER AND
Anja's return to Germany, I found myself, unable to sleep, squeezed
into the only nook of the mattress that Anja had not starfished herself across. She had chosen me over Uli, which made me happy, at
first. But as the joy settled into contentment, it slid from my attention, the way an aching tooth stops existing the day it stops aching.
Tonight, instead of thinking about how the girl I liked was sleeping
next to me, my brain was replaying all the lies I would tell when I
used to get high. I'd start a conversation with a stranger at a bar—ask
for a lighter or something—and then just start lying. Wherever the
strangers said they were from or whatever they said they did for a
living, I would, without thinking, respond, "I spent some time in
Wyoming," "I used to work the late shift at a gas station," "My mom
was actually a nurse." Then I'd make up a story on the spot—just to
talk, just to be heard. I loved the feeling of talking without fear or
purpose. I'd wake up the next morning plagued by memories, worried that I'd see the person again and not remember what stories I'd
already told them.

I wanted to hear Anja's voice and escape my memories, but she
was asleep. I remembered that she had the remnants of a liter bottle

of Coca-Cola mixed with vodka—the preferred drink of the Germans in my dorm—left in her bag. Without much thought between wanting it and taking it, I snuck out of bed, found the bottle in her purse, brought it to the bathroom, closed the door, twisted the cap off, heard the slight fizz, and took my first drink since I'd moved to Sweden. The vodka-Coke was room temperature, a little flat, and you could barely feel the burn from the diluted liquor. But it was there.

I drank until the bottle was empty, then tucked it behind the trash can under the sink. I curled back into bed and felt calm. It wasn't so much that I was drunk, but that, for the first time in forever, I wasn't agonizing over whether to do it. The decision had already been made. Now there was nothing required of me.

So I started drinking again and nothing terrible happened. I didn't take any drugs. Parties were easier to attend. People were easier to be around. Words were easier to speak and hear. Waking up in the morning was a little harder but not that bad. The only downside I noticed was that on the day after drinking, even if I woke up feeling okay, my ability to function eroded by the hour. By four in the afternoon, reading would be difficult, and I'd stare at the page until the words blurred. I'd scan through a text on the history of vernacular in the European novel, but no meaning would pass back to my brain. By seven in the evening I could barely carry on a conversation until I started drinking again. I certainly couldn't write—the *BuzzFeed* novel was going nowhere and the jellyfish story refused to be written. But I hadn't been able to write since I quit drugs, so it didn't feel like I was losing much there.

*   *   *

It was on a hungover Sunday night near the end of the term that I picked my first stupid fight with Anja. We had gone to a party at one of the student nations the night before, and I'd had eleven drinks. Anja had drunk a fair amount herself, but the difference was that, once we got to the party, Anja would stop drinking so she could dance, and I would drink faster so that I could dance. When we'd gotten home, we'd had fun rough sex, slept like drunks, and woken up sore from clenching the wrong muscles all night.

In the afternoon, I had taken the train up to Helsingborg to have lunch with family friends, and when I'd returned, in a bad mood for no good reason, I'd texted Anja to see if she wanted to come over. She'd written back that she was making dinner with three of the Dutch boys from our floor, but that she would come by later.

I knew that my anger didn't make sense. I didn't like making group dinners, and I had been the one who'd left for the afternoon without inviting Anja. She slept over most nights and would be doing so again tonight. But the anger refused to be wrangled by logic. I didn't like that she thought she could just have me waiting for her whenever she was done. I didn't like that she was favoring other boys over me.

When she came to my room a few hours later, she was all smiles.

"Hi!" She kissed me and asked me about my day, and I said it was fine, and she asked what I'd done, and I said nothing much, and she asked if I wanted to *Löffel*, which was not a verb but simply the noun for "spoon," and I said sure, so we lay down in bed and spooned.

"Is something wrong?" she said to the wall she was facing.

"No."

"Are you sure?"

"Yeah."

We lay there in silence for a while until I felt something wet on my arm.

"Are you crying?" I said.

"No."

I turned her over, took her chin between my fingers, and gently lifted her face up.

"You're crying."

"Not very much."

"What's wrong?" I said, trying to make my voice soft.

"I have been waiting all day to see you and you don't want to talk to me."

My anger had settled between us like a pouting child. "I do want to talk to you."

"No, you don't. I'm moving, and whenever I bring it up, you change the subject. And now you've decided that you don't want to be together anymore, and you're trying to make me break up with you. It's not very nice."

"It's not that." Though maybe it was partly that. She was right that I hadn't wanted to commit to a long-distance relationship. "I was just annoyed that you wanted to see your guy friends instead of seeing me."

"That's it?"

"Yeah."

She sniffled. "I thought it was much worse."

"No, that's it."

Then she punched me in the chest—very hard considering how little space there was between us for her to wind up.

"Ow!"

"You are such an idiot! You make me feel bad for something so stupid."

I said that she was right and that it was a stupid thing for me to be upset about. "But you don't have to hit me. I have soft bones."

"There is no such thing as soft bones."

I pulled her close to show that I could still be close. I told her that I wasn't trying to get her to break up with me. I shared a thought that I'd been toying with for a while: that we could meet in Hamburg—not too far from Lund or from her family's home in eastern Germany—for New Year's.

"Okay," she said happily. She was quiet for a while. "You will have a very good time in Germany."

"Of course I will—you'll be there." I kissed her. "Am I still an idiot?"

"Yes. But you are my idiot."

Getting out of the shower the following morning, I found that I had a small bruise on my chest.

"Look what you did to me," I said to Anja that evening as she pulled off my shirt.

"Oh my God!" She dropped the shirt and covered her mouth. "I am so sorry!"

"It doesn't hurt."

"I hit you and it bruised!"

"It's just a little bruise." I realized she was actually worried. "It's not a big deal."

"It *is* a big deal! I can't believe I hurt you."

"You didn't hurt me, Katze." I pulled her into a hug. "It's an affection bruise."

"There is no such thing as an affection bruise," she said, crying. "There is no such thing."

In Eugene, during my months of relapsing and editing memoirs, I had once brought home a girl from the Barn Light, who, after sex, wanted to massage my shoulders.

"I'm training to be a masseuse," she explained. Which made sense, since no professional would want to practice their profession in their free time.

"Train away."

She climbed onto my back. "Relax."

"I am relaxed."

"You keep clenching your muscles."

"Do I?"

"Take a deep breath. And let your shoulders sink." She waited. "See—that's what relaxing feels like."

"That is nice."

She kneaded my shoulders and I zoned out.

"You're doing it again! Relax!"

"The yelling is definitely helping with the relaxation!"

"Sorry." She sighed. "But it's like you think I'm going to hit you."

I'd never been worried that a woman was going to *actually* hit me. With Alexandra, she was so much smaller than me that, on the two occasions she tried to attack me, the righteousness I gained from her violence far outweighed any harm. But I was always bracing since I didn't know what would set her off. Finding out that I'd hooked up with one of her friends during one of our breakups, she wouldn't be mad for more than a few hours. But if I turned in a story to workshop that featured a narrator with a blond love interest, when Alexandra was a brunette, she would storm out of the classroom. Once she left a theater in the middle of a movie and drove off without me because I laughed at a scene she thought was degrading.

But she also had to brace for punches. Not knowing about the drugs, it must have been hard for her to know when I would be laughing and generous, and when I'd be distant or invite the attention of other women out of spite. An innocuous comment, if she made it in the middle of an oxy comedown she didn't know was happening, could close me off for the entire night. I never hit her, but the threat of my silent rages must have hung over her as much as the threat of her storm-outs and glass-breaking hung over me.

On the day that Anja moved back to Germany, I rode the bus with her to Lund Central. She cried when the train arrived. Sadness snuck up on me, unexpectedly, since I would be seeing her again in twelve days for New Year's. We kissed and waved and she was gone.

That night I got drunk alone, and the next day I sat in my room with the curtains closed, drinking, and scrolling through things I'd published when I was still writing. I wanted to figure out how I'd done it. I pulled up an essay I'd written about the literary depictions of hangovers.

The greatest hangover scene in literature? Is it from Cormac McCarthy's *Suttree*? Kingsley Amis's *Lucky Jim*? Or is the best hangover scene, as Amis himself suggested, from Kafka's *Metamorphosis*, when Gregor Samsa awoke to find that he'd turned into a bug and that people would not stop yelling at him to go to work?

The question of the best hangover scene is especially relevant to American literature because American writers love to drink. Tom Dardis argued that the Lost Generation of American writers had glorified alcohol in a way that writers from other countries had not. He argued that Prohibition had made getting as drunk as possible as often as possible a social statement, and that Hemingway, Faulkner, and Fitzgerald all partook. Once Prohibition ended and getting fucked-up was just getting fucked-up, the Great American Writers were already addicted.

If you went to grad school for writing, you heard the lesson repeated over and over from older writers: Alcohol does not make you a better writer. Drugs do not make you a better writer. I knew that Denis Johnson wrote *Jesus' Son* only once he got clean. That David Foster Wallace wrote *Infinite Jest* only after he quit drinking. That Cormac McCarthy wrote *Suttree* sober. The eccentric professor in Wilmington had told me about his days at Iowa with the great alcoholics and assured me that the tragic substance abuse you read about in biographies was not as charming in real life. The myth lost some of its luster when you were in a room with the great alcoholic and he was ruining the party—hitting on the female undergraduates until they cried and then pissing himself on the couch.

Even if the drunk didn't piss himself, he never wanted to listen. Every old barfly who sat down next to me in Lula's told stories upon stories, lies upon lies, without ever waiting for a response or giving me a chance to speak. Raymond Carver had told his students to write dialogue in non sequiturs because no one listened to each other anyway. Which was true—if you were a drunk. But one of the beautiful things about Carver's later stories, the ones he wrote after getting sober, was how his characters did listen to one another, and how this communication presented opportunities for connections—if only momentary—that you didn't see much in his earlier stories. When my dad would get drunk, before he left when I was fourteen, he would express gratitude through self-pity. My mom always refused to leave him, but she never hesitated to leave him with me when he was drunk. "You're the only person who's ever listened to me," he'd tell me. But whenever I tried to talk, he'd cut me off and then dive into a misty-eyed monologue about how his own father had never loved him, and his mother had hated him, and how he would never treat me like that. It was instructive to see that a person could feel so sorry for himself without feeling sorry for anyone else.

I skimmed the next few paragraphs of my essay (there should be a name for the sadness that comes from catching yourself skimming your own writing) until a sentence made me stop: *Since I've quit drinking, I've noticed that* . . .

I read it again. At the time I'd published the essay, I was drinking every night and spending every waking hour high. I had kept a bottle of tramadol on the nightstand to help me get out of bed in the morning. But here I had published a piece of nonfiction claiming to use the lessons I'd learned in sobriety.

It shouldn't have been such a shock to see it. I used to tell the women I brought home from bars that I was in the midst of quitting heroin, uttering these words while still high, sometimes on heroin but more often on pain pills. Sometimes I made up stories to tell them, but more often I hinted at tragedy I didn't want to share. The truth was too boring: My life, like all lives, regularly presented me with pain. When I found a drug that made the pain go away, I took it. I got high because I liked to get high. I drank because I liked to drink. Even during the last year of grad school in Wilmington, when my fellow aspiring novelist and drinking buddy had disappeared for two months following a breakup, and I'd had to go with two other classmates to pull him out of a motel room and carry him to the car to take him to rehab (thirty pounds lighter, skin bruised and yellow, he'd lost the ability to walk)—even then I had thought, *I'm not like that.*

I had always believed that the problem with alcoholics was not that they drank but that they drank in the daytime. I never drank in the morning and couldn't understand why anyone would do so—it was so exhausting. You ended up tired and headache-squinting and hangover-cranky before you even went to bed. But now, without drugs to relieve my hangovers, I began to understand exactly why writers drank in the morning. As I noodled around with these thoughts, I looked at the closed curtains of my room. I looked at my fourth Carlsberg Elefant Öl of the afternoon on the table.

I stood up and poured the rest of the can into the sink.

"I will not drink anymore," I said to myself. "I will not drink anymore in the daytime."

THE NIGHT BEFORE MY SWEDISH CLASSMATES LEFT TOWN TO visit their families for Christmas, I went to a little party my hipster friend from class, Bengt, was having at his place in Malmö. Bengt lived on the fifth floor of a block-long brick building on Sallerups-vägen, a busy street in the gentrifying blue-collar neighborhood of Värnhem. We'd go out for beers in Lund every week or two, but I'd never before been to his apartment.

"What's up!" he said in English, opening the door and giving me a hug. He wore skinny jeans rolled up to the ankle and a long-sleeved island-print shirt rolled up past his skinny biceps.

"*Tjena, grabben!*" I answered—some approximation of "Hey, buddy!" that I had settled on as my greeting for friends.

Bengt's studio was packed with people talking at drunk volumes. Karin, a cute girl Bengt had recently started seeing, was laughing loudly, and she gave me a big hug though I had only met her once. From class I saw Samuel, Jakob, Lennart, and Adam there, along with two girls and a boy that I didn't know, who I assumed were Karin's friends. We sat in a circle on the floor, as Bengt had no furniture besides a box-spring-less mattress. We drank warmish beer from the cans everyone had bought at Systembolaget before closing time.

We crowded around the windowsill to smoke out the window. They told stories in Swedish. I interjected a comment or one-liner here and there, but I couldn't yet manage a full story in Swedish.

I found myself smoking with Karin, who asked what I thought about something—a word that I had recently seen on the front pages of the Swedish papers without understanding what it meant. The headlines suggested that this word was a big deal, and that it had something to do with the nationalist Sweden Democrats and the center-right Moderates.

"What do *you* think?" I said.

Karin said that it was a fiasco, and that this was what happened when you—and then she said a few words that I didn't understand, sprinkled with a few words (*patriarchy, right-wing*) that I did.

My Swedish politics were confused at best. The previous summer, I had watched the conservative prime minister deliver a speech in which he explained that refugees would soon pour into Europe from the Middle East and that Swedes would have to "open their hearts" to these people, even if it meant cutting domestic spending. The amazing thing was that, outside of the extremist Sweden Democrats, all the conservative parties were on board with the sentiment. If to open your hearts and wallets to Muslim refugees was right-wing, then what was left-wing?

In the US, I was pretty far left. In Sweden, I thought I was center-left. I agreed with the Swedish left on opposing the privatization of schools and hospitals, which, according to my classmates, had proved disastrous during the previous eight years of center-right governing. But I was frustrated by the Swedish leftist feeling that everything that they disagreed with was the worst thing ever, given that the situation in Sweden was better than almost anywhere else in the world. I couldn't stand their tone of whining entitlement. But this scared the shit out of me, because when I said "whining entitlement," I sounded just like an American Republican.

I had been lost in the lead-up to the 2014 parliamentary elections in September, the first election that I had lived in Sweden and been eligible to vote in. In the US, I would know exactly what was meant by, for example, "family values," "integrity of marriage," and "real Americans," but in Sweden, I lacked the context to read between the lines and understand the meaning of each party's political language. I struggled to understand what words like *integration*, which was spelled the same in Swedish, meant. Only later did I learn that *integration* meant blaming immigrants for not learning Swedish quickly enough, while ignoring that the segregation in Swedish cities and the segregation of Swedish schools made learning Swedish a monumental task. I read party platforms and thought that almost all of them sounded reasonable, since I couldn't understand what they were really saying.

On top of that, Sweden had nine parties to choose from. I was used to a two-party system, in which what you were, Democrat or Republican, determined not only which news you read, but which world you lived in. I had tried to explain this to Swedes who asked about American politics. I'd used the split between the two realities to explain how America could support, for example, gun rights when so many Americans were being killed in mass shootings.

Swedish politics were polarized, but not in the same way as

American politics. Swedish voters would sometimes change parties from election to election based on the party's recent performance and current platform. Swedish newspapers even offered long questionnaires in election years to match you with the party to which you were best suited. In early September, I had spent an afternoon at my computer, reading the Wikipedia entries for each party, then filling in bubbles on the questionnaires.

The first quiz asked whether the government should impose an extra tax on jet fuel for flights within the EU. Twenty-nine questions later, the quiz told me I was a center-right Moderate. Unsatisfied, I found a second quiz, which asked if the state should require passing Swedish exams as a prerequisite for refugees to receive government benefits. My answers suggested I should vote for the Feminist Party. I took a third quiz, which had a lot of questions about the restrictions on hunting wolves, an animal I didn't even know lived in Sweden, and my answers indicated that I should be a member of the fascist Sweden Democrats. After eight quizzes—one of which asked if I would ever consider taking the last cookie from the plate at *fika*—I still couldn't find a party that fit my beliefs. I realized that this was partly because, once I was out of the either/or-ness of Democrat/ Republican, I found that I didn't know, specifically, what I believed.

On the day of the election, I had walked down to the polling place in the university building near my dormitory still undecided. It was crowded; Sweden had an 85 percent voter participation rate. In line, I began to sweat. It was as if I were about to take a drug test knowing I was just on the edge of what the internet said was the life span of oxy in the bloodstream. When I got to the front of the line,

I was informed that my address was still listed with the government as my cousin's apartment in Stockholm. I was told that I had to vote at my Stockholm polling place, three hundred miles north of Lund. Which was such a relief.

Bengt's party rolled into the morning. The nonserious drinkers left. It would be a week before I went to Hamburg for New Year's, and I was eager to find something to fill that time with. I wanted to write and publish something, anything, and I'd gotten it into my head that I should find a Swedish writer to study. I would read all their books over the next week, then write an essay about the Swedish writer, which I could sell to an American arts magazine or literary journal. The problem was that I didn't have any Swedish writers I liked. Swedes didn't study their national literature at the university level the way Americans did theirs. In class we were just as likely to be versed in American, British, French, or German literature as the Swedish canon.

"There aren't any Swedish writers worth reading," Karin said.

But the boys from class offered: August Strindberg, Selma Lagerlöf, Vilhelm Moberg, Tomas Tranströmer, Pär Lagerkvist, Moa Martinson, Harry Martinson, Lars Gustafsson, and Hjalmar Söderberg. I liked Söderberg's clipped delivery, Strindberg's cynicism, and Tranströmer's heart-stopping images. But the writer who piqued my interest was one that Jakob mentioned: Stig Dagerman.

Dagerman was the tragic wunderkind of postwar Swedish letters, Jakob told me. After World War II, from the ages of twenty-two to twenty-six, Dagerman published several books to great acclaim.

"But then he killed himself," Jakob said.

I was, despite my knowledge of how immature it was, still fascinated by prodigies, geniuses, and tragic figures who died by their own hand. The next day, before my hangover set in and the library closed, I checked out all the books by and about Dagerman that I could find. Over the coming days, I read Dagerman for as long as my hangovers would allow. I read about his suicide. Plagued by writer's block, guilt, and anxiety, he shut the garage door and started the engine. I tried to dig into the novels—which alternated between swirling stream of consciousness and nightmarish Freudian lyricism—with little success. What grabbed me was his essay collection, *German Autumn*. Dagerman wrote the essays at the age of twenty-three, on assignment from a Swedish newspaper to cover the conditions of German civilians after World War II. And much of the book took place in Hamburg—where I was going!

Dagerman had been a Swedish leftist and anti-Nazi activist, married to a refugee who'd fled the Nazis. But when Dagerman traveled through Germany in 1946, he saw a defeated population that the world had agreed deserved to suffer. He saw 7 million German civilians left homeless by Allied bombing. He saw families living in flooded cellars and subsisting on what dirty potatoes they could find. He saw mothers forced to prostitute themselves to foreign soldiers to feed their children. He wondered if it wasn't important to maintain the ability to feel for those suffering, even if they deserved to suffer.

Part of me admired Dagerman's empathy. But a part of me also wondered if it was real or if it was just a literary device. I figured the answer would come to me in Hamburg.

* * *

I did a solo Christmas in Lund, which I hadn't thought would matter, since I didn't even like Christmas. But the holiday was lonelier
when it was dark and snowy outside than when it was seventy degrees and sunny. If you ignored the golden tinsel hanging down over
the strip-mall storefronts, Christmas in California could be just like
any other day. In Sweden, Christmas was definitively Christmas.

On Christmas Eve, sitting in my room alone, I felt a little down.
I tried to call Anja, but she didn't pick up, as she was likely eat-
ing eighteen kinds of sausage with her big German family, listening
while her grandfather read a book to the children about Santa Claus
marauding through the forest and slaying the naughty. I tried to
call Stella, who didn't pick up either. But soon after, Stella texted
me a picture of her family and Zach, sitting around the tree in ugly
Christmas sweaters.

We miss you! the caption said.

The picture made me feel better, for a second, but then more alone.
Things were happening without me—people were growing. Stella
would probably soon marry Zach, and then my two college buddies
would be adults. I didn't feel homesick or want to return to the US, nor
did I want Stella and Zach to come visit me in Sweden—the thought
of visitors was exhausting. I just wanted time to stop for a while.

I decided that I should try to do something nice for someone
else. I went to the Save the Children website and bought a goat for
a family in Mali, which the promotional materials suggested would
help the family eat and survive for a year. I was a little disappointed
when I realized that I wouldn't get to see the family receive the goat.

After the goat purchase, I still had three hundred kronor, about $40, left in what I calculated to be my charity budget, so I biked up to the ATM by the student union, withdrew the money in hundreds, and biked down to the ICA grocery in the strip mall. A Rom woman always sat out front on the hard concrete, saying, *"Hej hej,"* to everyone who walked by, and clasping her hands in a thank-you prayer whenever someone dropped a few kronor in her cup. Today she wore a red scarf around her head. A long dress stuck out under a winter jacket.

She smiled at me when I approached. *"Hej hej."*

"Hej hej," I said, rolling my bike alongside me. I pulled a hundred-kronor note from my wallet and placed it in her cup.

"Tack, tack, tack."

"God jul." I wasn't sure what I was hoping for out of the interaction, but I felt kind of good afterward.

Then I biked—slowly and slippingly in the snow—down to Lund Central, where the other ICA was located. Usually a large Rom woman sat by the entrance in what looked like an uncomfortable position—one leg tucked under her, one stretched out in front. But today it was a younger girl, maybe in her late teens. I took a hundred-kronor note and placed it in her cup. Her eyes got big and she said something in a language I didn't understand.

"De nada," I said, for reasons that escaped me. But she smiled and bowed her head and I smiled and bowed my head and got on my bike. Now I was feeling really good.

In front of the nearly deserted entrance to the train station across the street stood a Middle Eastern man in a long ratty peacoat. He was holding up a copy of the magazine a nonprofit organization published for the homeless to sell.

"*God jul.*"

"*God jul,*" the man said back to me.

I handed the man my last hundred-kronor note.

"*Det kostar bara fyrtio,*" he said—it only cost forty.

"It's all for you." I waved off the magazine. "*God jul.*"

"I'm not a beggar. Here." He handed me the magazine. "It's only forty."

"I don't want one." I had bought an issue a few months earlier and found that it was maybe the worst magazine ever written. I handed the man the money. "It's a present."

"I'm not a fucking beggar!" The man waved his hands. "Give it to the Gypsy across the street!"

I walked back across the street and dropped another hundred in the cup of the young Rom woman in front of the ICA. Then I jumped on my bike without making eye contact and pedaled off, wondering why I hadn't just bought the magazine. When I got home, I drank until the memory of the failure faded away. Midway through my fourth beer, I began to think of all the acceptance letters from editors that would soon appear in my inbox. I could see the names of the editors and the congratulatory subject lines so clearly that it was strange waking up in the morning and remembering that I hadn't written anything at all.

ANJA MET ME IN THE ARRIVALS AREA OF THE HAMBURG AIR-port wearing a thick scarf and a puffy jacket. Her hair was tightly braided, and I felt a surge of happiness when I saw her big smile.

"Meine Katze." I kissed her.

"Mein Jonas." She kissed me back. "I am sorry, but I have a flu."

"Poor you," I said, trying not to recoil. I was sad for her that she had to be sick over the little time we had together. But I was also sad for myself that I would now be sick.

She drove us into the city in her mother's little black Renault. Once we'd settled into the apartment I'd rented for the weekend with my student-loan money, she looked so tired that I assured her it was fine if she just wanted to go to sleep. After lying with her until her breathing loudened and slowed, I rifled through my bag for the whiskey bottle I'd bought at the duty-free and drank half of it sitting in the chair in front of the window.

Anja felt a little better in the morning, so we went out in the city, where nearly every surface was covered in advertisements for *The Lion King*. *Lion King* buses on the outskirts of downtown, *Lion King* boats on the Elbe, and finally, across the river, a large yellow dome with a lion's head proclaiming DER KÖNIG DER LÖWEN.

As we walked along the water, Anja blew her nose and asked me what was wrong.

"Nothing," I said, realizing that I'd been quiet for a while.

"You're not having a good time."

"I am having a good time. I'm happy to be here with you." I squeezed her arm, trying to make it true.

During my time alone, longing for Anja, I had forgotten that relationships often involved taking care of another person at times when you didn't feel like taking care of another person. I was either feeling guilty about my failure to take care of Anja, annoyed at the need for me to take care of her, or both. Since my classmates had gone home for the holidays, I had only talked with cashiers and Christmas-charity targets, and I'd wanted to spend the weekend laughing with Anja, curling up next to her, and feeling at home while I gathered material for the great essay I would write about Dagerman and Hamburg. But I wasn't feeling what I wanted to feel for Anja or for Hamburg. Hamburg was not the dystopian ruinscape that Dagerman had described. It was just a boring city that inspired no literary insights. I thought about drugs and how they must be easier to find here than in Sweden. In Berlin, Bengt had told me, all you had to do was walk into a bar and someone offered you coke. It wouldn't be the same in Hamburg—but it wouldn't be too hard either.

As we rode the train back to the Nord part of the city where we were staying, I thought of a scene from *German Autumn*. Dagerman comes upon a train of German civilians who fled Essen for the Bavarian countryside during the Allied bombing. After the war ended, they were deported by the Bavarian government and told to return to their homes. But now they're not allowed back into Essen. The city is too ravaged to support even those who had stayed. They've been waiting outside Essen for a week in train cars deemed too leaky to transport "perishable" goods—refugees in their own country, suffering and dying while they wait for a green light.

The sick passengers beg Dagerman's German guide for help. The guide tells them that he's just here to give a tour to the nice Swedish journalist. Later, Dagerman wrote that he tried to impart kindness while gathering material to share the refugees' plight with the world. But he wondered what good it is visiting the suffering when one has no medicine to offer, only empathy.

"Journalism is the art of coming too late as early as possible," he wrote to a friend while touring Germany. "I'll never learn that."

Back at the apartment, I saw that the apartment owners kept a scale on the shelf above the toilet, so I took it down to weigh myself. The scale read 86 kilograms, which was too much. I took out my phone and converted the number to pounds: 190. When I'd left the US, I'd weighed 175. I stepped on the scale again and found that it read 86 again.

I came out of the bathroom and said to Anja that the scale must be broken. "It says I weigh eighty-six kilos."

"That sounds right." Wearing pajamas and a scarf, she was boiling water in the kitchen for tea.

"It's not right. I weighed seventy-nine when I came here."

"Well. You have gotten a little bigger."

"I've gotten a little bigger?"

"You still look good. I don't care."

"I'm going to get you some ibuprofen for your flu." I returned to the bathroom. I looked in the mirror. I lifted up my shirt. My belly protruded a little. When I turned, there was a crease in the skin down my side, between hip and rib. I *had* put on weight. How had I not noticed?

I found my big bottle of ibuprofen, bought from the Rite Aid back home, took it out of my toiletries bag, and brought it to Anja. "Take two."

"Thank you." But then she looked at the bottle in disbelief. "Five hundred pills? Why do Americans sell it in such a large bottle?"

"Convenience?"

"If you take forty, you will die."

"Don't take forty. Take two."

"Here you cannot buy more than twenty at a time. This is irresponsible."

"Can you buy a knife here? Because you only need one of those to die."

"It's different swallowing pills and cutting yourself with a knife. One is much more difficult. And what if you don't really want to die? If you have five hundred pills just lying there, and you feel bad, you can just take them. But if you have to go to two stores to buy them, maybe you have another thought on the way and you don't want to die anymore."

"I think people who want to kill themselves have stronger feelings than that."

"Maybe there are different levels to wanting to kill yourself."

I thought of Dagerman, whose suicide was not his first attempt. His biographer wrote that when Dagerman asphyxiated from the car fumes, he had been trying to get out of the garage, but had changed his mind too late and died while trying to escape his own decision. Then I remembered that this thought had nothing to do with my conversation with Anja, and that I had, for a moment, confused the things I'd read with the things I'd experienced.

"Do they have cars in Germany? Because you can easily kill yourself with one of those. Or household cleaning products. Or an oven. Or—"

"Okay, okay." She kissed me on the cheek. "I want to take a catnap now."

As she slept, I began to google neighborhoods in Hamburg to find the one with the highest crime rate, as that was the one most likely to have a drug trade. But I closed the window before I got too far. I would not leave my girlfriend sleeping in a rented apartment so that I could take a train to a dangerous neighborhood to try to buy heroin in German. I could barely order a kebab in German. Instead I finished off the whiskey I'd bought at the duty-free. During our ibuprofen argument, Anja had not once used her being sick to guilt me into not being such an asshole. I appreciated that and wanted to tell her, but she was sleeping, so I nestled next to her, stroked her back, and said, *"Meine Katze."*

When she woke up, I kissed her on the head.

"I'm sorry that I am sick and you aren't having fun."

"Don't be sorry. I'm sorry. I'm happy just being here with you."
And in moments like this, I was.

We kissed, then kissed some more, then she started to go down
on me. I didn't want her to do it when she was sick. But I didn't stop
her, at first because I could only imagine how bad it felt to be told
to stop when you were trying to fix something, and then because of
how good it felt for her not to stop. Afterward I went down on her
and she came with a long sigh. We cuddled and she seemed happier
and I was happier.

After she fell asleep, I tried to write about Dagerman. Outside
Essen, Dagerman sees a man console a hysterical girl from the train
by rolling her wheelchair around in the rain and mud. Dagerman
ends the vignette with this image of admirable consolation offered in the face of hopelessness. But by the end of his life, as he
sank deeper into depression, he began to categorize the temporary
consolations—the distractions from suffering that were the lifeblood
of *German Autumn*—as false consolations.

I wondered how much Dagerman had believed in temporary
consolations even in *German Autumn*—how much he'd believed that
his writing could change anything besides his reputation.

On the morning of December 31, I woke in my Hamburg bed with
a start. A bang outside the window. Then another.

I shot up. "What's happening?"

"Fireworks," Anja mumbled.

"What?"

She put her hand on my face and pressed my head into the pillow. "There are fireworks. Go back to sleep now."

I got up and looked out the window: Sure enough, people were shooting fireworks out their windows onto the street. It was 10:00 a.m. I dressed and put on a jacket, sat down on the single hard iron chair on the balcony, lit a cigarette, and took in the normality with which the Germans treated the chaos—the way they sidestepped explosions on their way to get their coffee. Pointy red silos with long wooden stems were scattered about the street. I made a note to remember this for my Dagerman essay. I had a headache. My muscles hurt. I couldn't remember the last time my body had felt good. Hamburg had not made me feel differently from Lund, but I determined that today I would have a good time and make sure that Anja also had a good time.

I went inside, put bread in the toaster, boiled some eggs, and put on water for Anja's tea. When the teakettle started whistling, Anja emerged from bed sleepy faced and sweatpants-ed.

"How are you feeling, Katze?"

She sniffled and stretched her arms over her head. "Much better." She put her arms around my neck and leaned into me. When I brought out the eggs and bread, she said, "Ohhh. I am so lucky."

It occurred to me that I might be in love with her.

After breakfast, we walked to the train and narrowly missed being hit by a firework. On the train, Anja rested her head on my shoulder and I ran my fingers through her hair. We got off in the city center, walked down the stairs, and saw German boys on the street shooting fireworks at one another, laughing, yelling in German what I imagined to be "I just hit you with a firework! Ha ha ha!"

We walked across one of the countless bridges that connected either side of the city's canals. Anja told me that Hamburg had more bridges than Venice.

"Suck it, Italy," I said.

"Yes, suck it, Italy."

One of the bridges was weighted with little locks that couples had bolted to the guardrail to commemorate their love.

"I should have brought a lock," I said.

"Very bad planning, Jonas."

I took off my left glove and tied the fingers around the railing. "There."

"A glove—how romantic!"

"Don't make fun."

Anja stuck her tongue out at me. But then she pulled out her phone and took a picture of the glove. We began to walk away, but she said, "Don't forget your glove."

"I'm leaving it."

"Why?"

"As a symbol."

"Of what?"

"Of a glove."

She punched me in the arm, but then put her gloved hand in my bare one and tucked her fingers between mine.

* * *

That evening, after sharing a bottle of champagne and having sex at the apartment, we took the train to the west side of the city to have New Year's dinner with her friends.

"Where do you know them from?" I asked her on the train.

"From university, in Greifswald."

"I picture that part of eastern Germany as a forest full of dragons."

"There are no dragons in Greifswald, Jonas."

"What does *Greifswald* mean?"

" 'Forest of the griffins.' " She paused. "I understand when I hear it that this does not strengthen my argument."

The apartment building was part of a rectangle of concrete apartment blocks with a shared courtyard. As Anja knocked on the door, I prepared for a night of smiling and nodding, and the occasional German phrase. But when the door opened, we were greeted by four blond Germans, two guys and two girls, speaking enthusiastic English. I tried to repay their English by being super interested in everything they said. I was ushered into the living room with the boys, while the girls pulled Anja into the kitchen. The boys asked me questions about Los Angeles and played me German rap while they readied a sort of long indoor grill on the table. The girls brought in plates of meat and vegetables, which I was told that you skewered like shish kebabs and then topped with slices of cheese.

Everyone gathered in the living room to watch an old short film called *Dinner for One*, which the whole country apparently watched every New Year's Eve. Around eleven, we all walked to the train to go see the fireworks by the harbor. On the way, I saw a yellow cat run across the street.

"*Katze!*" I yelled. "*Die Katze ist auf dem Strasse!*"

"*Ja, ja.*" Anja patted me on the arm, her friends looking confused. "Very good, Jonas. The cat is on the street."

We descended from the elevated tracks downtown to thick crowds of people, boats glowing on the water, and the biggest snowball fight I had ever seen. Except instead of snowballs everyone was throwing fireworks. I ducked my head and narrowly missed getting hit in the face.

"Look out for the fireworks," said one of Anja's friends.

We pushed our way through the crowd and found a spot by the railing overlooking the water. There we stood and counted down the seconds. At midnight, an orgy of fireworks erupted on all sides: from the decks of the boats, from the happy drunks standing next to us, from the windows of the train passing on the elevated tracks overhead. Anja and I kissed while everything whistled and popped.

I felt the cold on Anja's cheek as she leaned into my ear. "Happy New Year, Jonas."

"Happy New Year, Anja."

"When will I see you again?"

Despite myself, despite how happy I felt, I panicked. I didn't want to have a trip hanging over me—daily messages and check-ins and responsibility for someone else looming for weeks or months.

"We'll see," I said. "Soon."

* * *

After the fireworks chaos, we made our way to the Reeperbahn. The street was overfull. You didn't walk so much as rock forward with the crowd, then rock back a few steps when someone vomited or got hit by a firework, then rock forward again. Neon signs in the outline of guitars, elephants, and women lit up the sidewalks, and long queues from the clubs stretched out into the street.

Anja's friends had bought us all tickets to a club that would be open until eight in the morning. I was hoping Anja would get tired and want to go home before me, as I was always scared of being the boring one who wanted to go home. Even with alcohol, when I was clean, I couldn't maintain the energy to stay out all night. But if I took drugs, I could stay out all night. Then Anja would have a better time, too. And then I—

"Stop it!" I hissed.

"What did you say?" Anja yelled to be heard over the noise.

"Nothing."

When we got inside the pulsating room, I bought a round of tequila shots and reminded myself that no one here would have oxycodone and it wasn't worth giving up all that work for coke or speed, or for heroin, a bad batch of which could kill me. We made our way to a giant dance floor framed by fake palm trees. Behind a DJ stage was a massive clock, which was counting down to the New Year in Rio de Janeiro at 3:00 a.m. German time. We danced and I tried to not think about my dancing, but the tequila hadn't changed anything.

"I'm going to go outside to smoke," I told Anja.

"Do you want me to come?" Her cheeks were still red from the cold and she wore a cute black dress with tights. She was smiling the way she used to smile at me when I first met her.

"No, stay with your friends. You need to warm up if you're going to keep up with my dancing!"

She laughed and kissed me on the cheek.

I asked a bartender in bad German where I could find a smoking area, and he pointed to a narrow, glassed-off corridor behind some tables on the far end of the dance floor. It reminded me of the little glassed-off smoking room at the Atlanta airport, which, the last time I was there, had struck me as the most depressing place in the world. Out of oxy, I had taken two MDMA capsules on a flight from North Carolina to LA that connected in Atlanta, and it was in this smoking room that the pills started to hit me. They didn't land in that edge-softening way, but instead struck like a terror bolt. All the fat, solitary smokers, with their rolling suitcases and cell phones and futureless eyes, had scared the shit out of me. As I smoked in the little Hamburg smoking room, I tried to call up that feeling of terror from Atlanta and focus on it to subdue the craving.

I went to the bathroom, where a little stall had a metal toilet that looked like what I imagined a minimum-security prison bathroom might look like. I thought of how I used to sneak into bathrooms to take pills or bump lines of heroin, and I felt sad that my old self, the one who did these things, was gone. He didn't have to be gone, though. I could bring him back—if only for tonight. But then I remembered someone I hadn't thought of in a long time.

He was a guy from AA in Eugene whom I hated. He would say

things like "When I was loaded, I used to have to be the smartest guy in every room. And the problem was, I had the diploma to show that I was! That certainly didn't quiet my ego."

Like: "Trust me, I've spilled more in my life than you've drunk."

Like: "When I started AA, I used to think sobriety was sexually transmitted."

Yet this asshole had, in the parking lot once after a meeting, said something that stuck with me.

"You're how old?" he'd asked me without saying hello.

"Twenty-seven," I had answered, ambushed, at a loss for how to escape the conversation.

"I'm fifty-two." He'd paused. "And what's your poison?"

"Heroin."

"Are you rich?"

"No."

"If I told you that you could have a million dollars, but you'd wake up fifty-two years old, like me, would you take that trade?"

"No."

"Smart man. Twenty-five years for a million dollars is a terrible trade. That's only forty thousand dollars a year. But what if I said that I'd give you a quarter million dollars for just five years of your life. You wake up tomorrow, thirty-two years old, and you have a quarter million dollars in your bank account."

"I don't think I'd take that either."

"Smart man. Still not worth it. But how about this: How much money are you making now?"

"About twenty-four thousand dollars."

"What if I told you that I'd give you three times your annual salary—seventy-two thousand dollars—for just *one year* of your life? You wake up tomorrow seventy-two thousand dollars richer, but one year older."

I thought about it. I wouldn't have to worry about bills for a few years. I could just write. But nothing about the idea of the money made me happy. Nothing about the idea of losing another year made me happy. "Probably not."

"You wouldn't trade one year of your life for seventy-two thousand dollars?"

"I don't think so. No."

The guy stared at me, and for the first time, though I knew that this was as practiced as every other word he uttered, I felt as if he were actually looking at me instead of some interchangeable audience. "If you wouldn't trade even a year of your life for seventy-two thousand dollars, then why the fuck would you trade your entire life for heroin?"

The next morning, I woke before Anja. My head throbbed. But I hadn't gotten high. That was something at least. I got up and drank several glasses of water until my head felt better. I walked over to the window and saw the street sprinkled with glass and cardboard husks of fireworks.

I made coffee for myself and tea for Anja and brought them to the bedroom.

"Lucky me," Anja said, stretched out her arms, and rubbed her eyes in that lovely way she did when she'd had a good sleep.

I handed her the steaming cup. We drank, then cuddled, and I felt, if not good, at least content.

Then Anja sat up and said, "I do not think we should see each other after this."

I said nothing.

"I cannot be both together and not together."

She waited for me to respond. Part of me wanted to say that we should just be together, 100 percent. That I would come visit in a few weeks. Then she would come visit in a few weeks. It wasn't that far—it wasn't that expensive. But part of me was relieved that she was leaving me. That I wouldn't have to leave her. That I could be alone, with nothing required of me.

"It feels like I'm waiting for you to decide what you want," she said. "But I do not want to wait anymore."

I took a deep breath. I waited for the words to come out, but they didn't. I was remembering the moment as something sad that happened a long time ago. "If that's what you want," I finally said.

"Okay." She paused. "That's what we'll do." She kissed me on the cheek and got out of bed.

Malmö, Sweden

Spring/Summer 2015

Malmö, Sweden

IN MARCH, I DECIDED TO MOVE TO MALMÖ. SINCE RETURN-
ing from Hamburg, I'd spent the nights after class alone in my dorm
room and the weekends drinking heavily with my neighbor Laurent,
a nineteen-year-old French kid who seemed to admire me for some
reason. We would bike to the student nations to dance and drink,
then bike back, smoking and laughing about all the cheesy Swedish guys prancing around the clubs like aristocratic jeans models.
But in the sober afternoons, Laurent and I would once again be a
twenty-nine-year-old American and a French teenager with nothing
to talk about. Without Anja, I was lonely in Lund, and I was worried about the choices loneliness would inspire. Bengt and my other
classmates lived in Malmö. And Malmö was a city; it was harder to
be alone in a city.

At three hundred thousand, Malmö was the third-largest city
in Sweden. It was just across the Öresund strait from Copenhagen
and was twelve miles southwest of Lund, so I could easily commute
to the university. But while Lund was an ancient city of learning,
Malmö had a bad reputation. The city, which had sprung up around
the shipbuilding industry during the industrial revolution, had become Sweden's hub of immigration. One Swede told me, "If you've

seen Malmö, you've seen the world—if you know what I mean."
People in Lund said it was so dangerous in Rosengård, Malmö's no-
torious housing project, that the fire department wouldn't respond to
calls without a police escort. More than once I'd heard Malmö compared to a Swedish Detroit, but from my visits to Bengt's apartment,
Malmö felt more like a Swedish Oakland—across the bridge from an
international metropolis, other-ized by its neighbors, postindustrial-
izing in a hurry.

In the early nineties, as Malmö's shipbuilding industry was dying,
the city government began investing in culture. It renovated theaters
and concert halls. It built a sleek university downtown, the buildings
of which lined the harbor near the Central Station. In 2000, the
Öresund Bridge, connecting Malmö to Copenhagen and Sweden to
the Continent, was completed. The local paper started using the old
insult about the number of immigrants in Malmö, "If you've seen
Malmö, you've seen the world," as a marketing slogan. The city's promotional materials stated that 169 of the world's nationalities were
represented in Malmö. A grassroots group even aimed at bringing
residents from the remaining twenty-four UN-recognized countries
of the world to permanently live in Malmö, to make it the only city
housing citizens of every country in the world.

In the aughts, the city sold off the giant shipbuilding crane that
had hung over the western harbor like a gateway and in its place
erected a new symbol: a neo-futurist skyscraper called the Turning
Torso. The Turning Torso was a spiraling Epcot Center–ish tower
that, at fifty-four stories, was the tallest building in Scandinavia. It
was, unfortunately, surrounded by some of the most normal-size

buildings in Scandinavia—four-story luxury condos—and it looked like a very tall person in a room full of shoes.

But Malmö wasn't ugly. Glowing canals ran through the city center unextravagantly before emptying into the Öresund. Turn-of-the-century five-story apartment buildings with pastel turrets blended with the postwar concrete apartment slabs to make downtown blocks look like the offspring of Stockholm and the Soviet Union. Danes were moving to Malmö to save money on rent, commuting to Copenhagen by train over the bridge. Swedish writers, musicians, and artists were now moving to Malmö instead of Stockholm to save money on rent. Artsy undergrads and almost all the grad students from Lund were moving to Malmö to save money on rent. The word *gentrifiering* had recently been introduced to Swedish.

I, too, would save money on rent, as I told Stella when I emailed her about my move. Easily relatable news made correspondence easier, and in her return email, Stella told me how excited she was for me and insisted that we Skype. It was so nice to see her grainy face on the screen, telling me how exotic my life was. She and Zach had just moved back to our college town, San Luis Obispo, and she was working at a winery.

"But everyone there keeps talking to me about *wine*," she said. "It's so boring."

I also wrote to Anja to tell her of the move. We were trading emails that didn't say much but indicated that we were still thinking about each other. She would tell me about her studies and I would tell her about mine, and I would make up funny stories of things that hadn't actually happened to me, based on the things that had, in hopes of making her laugh. But the time between her messages was getting longer, first every day, then every other day, now every week or two. I missed her. But I couldn't tell her I missed her since I didn't know how long the feeling would last.

My new apartment was a spacious one-bedroom on the fourth floor of a drab concrete building with sky-blue balconies hanging off the side in a cheery addition. It was in the urban area of Värnhem, about a mile east of the Central Station, near Bengt's apartment, and cost thirty-five hundred kronor, a little less than $500, a month.

In the two blocks from the Värnhem bus stop to my new home were three kebab and falafel places, an African market, a neighborhood bar filled with alcoholics, a nautical-themed bar filled with alcoholics, a goodwill shop, and a Serbian bakery that displayed old bread in the window along with the sign FOR DISPLAY ONLY—BREAD INSIDE IS FRESH. The newer establishments included a locally sourced all-sourdough bakery, an upscale-grocery-chain store, a vegan Indian restaurant, and a fitness store that sold tank tops and protein powder and displayed yoga pants on window mannequins (whose asses I frequently caught myself checking out).

On the first night in the apartment, after Bengt helped me move in, I walked to the grocery store, bought my food, and returned to find that my electronic key wouldn't unlock the front door to the building. The keypad would turn green when you held the key in place and the door would click, but the lock wouldn't give. I lit a cigarette and waited for someone to come out. My street was just off a main artery, so I saw streams of traffic and city buses pouring by, but not a single car or person turned onto my street. I checked my phone, tried the key again, and smoked my cigarette. I waited. I'd only been standing there for ten minutes, but waiting when you didn't know how long the wait would be was almost unbearable.

Then three men turned down the street toward me. Two of them were wearing beanies and peacoats, and the one in the middle had on a big puffer jacket with his shaved head exposed. They were yelling to each other in what sounded like Arabic and gesticulating with their hands. Earlier in the day, lugging a box of my books from the bus, Bengt had told me to not stop for anyone who asked for directions at night. He'd been mugged at knifepoint in Folkets Park by two Middle Eastern guys who had pretended to be lost. I tried the key again. Again, it did not work.

The men approached. I lit another cigarette, not knowing what to do with my hands. I pulled out my phone and started pretending to check my messages, before realizing that pulling out an expensive phone was not a smart way to deter potential muggers.

"Hey! What are you doing?" the man with the puffer jacket called out in accented Swedish.

I drew hard on my cigarette. I put the grocery bags down in case I needed to use my hands. I was taller than them, but a fight would not go well.

"Are you locked out or something?" he said.

"The lock is broken," I said in Swedish.

"Hold on." The man in the puffer jacket pulled out his phone and made a call. Then he started yelling in Arabic. I heard a door open overhead. A man poked his head off the third-story balcony and yelled back in Arabic.

"My friend is coming," the man with the puffer jacket said.

The man from the balcony—short, with a shaved head, sharp beard lines, and an expensive-looking white-collared shirt tucked into designer jeans—emerged from the elevator and opened the front door.

"Thank you," I said to him. I held the door open for the three men.

"We're not going in," the man with the puffer jacket said.

"You just called to allow me in?" I continued in my unaccented but kind of weird Swedish.

"What were you going to do? Stand here all night?"

"How pleasant. Thank you."

"It was nothing." The man waved to his friend who had let me in, then walked away with the other two.

"Well? Come in," the man said with a slight accent and a little impatience in his voice.

"Thank you." I walked through the door he held open. "I just moved in, and the light turns green with the key, but I can't open the door."

I followed my new neighbor into the elevator, which was tiny in the way all Swedish apartment elevators are tiny, made to accommodate two or three people. The elevator itself had no door, but there were doors at every level that you could open once the elevator had come to a complete stop. When the elevator ascended, the empty fourth wall was exposed against the wall of the elevator shaft.

"I don't know how long I would have waited if not for your help."
I wanted to say something small-talky instead of something over-
wrought, but while I could now carry on conversations in Swedish
about literature and soccer, this we-just-met-and-we're-not-really-
going-to-say-anything talk was still difficult.

"It was so little." The man looked at his phone.

A sign hanging on the elevator wall warned riders against bringing large garbage cans into the elevator, since, in such a tiny space,
the garbage cans could catch on an edge of the exposed wall and
force the elevator rider's neck up against the back wall. The sign
showed a stick figure with its neck broken by a trash can.

"I guess you better not bring trash cans in here."

"No." The neighbor was quiet.

"Have you lived here long?"

"Ten years." He looked to be in his late twenties.

"Where are you from?" I asked, meaning where had he lived
before this apartment.

The elevator stopped at the man's floor. "Sweden," he said, and
walked off.

It was during those first six months in Malmö that I got my life
together. I decided to not drink more than once a week, and for the
most part I stuck to it, even if that one day a week still held more
drinks than it should have. I didn't take drugs. I thought about
them, but I thought about them less than I had in Lund. I went
for a run every weekday evening after school, ate healthier, and lost
ten pounds. I got a little better at Swedish small talk. I learned how

to say "Where did you live before?" In one of my emails to Anja, I asked if she would like to come visit. She explained that she had an exam coming up and couldn't make it; she didn't say that we should try another time. After that, the length between our messages grew even greater.

On Saturday nights, I'd go dancing at Grand or Moriskan with Bengt and the guys from class. Once every month or two, we'd go to one of the underground raves that you had to sign up for on private social media pages. You would prepay the cover charge and then receive a text at midnight with the address of the rave—usually an empty community center or warehouse in Sorgenfri. Sometimes on Fridays I'd meet internet dates for a drink that would either end in a polite hug or the kind of cautious sex you have when you're tipsy enough to initiate it but sober enough to be conscious of all the things that can go wrong. On Sunday afternoons, I went on long walks around the city, west through the old city and the harbor, out east to the blue-collar blocks of Kirseberg, south through the Middle Eastern enclave of Möllevången (which was being gentrified) and down into Rosengård (which was not), back up past the Louvre-looking glass train station building at Triangeln, and up through the warehouses of Sorgenfri back to my apartment.

After that first night of stupid fear, I never felt that I was in danger. Despite its reputation, I knew from internet research that Malmö had fewer murders per capita than Portland or Seattle and similar crime rates to Stockholm. But, as I saw it, three factors led to the Swedish fear of Malmö. The first was that, in Stockholm, the immigrant housing projects were located miles outside the city, in satellite towns that could be forgotten or used for punch lines. In Malmö, the housing projects were just south of the city center; from my apartment, you could walk to Rosengård in thirty minutes. The second was that over one-third of Malmö residents were foreign-born, and crimes committed in Malmö by men with dark skin were more frightening than those committed in Stockholm by men with white skin. Walking around Malmö at night, I felt safer than I had walking around Lund at night, as dark-skinned men smoking cigarettes and arguing outside kiosks were less scary than bands of white college boys, drunkenly eager to perform for their friends. It had also not escaped my attention that the only crime I had witnessed in either city was my own assault of the Swedish boy outside the nation.

The third, and the most well-founded, reason that Swedes were afraid of Malmö was that it had a high rate of explosions. Along with the culture, literature, and rave scene, Malmö had an organized-crime scene. Every now and again, somebody from one syndicate would try to kill somebody from another syndicate, and it would be big news in all the papers. But these syndicates were pretty good about only killing one another. More frequently, grenades or small bombs would go off in unoccupied buildings in the middle of the night, damaging property but not people. The fitness store down the street from my apartment had been bombed in the early spring, damaging windows and mannequins, apparently as a message from someone wanting money. The next day, the owner and his brothers had hung a giant banner that read EASTER SALE, OUR PRICES ARE EXPLOSIVE!

Even with all the sensational coverage in the news—every paper in the country would write about a Malmö crime, whereas the same incident in Gothenburg or Uppsala would only get regional coverage—the only crime that I'd heard of firsthand was Bengt's mugging in the park. But Bengt, I later learned, had also been mugged in London, Berlin, and Stockholm.

"People like to mug me," he explained at Moriskan one night. "I guess I just have that kind of face."

My classes in Lund met just three times a week, and I spent my off days at the Malmö University Library. The library was on the top floor of a five-story wavy-glass building in the middle of downtown. It had high windows with a panoramic view of the city, from which you could see the bridge, the old city, the Central Station, the Turning Torso, and, just across the canal, the boat from the Noah's Ark party.

At first I thought that it was the inspiring view that got me writing again, but I later realized that my inspiration might just have come from a lack of hangovers. Regardless, I started writing again in thirty-minute bursts that were short enough to keep me from hating my work but long enough to get coherent chunks of words onto the page. I soon completed the story I had long failed to write, about the immortal jellyfish and a teacher in his first semester sober, trying to balance sobriety with the affection he had for students who would soon leave. When it was done, I sent the story off to an editor at the *Sun* who had written me some encouraging rejection letters in the past. A few weeks later, she offered me $500 for it.

Sitting there in the Malmö Library, I read her email over and over, trying to record every little edge of the ecstasy so I could come back to it later. With every breath, I felt like a writer. I wanted someone to share my joy with—someone who would understand what it meant to be able to pay a *month's rent* with fiction—but whom could I call? My mother was teaching at a meditation retreat all month, off the grid. I hadn't been keeping up with my writer friends from grad school, and it seemed like kind of a dick move to write for the first time in a year to brag about being published. I could tell Stella, but with the time difference and her work schedule, it was usually hard to get her on the phone, and I didn't want to email her the news. I could tell my Swedish friends, but they would never have heard of the magazine.

But at least I knew. That was something.

Without the longing for drugs—which, aside from short, unexpected pangs, had settled down—and the near-constant hangovers, which had been relegated to two days a week following my drinking night, I found that I could get through most days without feeling trapped by the confines of my room, the vastness of time before I went to sleep, or the loneliness that couldn't be cured by other people. I was too busy for all that. I often woke up feeling kind of happy. Not jump-out-of-bed happy, but like I could open my eyes without groaning at the realization that my life was right where I had left it the night before. I would wake up and think, *Today you have to shower, go to the store, make breakfast, pack a lunch, take the bus to Lund, go to class, take the bus back to Malmö, write in the library, study, go home, make dinner, go for a run, and then be back here in bed by midnight.* Right back where I started but having accomplished one more day of life. There was no great excitement, but there was contentment. I rarely felt the need to escape my life or myself. It was the first time I could remember feeling this way.

One Sunday in late summer, I was headed down to the basement of my apartment building with a blue IKEA bag full of laundry in each hand. You saw these IKEA bags everywhere in Malmö: in the hands of Rom migrants gathering bottles and cans, Kurdish Swedish shop owners carrying tubs of garlic sauce to their kebab joints, and middle-class white Swedes riding the elevators down to their shared laundry rooms, avoiding eye contact with the neighbors they never talked to. It occurred to me, as I looked in the mirror of the tiny elevator, that I was starting to resemble one of those middle-class Swedes. I was twenty-nine years old. I had on leather boots and a red-and-black-checkered shirt tucked into jeans. And I was carrying laundry.

Back home, I'd always hated laundry, but in Malmö I came to love it. Swedish communal laundry rooms had sign-up sheets, which meant you had to schedule your time in advance and then stick to your schedule, as you might not secure another slot for a week or two. Going over your time was unforgivable. The Norwegian writer Karl Ove Knausgård had detailed this feature of Swedish life in *My Struggle*, which he had written while living in Malmö. Knausgård would forget his laundry in the machine, pissing off his neighbors to no end, and then rant against the tyrannical Swedish system of rules. "Set an alarm!" I would yell at the book.

In the US, the communal laundry room offered freedom. You didn't have to sign up. You could trot down whenever you wanted, laundry basket tucked under your arm, and always have the possibility of open machines. But there was no guarantee that you'd get a machine. Or that the previous user would empty his machine on time. You could spend a whole afternoon marching back and forth between apartment and laundry room without ever finding an open machine. In Sweden, there was less freedom. You did laundry on the day you signed up for it. But there was security. During your time slot, the machines would be yours. Everyone had an equal chance to wash their clothes, so long as they planned ahead.

My building was especially strict in enforcing the laundry schedule. Ever since some vagrants had been found squatting in the basement, the garbage rooms and laundry room could only be opened by electronic key. You scanned your key to sign up for laundry slots on an electronic board in the subterranean hallway, and your key would only open the laundry room during your slot. If you had the 1:00 p.m. to 5:00 p.m. slot, and you didn't make it back to the laundry room until 5:10, you'd be locked out, left to hope the next washer could let you in to get your clothes.

I walked down the foul-smelling concrete hallway, which was lined with the garbage rooms of Sweden's polynomial recycling system. When I reached the laundry room, a little winded from the weight of my IKEA bags, I found a distraught woman in a beige head scarf leaning against the door.

"I am so sorry," she said in heavily accented Swedish. "I didn't make it in time. I know the rules, but I just did not make it in time."

"It's okay, no harm," I said, which was the Swedish equivalent that I used whenever I meant "no problem"—though I wasn't entirely sure it meant "no problem." Everyday expressions were still tricky.

I let the woman in and she quickly emptied the washing machines of her wet clothes.

"There's no hurry. You may use the dryer—I'm not in need of it for another forty-five minutes. I don't mind sharing the room."

"No, no, no." She waved her hand. "Thank you."

"It would be pleasant to share."

But she apologized again and hurried out with her arms full of clothes, probably so distressed by her lateness that she had forgot to bring her IKEA bags. Her distress, I thought, must have come from past laundry room scoldings that she'd received from our neighbors. Almost the only circumstance in which I saw Swedes regularly talking to strangers was when someone failed to follow the rules: to take a number in line, to refrain from using cell phones in the quiet car of the train, or to abide by the laundry schedule. White Swedes, particularly older white Swedes, might grow irritated at the volume of the bus passenger speaking Arabic into his cell phone, yet would never say anything unless a specific rule was being broken. But when that number wasn't taken, that cell phone wasn't turned off in the quiet car of the train, or that washing machine was still spinning at 5:01, all their anger at the changing world—at living in a city where one out of every three people was from a foreign country, at having to listen to conversations in languages they couldn't understand, at being told that the jokes of their childhood were no longer funny— exploded in righteousness.

"This is the quiet car!" the old Swede would say, leaning in two inches from the Arab's face. He would point to the NO PHONES sign with an angry wave of the finger. "You may not talk on your phone here!"

Much as I felt bad for the woman who had to ask for my help to get her clothes back, I liked that the room was locked. I liked that neither she, nor anyone else, could come inside without my permission while I was doing my washing. I liked that she had to ask me to let her in. That I could put on my headphones and listen to podcasts without worrying about the sudden presence of another person saying hello, watching me, judging me. I liked that, in the laundry room, even Sunday-hungover and useless from my weekly night out, I was getting something done. In a few hours, the previously dirty laundry would be clean and ready to wear—there was no anxiety about it.

This evening, as I sorted the whites from the darks, I listened to a podcast in which a sportswriter was proposing that men's tennis matches be shortened from five sets to three, because the length of the matches was daunting for the viewer.

"Even when you're enjoying something," he said, "you can't wait for it to end."

The sportswriter said that he had never once avoided a book because it was too short—never once gotten to the end of a book and wished it were longer. I tried to think of a book that I had wished were longer but found that even my favorite short books had been precisely the right length. I had enjoyed them, in part, because I knew they would soon be ending. When I was reading a good book,

I couldn't wait to get to the end—to be done with it, so that I could think about it and maybe write about it. But when I started writing about it, I was so anxious to get the words out of my brain and onto the page before I lost anything that it wasn't enjoyment I felt but panic.

The same was true of relationships. I had only had the one serious relationship, with Alexandra, which now existed mostly in my memory as a blur of screaming, fucking, and crying. But besides that, all my monogamous relationships had been based on finitude. Back in high school, the only relationship I'd had was the summer before I was leaving for college. In college, a casual hookup turned into a short relationship once I knew I would be leaving town to move in with Stella and Zach. Part of me thought I fell for Anja because I knew she'd be leaving. In Hamburg, I'd been excited to see her. But I also couldn't wait to leave. Now I missed her terribly. But if she came to visit, the same thing would probably happen. There would be that perfect moment when I woke up next to her, or when she was trying to tell a story but laughing so hard that she couldn't get the words out, and I'd want to live inside that moment forever. But then the moment would end and she'd need something from me that I didn't want to give, and I'd either feel bad about withholding it or feel dread at having to give the thing I didn't want to give, and then I would, once again, wish to be alone.

Sex had become more fun since I stopped taking drugs, but the one-night stands I'd had after Anja were still anxiety producing, which meant that even sex was often more enjoyable retrospectively— thinking about it or jacking off to memories of it later.

I started the dryer and tried to think of something that I enjoyed more when it was happening than when it was over.

It took a while, but I finally came up with one thing: I enjoyed being high much more when it was happening than when it was over. I never wanted the high to end.

I sat on the dryer for a while and chewed the thought over.

IN EARLY SEPTEMBER, ALAN KURDI'S BODY WASHED UP ON THE shore of Turkey, then up on the front page of every newspaper in Europe. A little boy, facedown in the sand, wearing the tiniest shoes you'd ever seen. I first saw the picture when I was in line at the market. It filled the front page of three different papers on display by the registers. The boy was so small. I turned away. Looking would just make me feel bad and nothing would change. When I got home, I saw the picture again on social media. I stared at it for maybe thirty seconds. I closed the window and everything was tinted dark. I felt awful. But then I opened an NBA season preview. By the end of the article, the awful feeling was gone.

The picture kept popping up on Facebook, along with outraged captions. *How could we let this happen? How could we, in Europe, in 2015, let this happen?*

Then came the editorials. It wasn't enough to just post outraged status updates on Facebook. Alan Kurdi was just one of many who were dying on terrible midnight journeys from Turkey to Greece, one of the many dying in refugee camps in Jordan and Lebanon, one of the many stuck in a Syrian civil war too terrible for words.

When I read these editorials, I agreed with the journalists while also hating the journalists. I didn't feel that they cared about any of it. It was more as if they had seen an opportunity to correct some runny-nosed sentimentality and raise their own cultural capital with a few quickly googled facts.

Then came the picture from the Vienna train station: the information sheet welcoming refugees to Austria, explaining who to go to for services, and ending with the promise: *You are safe.* I saw the picture on Facebook ten times in a single day.

Next came videos from train stations in Munich and Amsterdam: white children welcoming brown children, Europeans giving water bottles and toys to Middle Eastern families, rows of whites standing on the platforms to cheer for arriving refugees. Finally, the videos started popping up from Malmö Central—Swedes lined up to high-five the Syrian men, women, and children passing through the gauntlet of applause.

I had mixed feelings. But I couldn't deny the lump in my throat every time I clicked.

One morning, I was sitting in the Malmö University Library, trying to read a work of literary theory written in English by a German academic. German academics wrote in an English that was more indecipherable to me than German. I was midway through my third attempt at a sentence (. . . *primarily in order to unmask interpellation in a postcolonial context vis-à-vis the master-slave dialectic* . . .) when I looked out the window and saw workers outside building something. Across the canal that separated the library from Skeppsbron, just behind the boat where the Noah's Ark party had been, yellow-vested workers were fencing off a little square by the canal with six-foot chain-link fences. The next day, they brought in massive shipping containers on a truck. They stacked them four containers long and two containers high, as if they were building an ugly two-story house. Then they put a porch swing out front and planted poles in the ground from which they hung white Christmas lights. Then police officers and people in Red Cross vests planted themselves outside. Then the workers hung a banner: REFUGEES WELCOME.

Over the following week, I sat staring out the window at families waiting outside the refugee processing center. They were ushered in by Red Cross volunteers, mothers lugging children and looking worried, children lugging bags and looking tired, and fathers nodding at the volunteers' words, keeping their heads up and trying to look in control. Despite the efforts to make the shipping containers look friendly, they were still shipping containers. A teenage boy sat on the swing staring at his phone, waiting. I saw him waiting the next day and the day after that, and I began to wonder what he was waiting for. It made me sad in a useless way. I wanted to walk up to him and give him my jacket. I wanted someone to see me giving him my jacket, film it, put it on the internet, and watch the video go viral, inspiring thousands to give jackets. But he already had a jacket.

That weekend, I went with Bengt to Moriskan, a large nightclub in Möllevången. This Middle Eastern neighborhood in central Malmö had recently become a hip place for young white people to live. The club was a long behemoth with domed Moorish Revival turrets that glowed whitely over Folkets Park at night. It was a caricature of a mosque, designed by an Eastern European architect as a dance hall for workers from the shipyards during the orientalist boom of the early twentieth century. It looked as if it were pulled not from Istanbul, but from a Las Vegas hotel called Istanbul, Istanbul.

Bengt and I paid our covers at the door, got our stamps, and checked out each of the club's three stages. A Yugoslav rock band was playing in the little dance hall on the left, a Brazilian samba party with a DJ was in the big dance hall straight ahead, and a Swedish jazzy-swing quartet was jitterbugging away in the pub area to the right. We bought beers and made our way into the big dance hall, where tall North African boys in tight white jeans stood on the peripheries of the crowd looking for dance partners. Eyes followed the Africans whenever they moved, regardless of whether it was to dance with a white girl, dance with a brown girl, or simply to get a drink at the bar. Bengt led me through the room confidently. I envied how he always looked like he knew where he was going. Even at a club where we didn't know anyone, he would push past people with confidence as if a big group of his friends were waiting for him just on the other side of the room. He would lead us to the DJ stage, which he would step onto like he was boarding a bus. Then he would salsa dance.

"Why are you salsa dancing?" I had once asked, struggling to be heard over the bone-jangling bass of the techno playing in the Sorgenfri warehouse.

"Because I know how to salsa," Bengt had screamed back, before resuming maraca-shaking his fists and solo-stepping in place on the stage.

This evening, when we got to the front of the room at Moriskan, I said, "Let's not dance on the stage," right as Bengt jumped onstage. It was a massive edifice with a DJ table in the middle and fifteen feet of open space on either side. I sighed and tried to act like I was comfortable at the foot of the stage, watching Bengt salsa his way through the Brazilian music. As always, I was surprised by the non-appearance of a bouncer to pull Bengt off the stage. If this had been America, Bengt would have been half-nelsoned to the ground in about two seconds. A drunk girl pushed past me and put one knee, then the other, on the stage. She unfolded her legs and strutted up to Bengt. They made eye contact. The dancing began.

I had once been uncomfortable with the ease with which Bengt attracted women. When I met a girl at a bar, it felt like a happy accident. I'd happen to sit down next to someone friendly on the smoking patio. A girl would accidentally take my debit card from the bartender instead of her own and a conversation would be struck up. There was nothing accidental about Bengt. He approached girls or they approached him. He never bragged about it or made a big show of it, the way some men did, which made me more jealous. If Bengt had been a showboating pickup artist, I could've just dismissed him as that sad brand of man who gets more joy from telling his friends about the hot girl he fucked than he got from the fucking itself.

I had wondered if I should be more confident and nonchalant, like Bengt. But if I did the things Bengt did—approached women with his recklessness—I would have suffered hangover shame so bad that I'd have to return to drugs. I had spent a lot of time thinking about what I could do to make women react to me the way they reacted to Bengt, until one day it hit me: Bengt was just better looking than me. He had a strong chin, blue eyes, and effortless hair that always settled in interesting ways despite appearing untended. There was nothing I could do about that. I never worried about it again.

Onstage, the dancing was not going well. The girl was trying to grind on Bengt, but he refused to stop salsa-ing. He kept trying to lead her with his eyes, and she kept grabbing him and rubbing herself on him. Eventually he hopped off the stage.

"Marry that girl," I said.

"I was trying to, but she kept grabbing me. I think she needed to hold on for balance."

We bought another round of beers and squeezed to the front of the Yugoslav rock room, watched the band for two songs, then squeezed through the crowd and into the pub room. No one seemed to care about our pushing and squeezing. In the pub room, the singer of the Swedish swing band, a small blond in flapper gear, was saying that this song was about how it was time to open borders. Everyone cheered.

"It's nice that you're all finally coming around to the idea of open borders," she said. "Though I don't know why it took so long. We've been playing this song for over a year."

Then the band cut into a trombone-heavy minor-key ditty with the chorus *We need to open borders / because we are all people*. It rhymed in Swedish.

I wanted to tell Bengt that I found this all a bit self-aggrandizing, but I didn't know how to say *self-aggrandizing* in Swedish.

I cupped my hand over his ear. "It's kind of gross, isn't it?"

"Yeah." Bengt made a face. "Swedes shouldn't play this kind of music."

I laughed. "No, I mean the message. It's kind of, I don't know. It's like they think they're Jesus or something."

"Absolutely," Bengt agreed, though I hadn't said what I wanted to say. "I'm not sure who they think they are."

We finished our beers and Bengt said, "You should come to the rally next week."

"What rally?"

"Torsten posted about it on Facebook. The Refugees Welcome rally in Stortorget."

"Oh, yeah?"

"I think it will be really good. Or it may be bad." Bengt looked up at the jitterbugging band. "But it can't be worse than this."

When I took the bus home that night—after leaving Bengt at the kebab stand with a girl who had dark hair and lovely eyebrows—I thought about the jitterbugging band. White people were using the suffering of others to raise their own cultural capital: through editorials, outraged status updates, train-station selfies, and, as it turned out, swing music.

But it wasn't helpful to stand on the sidelines criticizing people trying to do something they thought was good, no matter how oblivious or unhelpful the do-gooders' help was. Their self-aggrandizement was gross. Their minute-maid sentimentality did nothing for the victim. But Swedish borders *were* now open. One hundred thousand refugees would be welcomed into the country in 2015. Even if the cheering at the train station was fleeting, it was better to arrive to cheers than to the tear gas offered at the Hungarian border. It was better that Sweden was spending its money on building the refugee processing center by the canals than spending its money to take out ads in Middle Eastern newspapers telling refugees they were not welcome, as the Danish government had done. If the European white person used the Middle Eastern refugee to help himself, but the Middle Eastern refugee was also immediately helped—if also dehumanized—by the process, maybe it was a temporarily worthwhile bargain. But then the question was if the terms of the bargain could ever evolve.

I felt pride that I lived in a country that postered bus stops and train stations with the words REFUGEES WELCOME. But I also wondered: Which refugees were welcome? Over the past week, I'd been forgoing my schoolwork to read about Sweden's immigration history and the debate surrounding the Roma. The entry of Romania into the EU in 2007 had allowed Romanian Roma, often called Gypsies, free passage into other EU countries. At first, Swedes had felt sorry for the Rom migrants. Panhandling and homelessness had not been part of the Swedish welfare state, and to see a Rom woman sitting outside Systembolaget in almost every Swedish city, in a pose like the ones I'd seen on my Christmas charity tour—with a laminated picture of her children leaning against an empty coffee cup—was a shock. Her hands would be clasped in prayer, begging for coins to send home. Since these were the Roma that Swedes saw, it didn't matter how many migrants had paying jobs—they were invisible.

Since the seventies, Sweden had prided itself on one of the most liberal asylum policies in the world, opening its doors to Chileans, Persians, Kurds, Iraqis, Palestinians, Yugoslavs, Somalis, Eritreans, and Afghans. In the aftermath of the American invasion of Iraq, more Iraqi refugees had been relocated to the Stockholm suburb of Södertälje than to the United States and Canada combined.

But the Rom migration was different.

Smoking between classes one afternoon, Bengt said that while most Swedes could, in principle, agree that the purpose of the EU zone was not just for middle-class citizens to improve their lot, but for all EU citizens to have economic opportunity, Swedes disagreed on what counted as "opportunity."

"Does panhandling count as opportunity?" he said. "I don't know. You feel bad when you see them on the streets. You give them money, but you don't have enough to give to all of them. You wonder what's the best solution. But it doesn't seem like any solution is a good one."

The far left showed their righteousness by canonizing the Roma, and the far right played on the worst stereotypes about the Roma to bolster their anti-immigrant agenda, but those in the vast middle seemed to have an unspoken desire to find a way to get the Roma off the streets without passing any racist laws that made Swedes feel bad about themselves.

I told Bengt that I thought it was the dissonance between Sweden's identification as an open nation that welcomed those in need, and the actual resentment Swedes felt toward people who were so poor and oppressed that begging on a cold sidewalk ten hours a day was better than home, that had led to the shocking success of the Sweden Democrats in the 2014 elections.

"Sure," Bengt said. "When presented with evidence that you're not the person you thought yourself to be, the natural reaction isn't to look in the mirror. The natural reaction is to get angry at the person who robbed you of your delusion."

The rise of the fascists in 2014 had led to an anxiety Swedes were still struggling with in the fall of 2015. But the refugee situation in the Middle East might have been the cure for the country's psychic pain. The pictures of Alan Kurdi's body were easy to understand. This was the person we wanted to save.

After a few failed attempts to schedule another Skype date, Stella and I finally conquered the nine-hour time difference. When she popped onto the screen, her pixelated face lit up, and she yelled, "Jonas!"

I felt my shoulders relax at the sound of her voice.

I started to catch her up on what I'd been doing over the past few months but quickly ran out of things to say. Life felt so full, but it was either full of things that were happening only in my head or that required more backstory than they were worth.

"Oh, but I'm getting a story published," I said, suddenly remembering. "It's in a good magazine. I'm pretty excited."

"Oh my God! Asshole! Way to bury the lede!" She looked so happy on the screen. "I'm proud of you."

"Thank you." This was when we would have hugged, but without the hug I didn't know how to fill the space. "But what's new with you?"

"Well. Zach finally proposed. We're getting married."

"Oh my God! Asshole! Way to bury the lede!"

Stella laughed. "I know, right?"

I was happy for them. I'd never felt more at home than the year I'd spent with them in Austin.

Stella said that the wedding would be in the summer and that I *had* to come. I felt my stomach sink. I told her that I would try, but that money was tight. Which wasn't completely true—money would be tight if I spent eight thousand kronor on a round-trip ticket to Los Angeles, but I could make it work. I wanted to be there for her and Zach. But if I went back to the US, I might get stuck there and get stuck in drugs again. After we hung up, I thought of how there would be people at the wedding—people I'd known for years—who had no idea that they'd never seen me sober. How was I supposed to talk to them?

Word of the Refugees Welcome rally had been spreading on social media, and attendance was expected to number in the thousands—which was a high number for a pro-something rally, rather than the better-attended anti-something protests.

Bengt and I walked from Malmö Central on sidewalks crowded with lively young people. Stortorget was packed. Thousands of people held red-and-white banners and flags. I stood on the edge of the square, on the steps that held a large statue of a man on horseback, and snapped a picture of the crowd.

Bengt and I took a spot behind a group of teenagers holding up a banner calling for the destruction of the capitalist system that had created the refugee crisis in the first place. Two girls were holding up the banner. A serious-looking boy dressed in black patrolled back and forth between the two girls, lifting one girl's elbow, telling the other to hold the sign higher. I wasn't looking forward to two hours standing behind this boy. I wasn't looking forward to listening to political speeches. I wasn't looking forward to being part of an audience. But there was something happening here that mattered. Even if I wasn't a part of it, I wanted to understand it.

The opening speaker was a Chilean Swedish politician from the Communist Party. She told the story of when her family had escaped Chile to the suburbs of Gothenburg in the seventies. She said that her neighbors had all bought Spanish-Swedish dictionaries in hopes of making the newcomers feel more welcome. She got choked up when she said that her young son now wanted to go to the Central Station to give his toys to refugee children. Everyone cheered. I raised my eyebrows at Bengt as if to say, *That was actually good*. Bengt nodded in approval.

Next, an extremely Swedish-looking young professional wearing a blazer and jeans got onstage to talk about travel. He explained how the EU's laws stated that if an airline flew a passenger to an EU country and that person was denied entry into the country, the airline was responsible for paying for the passenger's return trip. So airlines wouldn't fly Syrians to Sweden, even if the refugees had the money, because the airline didn't want to risk paying for the return ticket if the asylum petition was denied. The guy in the blazer said that he'd talked to a refugee who had bought passage from Turkey to Greece for a thousand euros. On the night the refugee was to leave, the smuggler had left him and twenty others with just an inflatable raft—no navigational equipment or anyone to steer it—and told them to set out for Kos in the dark of night.

"Alan Kurdi's father," the speaker said, "paid over thirty thousand kronor for his family of four to board a raft that capsized five minutes after it left the shore. That's more than the price of four plane tickets from Damascus to Stockholm."

Murmurs ran through the crowd.

The solution, the man explained, was a venture to charter airline jets not currently in use to fly from Syria to Stockholm.

"If we can fly people to the moon," he said, "we can fly refugees to Europe."

The crowd cheered wildly. The idea of a business plan to combat the problem, complete with a pretty good tagline, was appealing. But I didn't like the guy. I couldn't put my finger on why. He wasn't naively sentimental. He was trying to implement a workable solution to a concrete problem. His solution, if successful, would not solve the refugee crisis. But it could make one terrible element of the terrible predicament less terrible. I applauded; but I was torn.

Next to the stage was an Iranian Swedish rapper and social activist who, I learned from Bengt, was a minor celebrity. The rapper was good-looking, dressed in a hoodie and backward baseball cap, probably in his early thirties. He said that he had come to Sweden with his family as a child. He talked about the museum in Småland dedicated to the emigrants who had left Sweden for the American Midwest by the hundreds of thousands in the nineteenth century.

"But where's the museum for the immigrants who *came* to Sweden?" he said. "Where's the museum for those who stayed to make this country a better place? Where's our museum?"

Then he performed an a cappella rap in Swedish about his family's journey to Sweden. I always tensed up at these public shows of sincerity and cries for approval—the slam poetry performance about a past trauma, the embarrassingly emotional acceptance speech at the Oscars. But the rapper's verses were, to my surprise, moving. I got chills.

Finally, a Syrian man who had come to Sweden two years earlier spoke, in halting but good Swedish, of his experiences.

He had been a lawyer in Syria; here he was a cook.

"The hardest part is forgetting." He paused. "But you have to forget the past so that you can live the future. And it is thanks to Sweden that I have a future."

He said that if you google *asylum* in Syria, the browser auto-fills in *Sweden*.

In front of me, a thin black man held up a sheet of paper that said *Thank you Sweden.*

I didn't know if I was feeling pride at living in a country that welcomed those in need, gratitude to the speakers for allowing me to share in their experiences, or warmth that came from real empathy— but whatever it was, I felt good. The speakers demanding crowd participation didn't bother me as they usually would. By the end of the rally, even the Communist boy in all black, his fist in the air every time the crowd cheered, didn't bother me.

One evening later that week, after a run along the canals, I was catching my breath on the couch, watching Swedish national television's weekly literature program. I had been thinking all day that if I finished six hours of research for school, did my grocery shopping, and ran three miles, I would reward myself with two beers. But now that I'd checked everything off my to-do list, I was no longer in the mood. I was already tired—the good kind of tired that didn't send you burrowing into your brain to investigate why you were tired— and had no need for the beers.

I thought about my run: my lungs pumping air, my heart beating blood, my feet crunching the gravel, my legs working the way they were supposed to. I'd watched the streetlights flickering on the canals and entertained the thought that 2015 was turning out to be the happiest year of my life. I couldn't say why. I was alone most of the time. I was going on thirty years old with no book publication in sight. On the rare occasions when I talked with friends back home, I didn't have any stories to tell. I suspected I was getting more boring by the day. I had little to show for my time on earth. But my days were full. Who knew that such happiness could come from the dumb filling of hours.

SOON AFTERWARD, I WENT OUT WITH A SWEDISH GIRL, LOVISA, I'd met on a dating app. I had written Lovisa my usual opener: *Hey there! Is English okay? Swedish is fine, too, but I'm 30% more charming in English.*

English is fine, she'd answered. *But Americans are usually only 20% more charming in English.*

As the conversation progressed, she seemed not only funny, but also warm and smart, and I thought that this could be more than another encounter that ended with morning awkwardness. I didn't want a relationship—something that could trap me in a place I wasn't sure I wanted to stay. But I thought that Lovisa might be the type I could share inside jokes with on lazy Saturday mornings.

I met her at Far i Hatten, an old pub in the park next to Moriskan, where she was already seated when I arrived. She was cuter in real life than in her pictures, with short brown hair, green eyes, and sharp cheekbones and a small chin.

"Oh, good," she said in English when I sat down. "You don't look at all like a murderer."

"Neither do you."

"So it's already going better than most of these!"

Everything clicked. Her English was excellent, and even if she sometimes couldn't find the right word or if it took her a second to understand the subtext of what I'd just said, she knew when I was joking and either laughed or added another bit to the joke. She told good stories. She asked good questions. She didn't check her phone too often. I found myself not hating the sound of my voice, which was usually what happened half an hour into a date.

When I returned from the bar with our second beers, I said, in Swedish, "It's unfair that we're just speaking my language. We should switch over to Swedish so you get a chance."

Lovisa smiled and started speaking more effortlessly than before. But slowly, yet undeniably, the spark of the conversation disappeared. With either language, one of us was at a disadvantage, like a correspondent with finger pressed to earpiece, waiting through a few seconds of satellite delay for the delivery of the anchor's message. When she fumbled in English, it didn't halt the conversation. Yet when I searched for the word in Swedish and lost the momentum of the story, or when it took me a second to understand the subtext beneath what she had just said, she seemed disappointed.

I excused myself to the bathroom, and when I returned, she started speaking English again.

After four beers, Lovisa asked if I wanted to go somewhere else. I thought she meant her place, but instead she took me to Babel, a nightclub a few blocks away that was housed in a converted church. The rooms of Babel were packed with Swedes dancing to the type of looping electronic music that I could never understand. Lovisa bought us beers and we danced sort of together but sort of apart. I would dance close and she would dance away. I'd check my phone and she'd pull me close. But every time I made the pre-kiss eye contact, she'd look away. I was okay holding off on sex. I actually preferred it. I had never liked sleeping with someone the first time I met her. I wouldn't have minded ending the night after Far i Hatten and enjoying the possibility of seeing Lovisa again later in the week. But now that we were drunk together in a club where it was too loud to talk, I didn't know what to do except start moving toward sex.

Eventually, needing air, I said that I was going to smoke and asked if Lovisa wanted to come. She shook her head. I walked out and found a spot in the crowded fenced-off area that separated the club from the sidewalk. I lit a cigarette and looked out at the wild night traffic on Bergsgatan. As I was watching a yellow commuter bus recklessly changing lanes, I was tapped on the shoulder. I turned and saw Ulrika, a girl I'd had a class with during the previous year. She had since transferred to the History of Ideas program at Lund. She was blond and beautiful in a way that felt more appropriate to TV than real life.

"How have you been!" she said in English, though she was Swedish, giving me a big hug.

"I'm good. How are you? How is the History of Ideas?"

"It's really easy compared to literature. Can I have a drag off your cigarette?"

"Of course." I offered it to her, but she leaned in and took a drag from it out of my fingers.

She was drunk and would have flirted as much with a large chair as she was flirting with me. But it was still nice to be standing outside, talking to a beautiful girl without having to guess at what she wanted, since I knew that she wanted nothing.

"We should hang out sometime!" she said, after I put out my smoke.

I gave her my number, comfortable in the knowledge that I'd never hear from her again.

When I went back inside, Lovisa was gone. I looked through all the rooms for her, circled back, and repeated this three times, then messaged her through the dating app. No answer.

I waited thirty minutes, but finally I gave up and walked out past the line of falafel joints on Bergsgatan toward my bus stop. I wondered why she'd left. Had she seen me talking to Ulrika? Had she gotten fed up with the ten minutes I spent outside? Had she found someone better? Had she been looking for an excuse to leave all along and simply found it when I went to smoke? I had a headache. I was irritated that I had spent over four hundred kronor on the night out. I missed Anja. I knew that if the date had ended better, I would not have missed Anja, and I knew that missing someone only when you were sad or lonely was not really missing them at all. But still, I missed her.

The following evening, lying on the couch reading, my brain staticky from the night before, I got a text from an unfamiliar number. It was Ulrika inviting me to a party she was having the following weekend at her house in Lund. I felt a smile spread across my face. How happy an unexpected text from a girl could make you.

* * *

Later, I lay awake thinking of Ulrika. About how sex with her would look. How talking with her after sex would go. I wondered if the conversation would take place in English or Swedish. I thought about the speed bumps that would come from either. In either language, she would get tired of me, but how quickly would this happen? Or how quickly would I get tired of her? What if she didn't think I was funny? What if she turned out to be dumb? What if I blurted out something personal on the first night and she was turned off by my neediness? Or what if I blurted out something personal on the first night and then found that I didn't have any intimate life details to share—that I'd used all my currency and had no way to pull her closer to me?

I ran through every problem that could arise. Then I ran through a perfect night—perfect conversation, simultaneous orgasms, eight hours of peaceful sleep, waking-morning smile, morning kiss, morning blow job, make her breakfast, sex again, totally in love. Then I found problems with that too. What would we do if we fell in love? Stay home and watch Netflix? What was there left to do if we had already found each other?

EARLY ONE MORNING, THE POLICE TORE DOWN THE ROM encampment in Sorgenfri, the industrial neighborhood where I had attended a few raves held in empty factory spaces. Since I'd moved to Malmö, a large vacant lot there had been filled with tents, cars, and motor homes. Sometimes when I'd walk by at night with Bengt, Rom men would be sitting by a tire fire, drinking beers and playing a guitar.

The police entered the lot at 4:00 a.m. and told the Roma to vacate. Some of the families folded up their tents or drove their cars out of the lot as instructed. Others were dragged out screaming. A few dozen activists stood out front yelling at the police. Nearby, a little cluster of Sweden Democrats, one of them sporting a swastika patch on a denim jacket, held a tailgate, drinking beers and laughing. In the press release that followed, the city government made clear that there would be no deportation of the Roma. But the city had chartered buses that would drive anyone who *wanted* to go home back to Bucharest for free. I heard all this information secondhand, at school the next day, smoking between classes with classmates who'd witnessed the action.

"The most disgusting part was the Swedes there, taking pictures for their Facebook pages, but not doing anything to stop it," said Torsten. He was Swedish, but was currently speaking English for the benefit of a German exchange student who was smoking in the circle. Torsten was short and skinny and wore tight dark jeans and thick wool sweaters. He was a Marxist who could navigate theory better than I could in both Swedish and English. He didn't run with Bengt, so I had never been out with him, but when he spoke in class, he was calm and attentive to the opinions of others. This was the most animated I'd seen him.

"How have we gotten to the point where police brutality is the norm in Sweden?" he said.

I prickled. Hearing the phrase from a Swede, when I came from a country in which police regularly shot people to death for no good reason, was a little irritating.

"It's a terrible situation," I said, opening my mouth though I had not intended to speak. "But was it really police brutality?"

"Removing people from their homes?"

"Removing people from private property."

"Semantics. It was a forcible removal."

"Really? How forcible was it? No one was beaten. No one was hurt. The Swedish police are, as far as I know, the gentlest in the world."

"The property that the Roma were living on is owned by a developer who's just let it sit for years. Do the police have to evict the people living there so it can just sit empty? The developer doesn't even need it."

"Who gets to determine need? Don't the Syrian refugees whose lives are in danger have greater needs than the Roma?"

"Are they moving Syrian refugees into the vacant lot?"

"I'm just saying that if we're looking at need, people who are escaping war have a greater need than the Roma, who just need money."

"But they aren't evicting the Roma for the Syrians—they're evicting them for a rich man. And just needing money is never 'just' anything when you're starving."

I rolled my eyes. How would Torsten, subsidized for his entire adult life by Swedish student stipends, rent stipends, and unemployment stipends, know anything about starving? "They're not starving. Nobody is starving in Sweden. The Roma are poor and they have difficult lives, but they aren't starving. Not here."

"How would you know?" Torsten sounded genuinely upset.

I knew from past arguments with Alexandra that once you had cut through the muscle of someone's logic into the tender belly of feelings, it was time to back off. "Maybe you're right. I'm sure you know more about it than I do. I'm just playing devil's advocate."

Torsten lit another cigarette, suddenly calm again. "*Devil's advocate*—what does that mean?"

I was surprised that Torsten, whom I'd heard use phrases like *socioeconomic hegemony*, didn't know what *devil's advocate* meant. "It's when you take a position that you may not necessarily support in hopes of furthering the argument."

Torsten thought about it—or pretended to think about it—for a minute. "It sounds like it means 'coward.'"

I pretended to laugh and asked Torsten if he considered protesting against the tyranny of the majority cowardly. Torsten, maybe sensing that he had cut through the muscle of my logic, said that perhaps I was right and that he was only joking. But we both knew that he had won.

The position of devil's advocate did exist to offer a reason to speak without the prerequisite of belief. It was a way to say something without having to face the consequences of having said it. When I thought about it, I had a hard time remembering when I'd heard anyone but a white male use it.

"The devil doesn't need a lawyer," my mom used to say.

I WOKE ON FRIDAY MORNING WITH A SURGE OF EXCITEMENT for Ulrika's party. I went to the library to work on a paper, but all I thought about was Ulrika. I was too antsy to get anything done. I showered early in the evening and tried on outfits with the blinds closed, not in fear of the across-the-street neighbors seeing me naked, but in fear of them seeing me trying on outfits. I was dressed and ready with an hour to kill. I wondered if I should invite Bengt. It would be comfortable to have a friend with me, and Bengt had brought me so many places that it would be nice to return the favor. But I also worried that Ulrika, upon seeing Bengt, would lose interest in me.

Eventually I texted Bengt to ask if he wanted to come.

Sounds great, but I'm on my way to Copenhagen for the night! Have fun!

I was happy to not have to worry anymore about whether to invite Bengt. For a moment, I wished that my old neighbor Laurent was still in Sweden instead of back in Paris. Even if he and I didn't have a lot in common, this was the kind of situation where we could laugh and drink and meet all these new people together. There was also a part of me that wanted to show off to him that a pretty girl liked me. But I told myself to stop worrying about what wasn't happening and look forward to what was. I still had time to kill, so I opened my email, then Facebook, and then the *Times*, where I clicked on an article about unaccompanied-minor refugees living in Germany. The article described the journey of a boy from Afghanistan who'd been separated from his family in a forest near the Macedonian-Serbian border. On his journey, the boy had been robbed and chased by police, but he had still made it to Germany on his own. He was seven.

Tens of thousands of unaccompanied minors had come to Germany in 2015 alone, the article said. Some of their parents had been killed in Syria, Afghanistan, or Iraq, or in the waters between Turkey and Greece. Some parents had been separated from their children on the journey to Europe. Some had sent their children away to continue their schooling after ISIS or the Taliban had closed their schools. Some had sent their children away to save them from forced conscription into ISIS.

The boys were making progress, one of the social workers at a home for unaccompanied minors said. They were learning German. They screamed less at night.

Few girls made the journey alone, apparently. The ones who did arrived with terrible stories. One girl had been raped so many times that the doctors in Germany found injuries weeks later. She was—

Just then, something shot up my stomach, up my throat. I ran to the bathroom and vomited. Hunched over the toilet, gasping for breath, I retched again. My stomach kept contracting until there was nothing left. When it finally stopped, I caught my breath, rubbed the water from my eyes, and stared down at the toilet. It was mostly orange bile. I hadn't eaten anything unusual. I hadn't even started drinking yet. I washed out my mouth in the sink, took a few deep breaths, and returned to my room. I didn't feel nauseous or dizzy. It was strange.

I sat down in front of the computer again and read of the young boy who'd lost his parents on the Macedonian border. He'd been in Germany for almost a year. He was now fluent in German.

The boy had been waiting for his mother, who the article said hadn't been heard from in a month. But the boy told the interviewer that his mother would come get him.

"She said she would come," he said. "She promised."

I ran to the bathroom and threw up again.

I took my second shower of the evening and tried to wash away whatever had just happened. I toweled myself off and stared at the mirror, my eyes still red from vomiting. I read about terrible things every day. Every time I opened the news it was a smorgasbord of suffering: another far right party's triumph, another study on the rapid decay of the planet, another UN report on rape as a weapon of war, another breaking-news bulletin of a terrorist attack. When I read the news of another mass shooting in America, I didn't even wonder anymore about the people who had been killed. I wondered about who had done the killing and what conversation would dominate the following week. Had it been a white man with a grudge (gun control) or a killer with Muslim roots (immigration)? Once, on the bus from Lund to Malmö, I'd read about the kidnapping and presumed murder of forty-three Mexican student protesters, while, in another window on my phone, I discussed with Bengt where we should meet for beers that night. Then I had climbed off the bus, put in my headphones, and not given another thought to the Mexican students. The outside world could sting for a second, but it couldn't hurt me. Only things that happened to me or to the people I cared about really hurt.

This didn't make any sense.

I put on my coat, put my beers in a cloth tote bag, walked to the bus stop, and tried to return to the good feelings of earlier in the day. I boarded the last commuter bus of the evening, the one that went straight to Lund without passing through Malmö Central, sat down in the back, pulled a tall can of Carlsberg from my bag, and drank it quickly. I still felt bad, so I drank another tall can. It wasn't working. I longed for pills.

I started imagining that I was working in the refugee home in Germany. I imagined that I gave up everything, learned German, and traveled to the border to help. I imagined that I would sit with the boy who was waiting for his mother, read him stories, play chess with him, and sing him back to sleep when he woke up screaming. I couldn't stop global warming or prevent mass shootings, and even when I fantasized about them, I didn't imagine fixing a problem so much as winning an argument. But I wasn't imagining an argument now. I imagined that I was the social worker the *Times* had interviewed. I pictured this life in Germany—playing soccer with the kids in the yard, teaching them English, making them laugh—all the way to Lund. When the bus stopped, I found that I was happy again.

* * *

I followed the map on my phone to a little yellow house on an old cobblestone street in the city center of Lund. Party voices hummed inside. I walked up five steps to the stoop and knocked on the door, but no one answered. I rang the doorbell and knocked again. Finally I tried the handle and, when it gave, pushed open the door. There, behind a row of coats branching out from their hooks, stood Ulrika in a blue cotton dress, barefoot, talking to a handsome Swedish man in a dress shirt and suspenders. When she saw me, she ran up and wrapped me in a hug.

"I'm so glad you came!" she said in English.

"You look very nice," I said in Swedish.

"*Tack!*" Continuing in Swedish, she said, "Jonas, this is Anders."

I shook hands with the man in suspenders, who had a sharp part in his hair and a canary watchband that matched his canary socks. I was feeling so good that I didn't even hate him for the shameless intentionality of his outfit. Anders introduced himself in English, then put an arm around Ulrika's waist, kissed her, and disappeared into the house. All the excitement fell out of me. I would have to drink a lot that night.

Ulrika led me to the fridge to store my beers and then into the living room, where poppy hip-hop was playing. Half a dozen broad-shouldered men who were far too tanned for early October were chatting with half a dozen long-legged women. Another man was hanging upside down from a stripper pole in the middle of the room, his shirt drooped over his head to reveal a six-pack. Ulrika was about to introduce me around, but then the front door opened and she ran over to hug the next party guest. I introduced myself, in Swedish, and the men small-talked with me until they had filled their politeness quota. I sought out Ulrika to ask where I could go smoke. Another girl saw the cigarette pack in my hand and said that she would show me—she was going out to smoke anyway. This girl, Eva, wore tight black pants with tall high heels that emphasized her muscular calves. As we walked down to the patio, I told Eva in Swedish that I was impressed to see her navigating rickety stairs in such heels.

"This is nothing—normally I dance in seven-inch heels."

"You're a dancer?"

She said that she had met Ulrika in pole-dancing classes. "As in competitive pole dancing, not stripping."

We sat down at a circular iron table on a narrow plot of fenced-in dirt, the chair cold from the cold. Eva rifled through her purse and loudly cursed the absence of cigarettes that had presumably never been there. "Do you think I could bum one off you?"

"Of course."

This rarely occurred in Sweden. Swedes didn't bum smokes like Americans. I'd had fewer requests for smokes since moving to Sweden than I'd get on a single Friday night walking down Front Street in Wilmington. Once Eva asked for the cigarette and I knew that her interest in me had been transactional, I relaxed and listened to her talk instead of trying to appear attentive while searching for hints about her feelings toward me.

"I did an exchange semester in Florida a few years ago," Eva said. "My roommate was this American girl who believed in creationism.

Which was so crazy to me! That someone like that existed in the real world, today, you know?"

"I guess it is surprising."

"I'm sorry—I didn't mean to say 'crazy.' It was just unexpected, as a Swedish person. If you believe in creationism here, people think you're an idiot. But the funny thing was that this American girl was intelligent. She believed in microevolution but not macroevolution—which I thought was like believing in rain but not clouds. But still. She was very smart."

Eva flicked the ash from her cigarette.

"Sometimes you meet people and they're very different from what you expected. They're actually people." She laughed. "Not the deepest insight! The cigarette must have gone to my head."

I liked what she was saying. And more than that, I liked how she showed awareness of the problems with what she was saying. It saved me the trouble of finding the problems with what she was saying and left me more space to just enjoy her company.

I went to the kitchen to get another beer. At the fridge, I was greeted by a girl with white-blond hair.

"I heard you were American," she said in English.

"You heard right."

"I was in Texas as an exchange student!"

Then she began telling stories, which weren't exactly interesting, but weren't insulting or confrontational either. She wasn't that type of party guest who, upon hearing that someone was American, liked to pepper the American with questions about the recent news that Donald Trump was running for president or say something like "Did you know that sixty percent of Americans think the Earth is the center of the universe?"

I smiled and asked questions. She touched my arm three times during the conversation.

As I was talking to her, a drunk boy came in and said in heavily Swedish-accented English that the girl and I were an "adorable couple" and asked us how long we had been together.

"No, she and I are together," said a blond Swedish guy. He was short and muscular, and he put his arm around the girl. She leaned into his embrace. "But we're very liberal." He looked at me and winked.

I assumed the Swedish boy was trying to assert himself. I wasn't trying to get in between a couple, so I went to the fridge, grabbed another beer, and asked Eva to tell me more about her time with the creationist roommate. But throughout the night, the blond boyfriend kept looking at me. One time he stared right at me, then said something to his friend, then laughed. I wasn't angry enough to do anything about it; but I didn't like it.

Later, the boy leaned against the counter I was leaning against and said, in Swedish, "Do you think my girlfriend is cute?"

"I'm sorry?" I said in English. "I didn't understand you."

The boy repeated his question in English.

"Jag fattar inte vad du säger," I said.

The boy tried again in both languages. He didn't get that I was joking.

Finally, after a third or fourth "Do you think my girlfriend is cute?," I answered, in English, "That's a trap."

The boy turned to his girlfriend and said, in English, "He thinks you're a tramp."

"No, 'a trap,'" I said.

"En fälla," Ulrika clarified, popping into the conversation.

"He thinks you're a trap," the boyfriend said in English.

"No, I think the question is a trap."

The girl blushed.

I escaped to the living room, where the girls had taken over the pole. They wore weight-lifting gloves, and the ones in dresses had put on bicycle shorts underneath. I watched as Eva climbed to the top of the pole, wrapped her legs around it, and slid down in a hands-free twirl.

"That's impressive," I said to the girl standing next to me, mainly so it didn't look like I was staring at Eva's ass. And I wasn't staring at her ass; I was looking at the space in front of me so I'd appear to be engaged in something without having to talk to another person. After the exchange in the kitchen, I was convinced that I was lost in a foreign place, and that if I kept talking, I would fall further and further away from the core of the party, with everybody making fun of me in whispered tones once I was out of earshot.

I wanted to return to the fantasy world in Germany in which I helped people.

But it was only midnight! How stupid did you have to be to leave a Swedish pole-dancing party so you could fantasize about saving refugees?

* * *

I stayed for another few hours, drank a few more beers, smoked a few more cigarettes, and had a few more conversations, which were mostly showcases for my conversational partners to demonstrate their mastery of English. Around 2:00 a.m., my drunk began to swell. When I was on drugs, the minute I felt the alcohol begin to overtake my behavior in a way that might embarrass me, I took more drugs. With another pill or another bump, my brain would either wake up or I would forget that I was terrified of embarrassing myself. But now, whenever that drunk siren went off, I would exit as quickly as possible, getting out before I said anything that would bring me shame in the morning. I finished the last of what I calculated to be my eighth beer, put on a sober face, thanked Ulrika with carefully articulated politeness, and headed for the door.

As I was putting on my shoes and jacket, the girl with white-blond hair and the passive-aggressive boyfriend came over to say goodbye. She gave me a hug and told me that it had been nice talking to me.

"Do you want to get a beer sometime?" she said.

"What about your boyfriend?"

"We're very liberal."

I paused. "It's okay for you to go out with other men?"

"I'm not looking for another boyfriend. But we're very liberal."

"Okay." I handed her my phone and she typed in her number. We hugged again, said bye, and I walked to the train station, as it was too late for the commuter bus.

* * *

On the train back to Malmö, I wondered if I should have tried to sleep with the girl. Or with Eva. Or with any of the other girls at the party. I didn't want to sleep with any of the girls besides Ulrika. But I wanted to have done it. I mostly wanted to wake up next to Ulrika. I wanted a new memory. Maybe. I wasn't sure; I was drunk.

The train car smelled like McDonald's fries; I was overcome by a desire for fries; I thought about how much I wanted fries. I felt sad, like something terrible had happened but I couldn't remember what. I thought of the leftover spaghetti and meat sauce sitting in a bowl in my fridge. What a nice thought. At home, I could take off my jeans and jacket. I could put on warm fleece pajama pants, heat up a bowl of spaghetti, eat it in bed, and stream the Clippers preseason game that had just tipped off in LA. How nice.

I got off the train at Malmö Central. I checked the departures sign on the platform. The bus back to Värnhem left in four minutes. How perfect! If I ran, I would get outside to the bus depot just as the bus was pulling up; I wouldn't have to wait even a single minute. Everything was waiting for me at home: the fleece pajama pants, the spaghetti and meat sauce, the basketball game. I charged up the stairs; they offered no resistance; the air felt cool on my face; I reached the top; I stepped in—

I was hit by silence. A complete wall of silence, completely out of place in a train station. I heard it before I saw it. Then: rows and rows and rows of sleeping bags. Against every wall, tucked under every bench, squeezed next to every sign. Sneakered feet sticking out, white socks sticking out, blue tarps draped over duffel bags.

Total silence. The drunk passengers who'd been yelling on the train were tiptoeing like teenagers who didn't want to wake their parents. Nobody spoke. I started to walk but measured every step to muffle the sound. I didn't want to kick a foot; I didn't want to look up. I'd been to the station in the days since refugees had started arriving. I'd seen a few families waiting on benches in the afternoon, children sleeping under blankets, fathers sitting anxiously next to backpacks covered in tarps. But I hadn't been this late at night. I hadn't been to the station in the time between the arrival of the night trains and the opening of the processing center in the morning.

A group of teenage boys were gathered in front of the Burger King. They were whispering to each other at the tables. One boy was staring down at his phone. Another was pacing little laps around the table. In the middle of their group sat an older man. He wore a green jacket and had thinning hair. He was staring at me. I smiled at him; he didn't smile back. He wasn't staring at me; he was just staring at the space that I happened to be walking through.

A boy came in through the doors that led to the bus stops; he smelled like cigarettes. His hair was cropped on the sides, but long on the top, combed over from left to right like a young Swede. He wore light jeans and a hoodie that was too thin for the cold.

I wanted to say something—to welcome him in some way.

I opened my mouth and whispered, *"Hej."*

The boy startled; he hurried past me back to the Burger King tables.

Of course he did—what kind of man whispers hello to a teenage boy in the middle of the night?

* * *

I missed my bus. I walked home along the canals and the thousand lights of the rail yards on the other side of the water. I tried to think about what I'd seen, but I couldn't focus my brain—or my eyes—on anything. I walked in a blur of sidewalk, streetlight, and water. At my apartment, I put on fleece pants, heated my spaghetti, and lay down in bed to watch the Clippers game. But when I turned it on, I began to cry; I couldn't stop crying.

I was so angry with myself. What had I seen that I hadn't already known? Why was I crying about a few hundred refugees who'd made it to Sweden—who were now safe—when there were millions in Jordan and Lebanon and Turkey and Greece who might be sent back, die waiting, or spend a lifetime in limbo, hoping to hear their number called?

I tried to stop, but I couldn't—I was weeping now.

I got out of bed and found the old book of literary theory with my reminder cards.

This feeling will not last forever.

One day you will be nostalgic for this day.

God will take away your pain if you let him/her.

Stupid cards for stupid nonproblems. I ripped them up and threw them on the floor. I cocked my fist back; I remembered that the walls were concrete; I pulled up; I did not pull up soon enough.

"Fuck!" I shook my hand and tried to shake the throbbing out. The pain pulsated up my wrist into my forearm. I had punched more walls than people; I wasn't good at punching either.

* * *

After a few minutes, the throbbing settled. The hand wasn't broken—I'd been able to stop that much at least.

I sat at my desk in front of the congealing meat sauce. I thought about the Refugees Welcome rally. One of the speakers was a spokeswoman from UNHCR. She had described a raft capsizing in the waters between Turkey and Greece. Refugees were swallowed up by the violent waves. A mother scooped up each of her four young children and clung to them in the raging water. But the waves struck harder and harder, until the sea ripped one of her sons from her arms. She screamed. Then it took one of her daughters. Then another. Then another. By the time the coast guard saved her, she was alone, wailing at the sea.

Malmö Central was filled with people who'd made it across the water, who'd made it to Sweden, and were now sleeping in a train station waiting for—for what? A lifetime stay in the guesthouse, if they were lucky. If they were allowed to stay, they'd be moved to housing projects separate from the cities. They would never learn to speak Swedish like a Swede, never get eye contact from a Swede unless they were breaking the rules. They would be safe, maybe, but never at home.

And this was the best possible outcome for those who made it out: Sweden or Germany. Britain barely wanted to let in five thousand. Americans had deigned to admit ten thousand Syrians after a two-year vetting period. In Hungary, police officers were teargassing refugees to stop them from passing through the country on their *way* to Germany and Sweden. Walls were going up all around Eastern Europe.

Just then, for some reason, my mom's former neighbor appeared in my head: a smiley, divorced, middle-aged Republican named Jim. He had started vulturing around Mom's apartment in the Valley after I left for college. Jim would stop by on occasion when I was home for break, hoping to show off his dad chops to my mom. He would shake my hand heartily and ask me about school and make jokes that only he laughed at. He would smile condescendingly when my mother said something he deemed liberal—like that a country as rich as America shouldn't have homelessness.

"Wouldn't that be nice?" he'd say. "But we have to live in the real world."

"We create the real world, you condescending fuck," I said out loud.

And then, instead of explaining economics to my mom back in 2005, Jim was right there in my bedroom in Malmö explaining why America shouldn't admit Syrian refugees. "Look, I sympathize with the plight of these poor people, but we have to consider American safety first."

"Safety from who?" I said. "These people aren't terrorists—they're *fleeing* terrorism."

"I'm not saying they're all terrorists." Jim took a sip of Diet Coke. "But there's no denying the increased risk factor there. And it's not just safety that has to be considered. Immigration is an immense strain on the economy."

"If immigration is such a strain on the economy, then why is it that the countries with the most open borders are the ones with the strongest economies?"

"Well, now——"

"Why is it that the xenophobes are the ones mired in economic depression? Why is it that America, the richest country on earth, is the one founded on immigration?"

"America's success is based on the free market, which——"

"You have more money than you'll ever need! You own an apartment and a car and have enough money in the bank to live on until you die of old age. You think people risk their lives and leave everything they know to come to a country that doesn't want them because they *want to*? Imagine what the alternative must be when that's the best option."

"Now look, Jonas, nobody gave me anything, I earned every cent——"

"Where's your empathy? Where's your decency? Where's your fucking humanity!"

I was punching the air, punching the world, about to punch Jim, when I saw myself in the mirror: eyes red, spit hanging from my lip, shirt stained with meat sauce, nothing but a weeping drunk in pajamas.

Malmö, Sweden

Fall 2015

It was at the Malmö University Library the following day, hungover, looking up every minute at the processing center out the window, that I saw the flyer. A little red square of paper under some brochures on a table: *Do you want to help a newly arrived refugee practice Swedish and English? Join the Malmö University Language Café!* The flyer said that speakers of Arabic, Dari, Pashto, and Kurdish were especially needed.

I typed out an email to the listed address, in English, saying that I was a former professor, proficient in English and Swedish. I admitted that I did not speak Arabic, Dari, Pashto, or Kurdish. I now wished that I spoke all these languages, even if this was the first I was hearing of two of them. I wrote that I'd be happy to help if they still needed volunteers.

I returned to the paper I was trying to build into my master's thesis. I was looking at Sara Ahmed's "A Phenomenology of Whiteness," which was about how whiteness enables bodies to move unnoticed, while dark skin attracts attention. I hoped to combine Ahmed's ideas with—something. I wasn't yet sure what. The week before, I had turned in a draft of a chapter to my thesis adviser, and reading back over what I'd written, I hated it. I hated that despite my efforts to sound academic (but still readable), my professor had scribbled in the margins, *Maintain academic tone.* I hated how going to class to study my favorite topic was starting to feel like a waste of time, since even if the books mattered, our conversations about them usually didn't, and I hated that I had nothing to add to the one conversation I'd encountered that did matter.

Ahmed ended "A Phenomenology of Whiteness" by relating an anecdote: She said that when she gave talks at universities, the first question was usually from a white professor raising their hand to ask what white people could do. *The sheer solipsism of this response must be challenged,* Ahmed wrote. The purpose of the white professor's question is to *re-position the white subject as somewhere other than implicated in the critique.* The white academics wanted to move from the uncomfortable position of being noticed (as a part of an inherently racist system), to their more normal state as the ones who noticed things (the people who diagnosed and described the problem). Everybody liked to conduct the experiment; few people liked being the subject of the experiment. I knew that moving from noticed to noticer was exactly what I was trying to do by writing this paper. I knew that listening was the most important thing for someone in my position. But I couldn't just listen—not if I wanted to get my degree.

I checked my email every five minutes.

Not half an hour later, I found that someone had responded to my message.

Thank you for your interest, wrote someone named Ali. He said they certainly needed more Swedish speakers. *We have many volunteers, but they are mostly exchange students from Germany or people from the Middle East (like myself) who are not very good at Swedish.*

The first meeting, Ali wrote, was tomorrow evening. He would be happy if I could join them.

At home, I googled the address Ali had sent. I looked at the street view of the map to make sure I knew exactly where it was: behind Malmö University, across the water from the windmill factory where giant sealed tubes were lined up like mega-blueprints. I wrote Ali to ask what I could bring—coffee, bread, cookies? He responded that they had all the food they needed. *Just bring yourself.*

I didn't want to show up empty-handed. I wanted a purpose to serve. But I didn't know how to teach Swedish. I imagined walking through the doors and finding more volunteers than refugees. I imagined pacing the edge of the room with nowhere to go, like a short boy at a high school dance. I imagined sitting face-to-face with a serious man from Syria who would, within two seconds of looking at me, realize that I didn't know what I was doing.

I wanted drugs. I could tackle any social situation when I was high. I checked my personal email, my school email, all my social media accounts, the *Times*, and *Dagens Nyheter*. I had no more internet errands to run, but I found that I couldn't close my computer. I googled *Syrian civil war*. I googled *Syrian refugees*. I googled *teaching Swedish as a second language*. With every search, I had to open more windows to accommodate the hits I wanted to investigate, so

I clicked back and forth, feeling not an accumulation of knowledge but a terrible anxiety at how much I didn't know. The unknowing grew and grew, until I shut all the windows and fell into bed.

The introductory meeting for volunteers would be followed by the first Language Café. The weather that day was angry and wet, and by the time I left the apartment, night was settling in to a sixteen-hour shift. I got off the bus at Anna Lindhs Plats and walked into a frightening headwind the two blocks to the student union. An umbrella tumbleweeded toward me; I moved aside to avoid it. I leaned into the wind like it was a couch I was pushing across the floor. Finally I made it inside, where about a dozen college students and one older woman were scattered across several four-chaired round tables.

I had barely sat down when, at 4:30 on the dot, a young woman stood up. Her blond hair reached down past her shoulders. She wore a thick winter sweater and jeans tucked into the type of knit socks that Anja wore. She reminded me of skiing.

"Welcome to the Malmö University Language Café," she said in English. "Thank you all for coming. My name is Katja, and I am an international relations student here at Malmö University. I'm from Germany but I have been living in Malmö for over a year."

She went on: "It's okay if you're not fluent in Swedish! I'm not fluent either. But we're going to be doing *Hej, hur mår du?* and *Jag mår bra*, and so on. The kinds of things you learn in a Swedish-for-exchange-students class."

She said that the idea of the Language Café was partly to provide the students with a comfort level with the Swedish alphabet before they started school, but also to provide them with a comfort level with Swedish people. "Of course, many of us are not Swedish people. But we'll do our best."

Katja told us that we'd be working with thirteen- to seventeen-year-old unaccompanied boys from Afghanistan, who were living in the transit home closest to the university until they were assigned more permanent homes.

I was excited. Teenagers were the exact age group I wanted to work with. But I had assumed the refugees would be from Syria.

"Will there be boys from Syria as well?" one of the volunteers asked.

"Ali, do you want to answer that?" Katja said.

A guy who appeared to be in his late twenties, with a neat dark beard, light brown skin, gray jeans, and a blue sweater, stood up.

"Hello, I'm Ali. I'm one of the organizers. While many of the refugees coming to Sweden are Syrian, most of the unaccompanied refugees are Hazara boys from Afghanistan. ISIS is a big problem in Afghanistan, and they still have al-Qaeda and the Taliban there. Many Hazara refugees escaped to Iran, but I'm from Tehran and I can tell you that it's not a good situation for the Hazara there."

The lone older woman in the room raised her hand. "Why is it only boys we're working with?"

"Because it's only boys that are living at this transit home," Katja said. "Families usually don't send girls unaccompanied."

"Because they don't want them to come here and be educated?" the woman said.

"Because they don't want them to be raped along the way," Katja said.

It was quiet.

"So now we're going to teach you some games that you can teach to the boys!" Katja said.

After Katja put us in a circle and taught us a meet-and-greet game, we sat back down and drank coffee from paper cups, made small talk, fidgeted, and waited for the boys to arrive. A little after five, they poured in with a roar. Smiling, laughing, joking boys—maybe forty of them, many with heads shaved on the sides and hair combed over the top, a few with hair that looked like it hadn't seen scissors in months. Their clothes had no unifying theme. Jeans of different colors, rips, and fades. Sweatpants and corduroys. Knit sweaters, hoodies, and long-sleeved thermals. Fake-leather jackets and puffer jackets. Infinity scarves like those the Germans wore and homemade scarves with maroon patterns. Some of the boys laughed with each other, pretending we weren't there. Some made direct eye contact, smiled, and waved. Most looked healthy, but none were fat. Behind the boys, clad in tight black jeans and a thick cardigan, I saw Torsten, the Marxist from class.

"*Tjena, grabben!*" I said, walking up to him.

"*Tjena*, Jonas! What are you doing here?" he said in Swedish.

"I'm volunteering. Do you work with the boys?"

"I just started. I have a bachelor's in social work, and they needed help at the transit home. There are supposed to be forty boys living there but they have two hundred and fifty. They're supposed to be there for a week, but they're staying for four to eight weeks."

"So you volunteered?"

"Well, not exactly." Torsten seemed ashamed. "I'm an employee. I get paid."

"That's great!"

"But *you* volunteered."

"Only for a few hours a week."

Ali called for everyone's attention in what I assumed was Farsi. "Dari?" he asked the class.

Most of the boys raised their hands. The ones who didn't raise their hands were elbowed by the boys standing next to them until they, too, raised their hands.

"Okay," Ali said to Katja. "They all speak Dari, so they can understand Farsi. I can translate." I had learned from a quick google that Dari and Farsi were both forms of Persian, and that the shared cultural roots were one of the reasons why the Hazaras were allowed temporary stays in Iran—even if it was, as Ali had said, "not a good situation there."

Katja introduced herself in English, and Ali translated into Farsi. She said that we were going to get into groups and play a game, then have some *fika*. "Which is a Swedish word you will need to know!"

Ali translated.

"*Fika*," several of the boys repeated.

"It means coffee and tea and sweets—Swedes have it several times a day!" Ali translated, and the boys laughed.

Then Ali went around the room assigning each boy a number, like a PE teacher.

"Two over here," Katja said, holding two fingers in the air. "Come on, Jonas, you're with me too."

I felt a little rush of warmth at being picked by Katja. I realized it was inappropriate—I should be focused on helping, not on a girl. But if I could use my wanting-to-impress-Katja energy on helping the boys, then I'd be a better teacher too. Everyone would win.

We organized seven boys into a circle and Katja explained the rules. You would say your name, then make a gesture—kick an imaginary soccer ball, do a spin, clap your hands, etc. The next person would say your name, do your gesture, and then say his name, do his gesture, and so on, until the last person was tasked with nine names and gestures. A few of the boys spoke English and helped communicate to the others.

After Katja finished explaining the rules, one of the boys raised his hand. He was almost six feet tall, with dark hair combed across his forehead, in the style that was fashionable in the Valley in the early aughts when emo was the rage. "When will we learn Swedish?"

"Soon!" Katja said. "But we thought maybe you wanted to have some fun first."

"Yes, this is fun, thank you."

"Thank you," several of the boys repeated.

"But we can begin the Swedish now. We are ready."

I looked to Katja. She wasn't prepared for students impatient to work. I tried to appease the boys with additions to the circle game, naming gestures and body parts in Swedish for them to repeat as they went along. If a boy used his leg for his gesture, I would point to my leg and say, *"ben,"* and they would all repeat the word. I applied this unpedagogical technique to every turn, pleased that I could contribute something and that I was impressing Katja. This feeling of pleasure grew and grew until I realized that it was about to be my turn and I had not processed a single name. I tried to concentrate. Then I began to sweat.

When it came to me, I said, *"Hon heter Katja,"* and high-fived the air. *"Han heter Sala . . . ,"* I stammered.

"Salahuddin!" the boys yelled, and laughed.

"Salahuddin." I made a peace sign. *"Han heter Osman."*

"No, I am Osman!" the tall boy with the emo hair corrected. More laughter.

My incompetence brought much joy to everyone, to the point where I even started enjoying it. I struggled through five names, with much help from the boys, one of whom patted me on the back in consolation.

After I finished, the next boy—a short kid with a guilty grin who was wearing a Russian fur hat—pointed to me and said, *"Han heter Salahuddin."*

The boys laughed thunderously.

I saw Katja shake her head and smile.

After the game, it was *fika* time. The boys lined up along the snack table, but when Katja got into the back of the line, a murmur of Dari ran through them. The boys punched each other in the arm and pointed at Katja. Then they began to step aside and motioned to her to go to the front of the line. One of them said something to the tall boy with the emo hair, Osman, who looked to be a group spokesperson—either due to his height or his English.

"Please, you go." Osman motioned Katja ahead.

"No, no—it's okay!"

Osman held his arm forward. "Please, my friend, you go."

So Katja stepped to the front of the line and filled her coffee with the embarrassment of someone who knows she's being watched.

She walked by me on her way to the back tables.

"Looks like they like you," I said.

She reddened and kept walking. I watched her as she walked away, then became conscious of my watching and looked down.

When Ali got in line, the boys repeated the same ritual of moving aside. After he'd filled his cup, he came over my way, stirring his coffee with a plastic spoon.

"They're very polite," I said.

"In Afghan culture, there is a great respect for your elders." Ali took a sip. "They say it lasts about two months once they get to Europe."

Several of the boys had gathered in front of a laminated poster of the Swedish alphabet that Katja had tacked up to the wall. They were holding up their phones to take pictures of the poster.

"They want a picture so they can practice the alphabet at home," Ali said.

"I've never had students like this."

"They're so eager to learn." Ali shook his head. "It makes you grateful for everything you have."

Had a white person said this, I would have cringed. But coming from Ali, who was here from Iran under circumstances I wasn't familiar with, I didn't know how to judge it.

Osman was sitting at a table with Arash, the jokester with the Russian hat. They were drinking tea and speaking Dari.

I crouched down at the table and said in English, "How's it going, guys?"

They both jumped up and offered me their chairs.

"No, no—it's fine. I don't need a chair."

"Please, my friend," Osman said. "Please."

"Thank you, Osman." I sat down. I wanted to be the adult and guide them through the conversation. But just as in my office hours, I didn't know how to do this. After a few moments of silence, I said, "How long ago did you arrive in Sweden?"

"Since four days," Osman said. "He around the same time. I was in Iran, with my uncle, but it is not good for us there. I walked through Iran. It takes fourteen days. But we can only walk at night. Then Turkey, then Greece, then Macedonia, then Serbia, then Hungary, then Austria, then Germany, then Denmark, and now Sweden." Osman counted the countries off on his fingers.

"How long did it take?"

Osman said something to Arash. Arash said two things in Dari, each with the inflection of a question, then shrugged.

"Forty-four, forty-five days?" Osman said. "Once we walked for three days without stopping."

"You must be tired," I said stupidly.

189

"We are fine."

"Welcome to Sweden."

"Thank you," Osman said.

It was quiet again. I felt the silence as something I had to fix.

"Is your family still in Afghanistan?" As soon as the words left my mouth, my internal elevator plunged. But it was too late.

"No," Osman said. He took a long sip of his milk-whitened tea.

I sipped my coffee and hoped he would say something else. He did not. I noticed, with surprise, that I was suddenly angry at Osman. Then angry at myself for feeling angry at a child when all he had done was sidestep a thoughtless question that could be uncomfortable for us both.

Here was the rare conversation in which I actually wanted to hear the answers to my questions—where I wasn't just asking *Where are you from?* or *How's work?* to be polite. But I wanted to ask questions like a friend, not like a thief. More than anything else, I wanted not to ask about dead family members.

"Excuse me, my friend?" Osman said. "How do you say, 'Thank you for the food'?"

"In Swedish?"

"Yes. The woman who serves food at the home doesn't speak English. We don't know what to say when she gives us food."

"You say, '*Tack för maten.*'"

The boys repeated the sounds, bending them into foreign shapes from the backs of their throats. I repeated the sounds back until they blossomed into intelligibility. Then Osman pulled a crumpled sheet of paper and a pen from his jacket, wrote down the sounds in

Dari script, and held the paper up so he and Arash could ground the sounds in writing.

"*Tack för maten,*" they said.

"*Bra!*" I said. "That means 'good.' You are *bra* at Swedish already. You'll speak the language in no time."

Osman smiled in an unguarded way that I wasn't used to seeing in someone his age. It was the kind of smile that tended to die at puberty. I was so happy to see the smile that I didn't immediately notice how expertly Osman had guided the conversation back into the realm in which I felt comfortable. It was either conversational aptitude, kindness to me, or pragmatic knowledge that keeping me happy might be good for him.

"I went to eighth class," Arash said in surprisingly clear English, adjusting the fur hat on his head. "In Afghanistan."

"I can tell. You speak good English."

"Yes. I lived alone. My uncle came every week to see me, but I lived alone in a big house. Very big. But the Taliban saw the big house and they came for money. I said, 'Okay, fine, I have a big house, I have money, okay. I will pay them.' But then they started coming two times in a week. Three times in a week. Then they came every day. That is when I said, 'Enough of Afghanistan. I will come to Sweden.'"

As Arash talked, Osman's eyes widened. It looked as if he wanted to stop Arash—either because Arash was lying or because Osman thought the story would give me the wrong impression—but was worried that saying anything in front of me would hurt them both.

The Iraqi writer Hassan Blasim wrote a short story about a refugee arguing his case for asylum to an immigration officer in Malmö, in which the narrator says, *Everyone staying at the refugee reception center has two stories—the real one and the one for the record.* It had occurred to me that the boys might exaggerate their stories, seeing as they were trying to get residence permits, and the more cogently horrible your backstory, the likelier you'd get to stay. But I also thought the boys might exaggerate their stories because everyone exaggerated stories from their past, even if they weren't trying to get a residence permit. I exaggerated the stories from my American past when I told them to my Swedish classmates, sometimes to impress my listeners, but more often it just happened without my even thinking about it. Maybe it was the leftover good feelings from when I'd seen Osman's unguarded smile, but listening to Arash, I didn't care how true his story was. I didn't care if the boys had walked through the desert for three days straight or three hours straight. I didn't care whether ISIS had threatened their families, their schools, or their cities. I didn't care if they had escaped Taliban extortion, al-Qaeda violence, lack of schools, oppression, poverty, or something I hadn't even considered. Whatever the reason, the boys were here now. And being here now, alone, was difficult enough.

"I want to go to school here," said Arash.

"What would you like to study?" I said.

Arash looked to Osman, but Osman didn't understand.

"I'm asking what subject he's interested in," I said to Osman.

Osman looked confused and said something to Arash. Arash said something back.

"Yes," Osman said.

I couldn't think of a gesture that would communicate the question. I began to sweat a little. Every silence was a failure on my part.

"School is very good here," I said. "You can go to university here for free."

Osman nodded, concentrating hard. "You are from Sweden?"

"I'm from Los Angeles."

"Los Angeles?"

"In America."

The boys murmured, impressed.

"You are rich?"

"No." I laughed, thinking how I'd never made more than $24,000 in a year and was falling ever deeper into student-loan debt. Then I remembered myself and stopped laughing.

"Do you know movie stars?"

I didn't know any movie stars. "Once I met Michael Keaton."

The boys looked puzzled.

"You know, Batman?"

"Christian Bale?" Arash said.

"You know Christian Bale?" Osman said.

"Yes. I know Christian Bale."

The boys giggled and talked in Dari.

"America is good," Osman said. "I would like to go there."

"I hope you will one day."

Osman nodded and got a look of concentration. I worried that he thought I was testing him, deciding if he was good enough for America.

"Do you want to know how to ask where someone is from in Swedish?" I said.

"Yes," Osman said. "Thank you."

As Osman copied down the Swedish words in Dari characters, I saw a boy walking around by himself, away from the minigroups that had formed, staring down at the floor. He was skinny and handsome. He wore sweatpants and sandals with a crew-necked sweatshirt that was wet around the shoulders, not yet dry from the rain.

I called him over. "Would you like to learn some Swedish?" I said, brimming with confidence.

The boy stared at me.

I asked Osman to translate.

"No, I understand," the boy in the sweatshirt said in English.

"Good. If you want to ask somebody where they are from in Swedish, you say, '*Varifrån kommer du?*'"

"I do not want to do that right now," the boy said.

Osman growled something in Dari.

"I am sorry," the boy said. "I can learn Swedish."

"No, it's okay," I said. "You don't have to learn it now."

"Thank you." He walked away.

I watched him crouch down next to the restroom door and pull out his phone. I wanted the sinking feeling inside me to be from tenderness and care, but I suspected it was more embarrassment at my mistake.

"He is, you know . . ." Osman tapped his head with his index finger. "He wants to live in his phone. But we want to learn."

I gave Osman and Arash another Swedish phrase, listened to them practice, and said, "Good! Now I'd like you to teach it to three other boys."

Osman and Arash nodded and hurried off to a group of other boys.

I went to talk to the boy sitting by the restroom.

"I'm sorry about that," I said in English, leaning against the wall and lowering my backside to the floor.

The boy looked up at me.

"I shouldn't have been trying to teach you Swedish on your break. Breaks are for relaxing."

"I can learn Swedish on my break. I was just thinking about something else and it felt difficult to start learning something new when I was thinking about that."

"That makes sense. It's difficult to switch between thoughts."

We were quiet for a moment. The boy ran his thumb over the screen, though the phone was locked.

"What were you thinking about?"

"I was thinking about my family. But I would like to learn."

"We don't have to learn Swedish now. You have all the time in the world." I smiled. "What's your name?"

"Aziz."

"Jonas." I offered my hand and Aziz shook it limply. I was about to ask him where his family was, but I caught myself before salting any more wounds. "You were thinking about your family?"

"Yes. They are in Tehran. My mother and my sister."

I nodded, thinking of how to move forward without accidentally asking about someone who might have been killed. "Is your sister older or younger than you?"

"I am the oldest." He paused. "Would you like to see a photo of my sister?"

He unlocked the phone and showed me a picture of a toddler with a blue bow in her hair, sitting on a baby-blue blanket in front of a photographer's blue backdrop, smiling with her whole face.

"Her name is Najma. It means 'star' in Arabic."

"That's beautiful. You must miss her."

"Yes. She needs me." He tensed up. "But it is not good in Tehran. We left because it is not good. We did not just want to go."

"I know," I said, though I didn't know at all. But I suspected that you wouldn't send your son on a three-thousand-mile trip, alone, to a country where he didn't know anyone, if things were good at home.

Aziz was looking down again.

"Your family must be proud of you," I said.

"I don't know."

"I'm sure they are. Many people try to make it here. Most don't make it. And you did it all on your own." I reached my hand out to his shoulder. "Your mother must be very proud."

The moment my hand touched the wet sweatshirt, I realized how inappropriate it was—how likely it was that he didn't want to be touched by a stranger. I was about to pull the hand away when Aziz looked up and smiled a tired smile. So I left it there for a second.

"You pronounce it *Najma*?"

"Yes, *Najma*," he said. "Like a star."

*   *   *

On the bus ride home, I felt pleasantly worn-out. But I also longed for drugs. I wondered why doing something good—even with the clumsiness of a drunk trying to fit a key in a lock—would make me want to get high.

"Because *everything* makes you want to get high," Duke had said.

But not everything made me want to get high anymore. I still thought about drugs at least a few times a week. I still longed for them—especially when I was hungover. But there were times when I felt happy or proud or good without explanation. It was strange: feeling good without knowing where the good feeling had come from or when it would end.

AT THE SECOND LANGUAGE CAFÉ, AZIZ LOOKED LIKE A DIFferent person. He wore a rain jacket and boots and wasn't soaked at the shoulders. He called out, "Jonas, my friend!," before I could even think of the appropriate greeting.

He reached out and shook my hand in several elaborate steps. "I heard that you are American!"

Which explained the handshake. "I am. But not too American, so don't worry. Did you get a new jacket?"

"This? No, I simply misunderstood Torsten last time! I thought we were just going downstairs, but then we walked ten minutes in the rain! But now I am ready for the Swedish weather. Tell me, did you see the American Music Awards last night?"

"Were those yesterday?"

"Jonas! I thought you were American!"

"I'm a failure. Did you see them?"

"I read about them on the internet."

"Who won?"

"Taylor Swift. I like Taylor Swift."

"Me, too. She seems like she's a nice person."

"Very nice! And Justin Bieber won."

"I'm not a big fan of Justin Bieber."

"I am also not a big fan of Justin Bieber. And One Direction won. But do you say di*rec*tion or *di*rection? The second way is British, right? You would say it the first way, because you are American?"

"That's right. You're very good at English."

"Thank you."

It was a strange kind of small talk—normally empty calories that today felt substantive.

"How is your sister, Najma?"

"You remembered! Very good, Jonas. She is well. I Skyped with her on Tuesday. She is already bigger than I remembered."

Ali whistled that it was time to start.

"I'll talk to you afterward," I said, and we performed another long handshake.

After the first Language Café, I had asked Ali to teach me to say, "Hello. My name is Jonas. I'm from Los Angeles. That is all the Dari I can speak." He had repeated the words until I got them right, and I had copied them into a notebook I kept in my pocket. Now, as the boys assembled in a semicircle readying for the day's directions, Ali suggested that I offer my Dari/Farsi introduction as the welcome speech. "The boys have probably never seen a white person speak Farsi before. It'll be fun for them."

I felt a surge of pride. But there was a wrinkle in the plan.

As we soon learned, a new group of boys had arrived from Syria who spoke Arabic, not Dari. Muhammad, a volunteer who had come to Malmö from Syria two years earlier, jumped up to translate for the Arabic group.

I stepped forward and said in Dari, "Hello. My name is Jonas. I'm from Los Angeles. That is all the Dari I can speak."

The Dari speakers applauded—Aziz whistled—and I took a joking bow.

"What did he say?" Muhammad asked Ali in English.

"He said that his name is Jonas and that he is from Los Angeles and that he doesn't speak Dari," Ali yelled back in English.

Muhammad translated into Arabic that my name was Jonas and that I was from Los Angeles and that I didn't speak Dari. When Muhammad stopped, scattered, confused applause came from the Arabic-speaking boys. But I still felt pride.

"Welcome to the Language Café! We're so glad you came," I said in English. Then I waited for the simultaneous translations to finish.

"How is it at the home?" I asked Aziz at *fika* break.

"It's good. We eat. We go to the Central Station to use the Wi-Fi. We sleep. Then we do it again."

"That sounds hard."

"It is a little hard to wait. I want to start school." He paused. "Do you know when we will start school?"

"I don't know. I think you start school when you get moved to your more permanent home."

"When will that be?"

"I don't know exactly. But I think it takes a month or two."

"Oh." Aziz looked down. "I went to school at home."

"I can tell. You speak very good English."

"Thank you. I went to ninth class. But then, Daesh—you know Daesh? ISIS?"

"Yes."

"Daesh closed my school."

"I'm sorry."

"Yes, it was bad. Then I couldn't go to school in Iran." Aziz paused. "Do you think I can start school sooner if I learn Swedish?"

"You're doing very well with the Swedish—that's not why you have to wait."

"Yes." He nodded. "Then why?"

"They have to find you a home."

"But I could go to school while they look for a home."

"They don't want you to start a school and then have to start a different school two months later."

"Why not?"

"It'll be hard for you to leave."

"But that's stupid. I have already left."

"I know." I sighed. "I don't make the rules."

"No, of course. That was rude of me."

"It wasn't rude at all. It's very difficult to wait." I tried to think of something to say. "The thing to remember is that once you start school here, you can go for as long as you want. You can go to university for free."

"Yes, that will be very nice." Aziz forced a smile.

I thought of Dagerman showing up at the refugee train outside Essen, empty-handed except for his notebook and his consolation.

"What do you want to study?"

"I would like to study medicine. I want to be a doctor." Aziz looked at me. "But what is needed here?"

"What do you mean?"

"Do they have enough doctors in Sweden? Or do they need barristers? Or architects? What is needed?"

"Doctors are always needed here. I can never get an appointment. You'll make a great doctor."

Ali whistled for class to start and Aziz pulled my hand into a shake, then a fist, then a bump, which, by now, we performed in rhythm.

Besides a brief mention I'd let slip to Bengt after the first meeting, I'd managed to keep my volunteering to myself. It was all I wanted to talk about, but I didn't want to sound like a Habitat for Humanity spring-breaker just returned from the Ninth Ward to explain poverty, and I had to keep reminding myself that I couldn't preach about the boys since I knew nothing about them. But I still wanted to show Aziz around. Take him by Universitetssjukhuset in Lund so he could see Swedish doctors in action and understand that it wasn't that hard to become one. Give him a tour of Malmö. Maybe bring him to the grocery store and go over which milk was the regular milk and which was the *filmjölk*—the sour, watery yogurt that needed to be covered in müsli and sugar before it was edible. At least take him out to lunch.

Between the second and third Language Cafés, having spent much of the night before thinking about what I could do for the boys, I started writing a message to Torsten to ask if I could meet up with Aziz outside of class. But I couldn't figure out the right phrasing in Swedish. How could I write the message with the right amount of humility and respect, but also enthusiasm? Then I thought about how the other boys would react if I came by and took only Aziz to lunch. Osman might think he had answered some question wrong or not learned Swedish quickly enough. I could take them both out. But what about Arash? What about all the other boys? Torsten had said there were 250 boys at the home. My savings were drying up and I calculated that I could spend at most three hundred kronor on extra expenditures that week. I couldn't take 250 boys to lunch.

Maybe I could bring them books in Dari? Or books that taught Swedish with Dari translations? I got on the computer and checked the websites of local libraries, Swedish booksellers, and the resources offered by Migrationsverket, but I found no books that taught Swedish from Dari. Even the Farsi offerings were scant and expensive.

Then it hit me: notebooks. I had seen Osman and other boys taking notes on torn sheets of paper they carried in their jacket pockets. I could give them notebooks and pens to write phonetic spellings of Swedish words. Torsten had said the boys were mainly waiting around most of the time.

"It's hard to have too much time to sit and think about things," Torsten had said. "Especially considering that they have so many unhappy things to think about."

I went down to the grocery store, IKEA bag in hand. I bought forty notebooks and forty pens for eight hundred kronor, which was more than I had planned on spending, but I wasn't going to give notebooks to only half the boys. I carried the heavy IKEA bag home and thought of how these would be their notebooks to keep. Maybe we could encourage the boys to write about their memories, their experiences, in Dari or Arabic, to have an outlet. With a journal, they could write whatever they wanted, and no one would read it. They wouldn't have to impress the Europeans with the tragedy of their pasts in hopes of being granted permanent residence. They could write their impressions of this new country. We could emphasize the importance of what the boys were doing—highlight that their experiences were worth recording. We could emphasize that, even if they didn't have a museum, they were a part of history.

When I got back home, I sat down at my desk and began making a four-column worksheet. The boys had made it clear that they wanted to learn Swedish, not play games, and the worksheets that Katja and Ali had brought to the second meeting were ancient photocopies that taught phrases like *I am a stonemason.* I wrote Swedish phrases on the left: *Hej! Jag heter _____. Vad heter du? Jag kommer från Afghanistan, varifrån kommer du? Jag har gått vilse, kan du hjälpa mig?* I translated the phrases into English in the second column: *Hi! My name is _____. What's your name? I am from Afghanistan. Where are you from? I am lost, can you help me?* I left a third column blank for Dari and the fourth blank for Arabic.

I tried to translate the Swedish into Dari online, but I was met with the left-to-right problems. Dari script was read from right to left, but my word processor flipped the Dari phrases as soon as I pasted them from the translation engine. Even though I couldn't read any of the Dari characters, I could see that they didn't look the same in the word processor as in the translation box. I downloaded a Dari keyboard for the word processor, which fixed the right-to-left problem, but since I didn't know what any of the characters meant, I couldn't check if my question read, *Where are you from?* or *Where you from are?* The translator copied the question mark from my Swedish into Dari. Were there question marks in Dari? Or was the translator just copying an untranslatable character?

There were so many little obstacles—so many fences between Dari/Farsi and English/Swedish. Verb construction was completely different. Prefixes were suffixes. Left was right and right was left. And then there was an entirely new alphabet. I imagined trying to learn Swedish and being told that the *k*, which was a symbol you may never before have seen, sounded like a hard *kah*, unless it was followed by a *y*, in which case it was a shushing *sh*. But now, as I thought about the sound of Swedish words, I realized I was using English sounds as a frame of reference. Describing the *ky* sound to a Swedish child learning to read, I would compare it to the *sj* sound in Swedish—but I couldn't explain the *sj* sound in English because it had no English equivalent. I couldn't imagine what the Dari equivalent to any of this was.

Once I finished the worksheet, I posted it to the group page for the volunteers, along with a note asking Ali if he could proofread it since, if Farsi was mutually intelligible in speech to Dari, I assumed it had to be even more so in text. Ali had said Farsi and Dari were like Swedish and Norwegian, and I could read Norwegian much better than I could understand spoken Norwegian.

I stared at the screen and waited. Nobody responded to my post.

Five minutes. Ten minutes. I saw that Katja had seen the post, but she left no reply. Regret spread like a rash. I had overdone it. Nobody had asked me to make a worksheet. It was presumptuous. I wasn't one of the organizing members of the group like Ali and Katja—I was just a volunteer. I had probably mangled the Dari. The arrogance! To think I could just google-translate my way into a language that, up until a few weeks ago, I hadn't even known existed. The jitters were like caffeine shakes. I thought about deleting the post. But Katja had already seen it. If I deleted it, she would know that I cared whether she liked it or not. With pills, I could stop worrying about this nonsense. All it would take would be two or three white ovals of oxy to send me on an ecstatic walk to nowhere in particular. I could just walk until I found someone to talk to—a bus driver, a bartender, or anyone else with two ears who couldn't leave.

Then a blipping sound from the computer brought me back. A little text window informed me that Ali had liked my post. A comment appeared.

Great, Jonas! I'll get right on it!

A wave of relief washed over me. I reread my original message with pride. I had taken the initiative to do something good.

Five minutes later, Ali posted a revised doc.

Very few errors. Good job. I'll get Muhammad to do the Arabic column. We will use it next week. Meet tomorrow to discuss exercises?

I wrote back, *Sounds good!*

What's a good bar to meet? Katja asked.

How about Balthazar? I wrote.

See you there! Katja wrote.

Everything was better. I lay down and thought of Katja lying next to me, her cheeks happy and red as she laughed at my jokes.

The following evening I took the bus to Balthazar, a small bar in Möllevången, in central Malmö. To Swedes outside Malmö, Möllevången was a lawless ghetto. The Swedes I knew who were born in Malmö said that, when they were teenagers, whites didn't go to Möllevången. But postgentrification, it had become the heart of the city's nightlife.

Balthazar was just off the main square, behind a row of potted bushes that blocked off the bar's patio from the sidewalk. Inside, a single candle sat on every table, without which you wouldn't have been able to see the person sitting across from you. Bengt had brought me there for a beer shortly after I moved to Malmö, and as I'd sat drinking with him, I'd imagined future evenings when I would show the bar to visitors as if it were my own spot.

Katja and Ali were waiting by the door when I walked in.

"This is a cool place," Ali said, shaking my hand.

"I've walked by it many times, but I never saw it before," Katja said after giving me a hug.

I ordered the cheapest tap beer, in Swedish, and Katja and Ali followed my lead. Occasionally I found myself in one of these situations where I was the most Swedish person in the group. I would know which beer was on tap so you got forty centiliters in a glass instead of thirty-three centiliters in a bottle. I would know where to buy your train ticket or which bus to take. I would feel good and valued, until the moment I talked to another Swedish person and found myself using the wrong phrase or struggling through a punch line that lost its punch in the five extra words it took me to get there.

"Good job on the worksheet," Katja said, as soon as we sat down. "I can print out copies in the student union for the boys."

"I didn't mean to overdo it with that. I'm sure you have lots of worksheets to use. I just thought the boys might want something more current."

"Don't worry," Ali said. "We're not Swedish!"

We all laughed. Swedes had an old saying: *Tro inte att du är nåt*— "Don't think you're anything special." It was more common in the previous generation than in mine, but you could still see remnants of it in Swedish group dynamics, which, on the one hand, were governed by respectful communal decision-making and, on the other hand, took forever. In a skit by a Swedish comedy troupe, a group of Swedish soldiers under machine-gun siege try to schedule a meeting to get everybody's input before they decide on a course of action.

"I was telling some people about the Language Café," I said, "and I was offered a donation of journals. I thought that might be good? For the boys to have something to write in?"

"That's fantastic!" Katja said.

"Very good," Ali agreed.

"I was thinking that maybe they can write down the phonetic spellings of Swedish words and copy the alphabet in there?"

"Absolutely," Katja said.

"And I was thinking they could use their journals to write about their experiences and their memories."

"In Swedish?" Katja said. "That might be a little too hard."

"No, in Dari or Arabic. Not for language practice. Just for an outlet. Torsten said that they have so much time on their hands, thinking about the past and all that. I thought it might be helpful for them to do something else instead."

It was quiet for a moment.

"But how would writing about the past help them stop thinking about the past?" Katja said.

"It wouldn't help them stop thinking about it. I just mean that sometimes it helps to put it on paper instead of holding it all in."

"Sure." Katja paused, maybe trying to find the right words in English. "My concern is that we are not trained psychologists. What would we do if we tell the boys to start recording their memories and then we don't know how to help them with that? We don't know what's going to come up or what effect it's going to have. And we also don't know the pressure they might feel to process things that we cannot support them with, since we only see them for a few hours a week."

As she was speaking, it dawned on me how naive my idea was. How condescending, too—as if the boys needed an inspirational teacher to tell them that they could write down their thoughts.

"You're right. That was stupid of me to suggest."

"Not stupid," Ali said. "It's great to have the notebooks. Maybe we just say they're for Swedish practice?"

"Absolutely. They should use them for Swedish practice."

"It's great that you got the donation." Katja reached over the table and touched my hand. "Really great."

It was painful to receive consolation for something like this from a girl I liked—not consolation for my tragic past but for the dumb thing I had just said.

"So how long have you guys been living in Sweden?" I asked, trying to sound unfazed.

"This is the second year of my bachelor's degree," Katja said.

"That's right—I remember you said that at the introduction meeting. And you're studying international relations?"

"Yes, they have a really good program at Malmö."

"What about you, Ali?"

"I've been here about a year and a half." He took a sip of beer. "I'm finishing my master's. And then maybe I'll stay."

"Stay here permanently?"

"If I can."

"Did you move directly from Iran?" I said, tiptoeing.

"I left Iran when I was eighteen. Then I moved to Ukraine, and then to Malaysia, and now I'm here."

"What makes you want to stay here?"

"No one has ever been racist to me here." Ali laughed. "It sounds stupid, I know. But it's not good in Iran. And in Ukraine, everyone called me a terrorist. And in Malaysia, everyone *really* called me a terrorist. And it's silly, but it still hurts when people call you that all the time. And no one says that to me here."

I didn't know whether to chalk up his directness to the difficulty in maneuvering around emotions in a second language, or to the lack of a need to maneuver when you have something substantive to say. Either way, I was impressed and a little intimidated—to say something so personal, so directly.

During my last month in the Lund dormitories, after Anja and I had split, I had spent a lot of time drinking with Laurent. When we were out at the student nations, he was all teenage strut, but when we were alone and he was speaking broken English, he sometimes expressed himself with such tender directness that I didn't know how to respond. When Laurent was to return to Paris at the end of his exchange program, he'd given me a hug and said, "Man, I will miss you." Not *We're going to miss you around here*, as I had been planning to say, but "I will miss you."

I was touched but had found myself unable to say, *I'll miss you, too*. Instead, I'd said, "I think you'll do just fine back in Paris," and patted him on the back.

I wanted to say something that made Ali feel cared for in the way Laurent had made me feel cared for when he said that he would miss me.

But before I could try, Ali said, "And the girls—the girls are prettier here than anywhere else."

I laughed.

"You like the Swedish girls?" Katja raised her eyebrows at him.

"I only like you." Ali reached for her.

"*Ja, ja, ja.*" Katja fake-pushed him away. Then she relented to his kiss.

On my ride home, the bus passed the colorful lights of Möllevången's falafel joints and pizzerias and turned onto Drottninggatan, where the canals separated the street from the gravel jogging path. I thought about what a nice evening it had been. The momentary disappointment over seeing Katja and Ali kiss had soon settled into relief that I wouldn't have to ask Katja out.

I liked Katja and Ali. They were kind. They were easy to talk to. And it occurred to me, sitting there on the bus, that they had not once asked me about Donald Trump. For the past few months, since Trump had announced his candidacy for the Republican nomination and the Swedish media had discovered that he made for great copy, I could hardly be introduced to someone without being asked about Donald Trump. Classmates. Friends of friends. Any drunk person, once they found out I was American, wanted to know my thoughts on Trump.

I hated having Trump conversations. I could say that Trump was an embarrassment and a joke, but I had trouble talking about it in a way that avoided the anthropologist-studying-the-natives tone you heard in every NPR report on Trump voters. If I talked to a Swede about it, I would have to not only outline my own opinions, but also explain primaries and electoral procedures that I didn't totally understand (what was a caucus?), then finally deliver a short lecture on why it would be impossible for Trump to win the presidency. I'd almost always find myself defending America against a Swedish jab, despite being so deeply troubled by my country's direction that every time I closed the news I felt shaky and depressed, like I was coming down from a cocaine high.

Given that the Language Café was designed to provide a warm welcome to Muslim refugees driven from their countries by war and fundamentalist terror, it wouldn't have been strange to ask the American volunteer what he thought about the xenophobic American presidential candidate who appeared to suspect Muslims were terrorists until they were proven otherwise. But Katja and Ali never brought it up. For this, I was grateful. My hope was that newspapers and news sites and TV stations would just stop talking about Trump, and then people would stop talking about Trump on social media, and then everyone would stop talking about Trump altogether, and then he would just disappear, and the Republicans would nominate the more quietly toxic candidate, who'd lose to Hillary Clinton without embarrassing the nation too much in the process.

In the morning, I took the bus back down Drottninggatan to get a haircut. My barber, Mahmoud, like every barber I'd visited in Sweden, was from Iraq. I sat down in the chair. Mahmoud, clad in an Easter-green polo and white chinos, asked me in Swedish what I wanted today. I held up about two inches and said, in Swedish, "Make me look pretty."

He gave me a thumbs-up in the mirror. "The prettiest."

I felt the triumph of successful Swedish banter.

Mahmoud started snipping at my hair, which reached nearly down to my shoulders. He said that he was taking a trip to New York with his family in the spring, and knowing that I was American, he wanted some tips.

"The hotel rooms in Manhattan are so expensive. Is there anywhere else you can stay without being too far away from everything?"

"All my friends in New York live in Brooklyn. You can take the train to Manhattan from there in half an hour or so."

"Isn't Brooklyn dangerous? That's where all the black people live, no?"

"Brooklyn isn't . . ." I stopped. "There are . . ." I stopped again. "Brooklyn has changed a lot over the last ten or twenty years. It's a sought-after place to live. It's diverse and not dangerous."

The bell on the door rang, and a girl in her early teens walked in.

Mahmoud said something to her in what I assumed was Arabic, and she answered, then walked through the curtain separating the shop from the back rooms. The girl emerged again with a can of soda.

Mahmoud told her something, and she said, *"Okej, Pappa,"* in annoyed teenage Swedish.

"What language were you speaking?" I asked after she left.

"Arabic."

"Your daughter speaks it fluently?"

"Oh, yes. She's proud because her older brother isn't so good at it. But I speak it with her so that she'll remember. She doesn't resist like my son always has."

"My mother did that for me with Swedish in the US. I didn't appreciate it then, but I appreciate it now."

I asked Mahmoud if it had been hard for him to learn Swedish when he came over.

"No, because I already spoke English, so I knew most of the alphabet." He said he had met his wife at the adult-learning center, and that she had helped him a lot with the language.

"Love is the best way to learn a language," I said, slightly editing the cliché *the bedroom is the best place to learn a language.*

"It is!" He laughed and measured out my hair by lifting a handful of it straight out, then dropping it to the side. He unsheathed a second pair of scissors. "There was a woman in my Swedish class from China. She knew English, so she learned Swedish quickly. But there was another woman from China who didn't know the alphabet, and she had to learn it from scratch. It took her a very long time. Actually, I'm not sure that she ever learned Swedish."

"I imagine it's difficult when you don't know the alphabet. I'm working with refugees from Afghanistan, and I can't imagine how difficult it is for them to pick up on the sounds and appearance of all the new characters. They seem to be good at it, though."

"You work with refugees?" Mahmoud stopped snipping and looked at me in the mirror.

"I don't 'work' with them, exactly." I felt my face heat up. I hadn't meant to say it. Only a few weeks in and I was already using it as capital. "I only volunteer a little bit. And I just started. I don't know anything about it. I was just thinking about how, when I hear you speak to your daughter, I can't hear where one word ends and the next one begins. It must be hard to learn a language when you can't see the boundaries between the words."

"My son is also working with refugees."

"Is he? And he's only a teenager? You must be proud."

"Yes, he's a good boy. He's working with refugees from Afghanistan in Rosengård," Mahmoud said. "These boys, they come here and they have nothing. It really makes you appreciate what you have."

"Yeah."

"But it worries me, too. After you have everything taken from you, it does something to a person. I don't know if it can be healed.

When I go back to Iraq, the young people there—they're frightening. They think that you want to take something from them. You have to convince them otherwise before you start a conversation." I watched Mahmoud shake his head in the mirror. "It's good that my son is working with the refugees. But when he comes home, he doesn't feel good."

"You're exhausted afterward."

"No, not because of that. It's something else."

"I mean emotionally exhausted. It's emotionally painful."

"Yes, exactly. Emotionally painful." Mahmoud pulled the cape off and shook my hair onto the floor.

As I was coming back from Lund after a three-hour lecture on Derrida, which I had struggled to understand or care about, my bus passed the farm country between Lund and Malmö, where the rapeseed flowers would burst the now-icy fields yellow in the spring. I began to think about how I used to get high before the lectures I attended in grad school back home. How I used to drink liquor from a travel coffee mug and pop pills in bathroom stalls. I would talk and talk in class and no one would stop me. Sitting on the bus, I didn't feel the desire I normally felt whenever I thought of drugs—the desire for drugs I'd feel even when I read of an aid worker caught stealing morphine from an understocked civil war hospital in Sudan. Instead I felt shame. But I didn't long for pills to hide the shame, as I always had when ambushed by the shame of last night, last week, last year. It was comforting: to feel pain, knowing it would pass.

THE NOTEBOOKS WERE A HIT. WHEN WE PASSED THEM OUT, the boys called out a happy clamor of "Thank you," *Tack*, and what sounded like *Shook ran*. During the lesson, I looked over their shoulders as they wrote out the phrases in their notebooks in Dari or Arabic. I listened as they voiced my Swedish words sharper and throatier than I had, sounding like a tape recording of a tape recording. When they finally got the phrases right enough to be understood, I patted them on the back and said, *"Bra!,"* and they smiled.

"Jonas, my friend!" Aziz called out, walking toward me from his group.

We performed our elaborate handshake.

"How's your week going?" I said.

"It's going very well. We went to Rosengård to see Zlatan!"

Malmö's favorite son, Zlatan Ibrahimović, had just led his current team, French giants Paris Saint-Germain, to play against his boyhood club, Malmö FF, in the Champions League. It was a big deal. The Malmö city government paid for the match to be shown on a big screen in Rosengård, the projects where Zlatan was born and where football fields were named after him. I had gone with Bengt and stood watching with thousands of fans, mostly young boys speaking immigrant Swedish, the crowd divided on whom to root for, Malmö or Zlatan.

"I was there!" I said. "But I didn't see you."

"How is this possible?" Aziz said.

I laughed. "I guess there were a few other people there, too."

"Yes." He laughed. "But Zlatan did not play well."

"That header went right over the bar! I think he was nervous."

"Nervous? But he's Zlatan."

Zlatan was known among soccer fans worldwide for his self-confidence. As a young man, the son of Bosnian and Croatian immigrants, coming up through the ranks at Malmö FF and in the Swedish national team, his bravado had made him hated by white Swedes and beloved by immigrants. You weren't supposed to dance around with the ball like that. You weren't supposed to say that you were the best. One Swedish player had said that he always felt as if Zlatan got more joy from humiliating defenders than he did from scoring. But then Zlatan started really scoring. He became the star of the national team and was now Sweden's all-time leading scorer. When old white Swedish men talked about the national team now, they said, "They aren't giving Zlatan any help! How's he supposed to do it all by himself?"

"Zlatan gets nervous too," I said. "He's playing against his boyhood club. Everybody's watching. Can you imagine the pressure?"

"Yes, I see that. Do you think they will show the return match on the big screen?"

"I'm not sure." I wanted to add, *If they do, we should go watch it together*. But Ali whistled to signal we were starting up again. Aziz and I shook hands once more and returned to work.

A FEW WEEKS LATER, I WENT TO AN INFORMATIONAL MEETING that Katja had organized about becoming a mentor or foster parent for a refugee. When I first received the invite, I hadn't planned on attending, but then I'd read an article about how many refugees were stuck waiting for work permits that wouldn't arrive until their asylum request was approved, unable to start working or studying or building their new lives without the permit. These asylum requests took a long time to process, and many refugees would be sent back if Sweden deemed that their lives would not be in danger upon return. When Aziz had asked me about Swedish universities, I had assured him that he could attend for free, thinking that all the boys would receive the benefits of temporary citizenship. Now it turned out that he couldn't attend university without a permit, which he might never receive. At each of the last couple Language Cafés, I had found a reason not to invite him out, and with every passing week, I could see him getting antsier at his situation. At the last meeting, he had snapped at a new German volunteer—who had incorrectly explained a Swedish phrase—that if she didn't speak the language, she shouldn't teach it.

I wondered if I couldn't at least provide him with a place to stay, a place where he could have a little breathing room, until he learned what would happen next. It was a ridiculous thought. But the more I thought about it, the more it felt reasonable. It would have been ridiculous for me to offer a home to one of the other boys with whom I couldn't converse for more than a minute or two. But Aziz and I got along easily. Even on the day he'd snapped at the German girl, after he'd told her how sorry he was and how much he appreciated her volunteering, he had asked me if there was something he could do to show her how sorry he really was. After my assuring and reassuring him that the volunteer had already accepted his apology, he finally believed me, and we had filled the rest of our conversation effortlessly talking about movies. I imagined having him stay with me would be like having a roommate who didn't pay rent.

I took the bus down to Anna Lindhs Plats and walked to the student union, hood pulled up against the rain that fell unpleasantly in the thirty-five-degree November gray. Inside the student union, the same place where we held the Language Café, about a dozen people were gathered around tables facing the front of the room—mostly women but a few gentle-looking husbands. I was the only single male I could see. Katja was in conversation with a young woman; Ali wasn't there; I sat down at an empty table. A few minutes later, another unaccompanied white man plopped down at my table. He was fortysomething and heavyset, but confidently so, like he owned a boat. He removed his leather gloves but kept on his designer peacoat and leaned back with an air of authority.

Katja stood up and introduced the woman she'd been talking to, who was a social worker with the city. The social worker looked to be in her midtwenties, dark haired and sweet looking with big silver hoop earrings. She introduced herself in Swedish, pulled down a screen, and brought a PowerPoint to life with a click of a button. It was the first time that I'd seen a public PowerPoint presentation begin without any group brainstorming on how to get it to work. The first slide read, *What does it mean to be a foster parent?*

"To be a foster parent, we don't have any requirements as to marital status or sexual orientation or gender," the social worker said. "We are only assessing your suitability as a parent and your ability to provide a safe and nurturing home for a child in need."

I was unequipped to care for a child. I didn't even really know him. But it wasn't like I was asking to adopt him—he could just stay with me for a few weeks.

"The first question is," the social worker said, "have you had any major life changes in the previous year? A major life change means that you, for example, recently ended a serious relationship, got married, had a biological child, suffered the death of a parent, lost your job, and so on. We find that people who have made major life changes recently are much less able to make decisions far into the future. So maybe you think you want a foster child now, but in three months, you realize that's not what you want at all. And then the child is the one who gets hurt."

I hadn't had any major life changes in the past year. It had been more than a year since I'd moved to Sweden. It had been more than a year since I'd quit drugs. In the past, I would have had to load up on oxy, or at least tramadol, just to be able to attend this meeting—just to be around people. Now I was here, sober, doing no harm. Maybe it wouldn't be the worst thing for Aziz to live with me.

"The second question is: Do you have a stable living situation, with at least two bedrooms in your house or apartment? Unfortunately, if you don't have a separate room for the child, you will not be considered at this time."

I did not have an extra bedroom. I could have slept on the couch. But the social worker said two bedrooms. The answer was no before I'd even asked. The social worker clicked the next slide. I was disappointed. But then a feeling of lightness came over me—a stupid feeling of lightness, since I'd been relieved of asking to take on a burden that no one in their right mind would want me to take on in the first place.

The social worker explained that if you were interested in foster care, you filled out an application and met with a caseworker. Then, if you were a suitable candidate, you had to undergo an interview with a psychologist.

The confidently fat man next to me raised his hand. "What is it they're looking for in this psychological examination?" He spoke in a posh Stockholm accent.

"That's a good question. The psychologist will want to gather information about how suitable you are to care for children. They will want to make sure, for example, that you haven't been victim to a serious trauma that would impair your ability to raise a child."

"But we're all victims of trauma." The man leaned forward.

The social worker smiled. "Of course, in a way."

"No, really, that's how it *is*," the man insisted, motioning to the room for their support.

The social worker nodded politely.

"And why all the bureaucracy? Shouldn't you lower the requirements when there are so many of them?"

"That's a good question. But even with so many unaccompanied children coming to Sweden, we'd rather the children live in group homes with trained professionals where we can make sure they're cared for than have them placed in unsuitable homes."

"So it's better for them to have no homes?"

The social worker waited a moment, maybe trying to find the right words. "It's not uncommon for a person to see a report on the news or read a story in the paper and feel intense sympathy, and feel the need to do something, and want to adopt a child from a conflict zone. But the problem is that this feeling doesn't always last long. It often wears off once the child turns out to be a real person with real tantrums, real demands, and real problems. And, again, in that situation, it's the child who gets hurt. It's difficult for someone who's already been through so much and lost so much to be placed in a home and then be rejected by their host."

The man shook his head. I knew that it was difficult for the boys to stay in transition homes. But the difficulty of the transition homes came from boredom, overcrowding, and understimulation, which was nothing compared to the damage that self-righteousness could do.

The next speaker was a middle-aged white woman from the Association for the Unaccompanied, a group that was started by unaccompanied minors arriving in Malmö. The association had an office three blocks from my house, and I had seen a flyer on their window advertising a talk by the actor who had played the Hazara lead in the movie adaptation of *The Kite Runner*—the book that was, for many Americans and Europeans, the source of all our knowledge about Afghanistan. The young actor, Ahmad Khan Mahmoodzada, had become a refugee after the movie's portrayal of his character's rape by a Pashtun boy had made him a target in Afghanistan. After years in limbo, he had finally settled in Dalarna, the mountain province north of Stockholm. He had recently appeared in his first TV commercial in Sweden.

The woman from the Association for the Unaccompanied said that she was here to talk about their mentoring program. They wanted to get Swedish people to mentor young refugees because, without fail, she said, when you asked the children who arrived here what they most wanted, they had two answers. The first was a family to live with. The second was to know a young Swedish person.

"We have young people in our organization who have lived in Sweden for five years and have never been in the home of a Swedish person."

A murmur ran through the room. Someone said, *"Herregud."*

The man next to me raised his hand again. "I'd like to start a group for unaccompanied refugees."

"How do you mean?" the woman said.

"I already lead a theater group, and I could lead a group for them to talk."

"Talk about what?"

"About being a refugee. You know, share their experiences, work out their problems."

The woman was quiet for a second. "I don't know if they need to talk about being a refugee. They probably already know what that's like."

"Not just *what it's like*." The man rolled his eyes. "Digging a little deeper, you know? Really getting in there."

"That's very nice of you," the woman said, clearly trying. "But we just need people who can volunteer to spend some time, one-on-one, with kids who are new to Sweden."

The woman then called on another raised hand, and the man leaned over to me and said, "These people—it's like they don't even want any help. No wonder it's a crisis."

"Are you offering to help?" I said.

"Didn't you hear what I said?"

"Who is it that you're offering to help?"

The man stared at me for a second, harrumphed, then loudly backed his chair up and walked out. Here was a man who wanted to save everybody with a talk-therapy group he thought he was qualified to lead because he had done theater. (And maybe he could gather some stories in the process.) But not that long ago I had wanted to save the boys by telling them to write their memoirs in grocery-store journals. (And maybe I could gather some stories in the process.) It occurred to me how difficult it was for men to join in the day-to-day slog of helping strangers without the promise of attention and praise. The thought made me uncomfortable.

The afternoon's final speaker was a middle-aged Iranian Swedish woman who wore a gauzy shawl and olive-rimmed glasses. She looked like a visiting professor and spoke grammatically flawless Swedish with a Middle Eastern accent.

"My name is Laleh, and my husband and I are foster parents. Over the last twenty years, we have had eighteen foster children stay with us."

We were all leaning forward in our seats. It had been a bit of a letdown that the Association for the Unaccompanied had sent a white representative.

"My husband will let the boys get away with anything. If Hitler came running into our living room crying, my husband would put his arm around him, and say, 'It can't be as bad as all that, little Adolf.'" She paused for polite laughter. "I give the boys hugs and I'm sweet to them. But I also hold them accountable. One of the boys, the first evening he came to my house, he walked in the living room, and without looking at me, he sat down on the couch, leaned back, and put his feet on the table. I said, in Farsi, 'Is that how you walk into a room? What would you do if your grandmother were in this room?' He got up right away and kissed my hand. That's how a boy greets his grandparents in Afghanistan. And then he sat up straight and behaved himself."

She paused. "You have to have rights *and* responsibilities. When the boys come here, they immediately have rights they've never had before, which is good, of course. But they forget the responsibilities they've had their entire lives, because nobody holds them accountable. Afghan boys are very well mannered, but they forget. And do you think that's good for them? That it makes them comfortable to have no rules?"

I wrote down in my notebook *rights and responsibilities*.

"Sometimes the boys who come over are damaged. They have seen things that children shouldn't see. And I'll be honest—it can be difficult. We had a boy in our house who was nine years old. One day, I walked down into the living room and saw him on the family computer watching a YouTube video of ISIS beheading a prisoner. He was laughing."

She paused.

"For me, as a victim of torture, it was difficult to watch a child laughing at someone else's execution. He didn't turn the screen off when I came in the room because he wasn't trying to hide it. He wasn't trying to hide it because he didn't think he was doing anything wrong."

She paused again.

"But this wasn't about me. It was about him. You must consider these boys' environment, what they've experienced, what they're going through, and you must create some kind of normal. Your kind of normal. That's the only hope you have."

Her speech had such substance; I was moved and jealous. To be able to say something like that and have the force of experience behind your words. But I could only imagine the credibility, not the weight, that came with the experience.

"Let me end with one short story. A few weeks ago, our birth daughter was explaining to her foster brothers that she was getting married. She told them how the ceremony would go and that they would be seated at tables with cousins and children their own age. Our youngest boy, who is eight, stood up, crossed his arms, and yelled, 'No!' "

Laleh laughed. "We were shocked! He had never raised his voice before. We said, 'What's wrong?' He said, 'I'm not going to sit at a *table* at my *sister's* wedding. I'm going to wear a tuxedo and stand by the door and greet the guests when they come in!' Because that's what brothers do at Afghan weddings! And he wanted to show that he was not a guest, not a charity case—he was her brother. He was going to participate. He was going to help."

The whole room laughed. What a relief to unclench the muscles tensed in preparation of stories of rape or beheading or horrifically creative evil.

"When we're giving, it's easy to get wrapped in the giving. It's easy to get wrapped up in us being the givers and them the receivers. But it's important for the boys to feel like they can give as well. It's important for them to participate. Thank you."

After the speech, I shook Laleh's hand, thanked her, said bye to Katja, and went home to work on my master's dissertation on the phenomenology of whiteness. The paper had spread out unmanageably. It was now mostly a list of the stoppings and killings of black men by American police. I had no idea what my thesis was. It didn't have much to do with literature. I was only attending about half my classes, and it would be a miracle if I graduated. I couldn't concentrate. I kept thinking of Aziz and Osman and Arash and the rest of the boys coming to Sweden smart and kind and capable and eager to learn, and being ruined by Swedish indifference.

I decided to ask Torsten if I could mentor Aziz.

As soon as I reached the decision, I knew it was the right one, but then I started running laps in my head in search of what I could do with Aziz if Torsten said it was okay. I could take Aziz to an Afghan restaurant in Möllevången. But that might just make him sad. If I were homesick, I wouldn't want a Swede to take me to the TGI Fridays in the city center. We could go to a Swedish restaurant. But not many restaurants served traditional Swedish cuisine—beef and fish and potato dishes. Swedes could make Swedish food at home. When they went out, they wanted Thai food, tapas, hard-shell tacos, or American barbecue. In my time in Sweden, I had only been to four or five sit-down restaurants. If I were to be honest and give Aziz an accurate picture of my Sweden, my version of normal, we would cook together.

I got out of bed and opened the door to the balcony. Sweat had soaked through my shirt. The black night air blew in cold. I could show him how to make Swedish meatballs. Would that be fun?

I wanted to give Aziz something nice. If only I knew what that something was.

BEFORE THE SIXTH MEETING OF THE LANGUAGE CAFÉ, ON AN unseasonably mild November evening, I was smoking behind a planter near the student union when Ali walked up.

He made a pretend-shocked face. "Does Mr. Anderson *smoke*?"

"Unfortunately, he does."

"Have you got a fag?"

"You probably don't want to say it like that. But you are welcome to a cigarette."

He thanked me. "Are the Lucky Strike organics better than the regular Lucky Strikes?" He examined the paper-bag-colored pack I'd handed him.

"If you blindfolded me, I couldn't tell the difference. But they cost the same and I like the way the package looks."

"It's funny that you say that. Because if somebody says, 'Lucky Strike organics taste so much better than regular Lucky Strikes!,' then everyone will want to trick him into revealing that he can't actually tell the difference. But you've said that you can't tell the difference before anyone else can accuse you of not being able to tell the difference."

I laughed. "I try to reveal my flaws before anyone else can."

"Excellent strategy." Ali pulled out a cigarette, lit it, and handed the pack back to me.

"I've been thinking a little about how we should organize the lessons." I told him about Laleh's speech on rights and responsibilities—about setting up rules to make the boys feel safe. I repeated the anecdote she'd shared about the boy who put his feet up.

Ali took a long drag off the cigarette. He looked out at the windmill factory. Then he said, "That's bullshit. The kid just came to a foreign country, away from everything he knows, his father's head probably rolling on a street in Kabul, and she's making him kiss her hand? I know that kind of Persian—I've met them back home. They try to act like they know everything about Hazara, but it's superior, racist bullshit."

I made a mental note to cross out my previous note.

The boys entered in a wave of laughter and yelling, with Torsten behind them, shouting halfhearted directions in English. I looked for Aziz but didn't see him. A new boy caught my eye because he looked about twenty-five. He wore a faux-leather jacket and sported a five o'clock shadow. He was joking with a boy in shapeless clothes and a bowl cut, who looked prepubescent. I saw Osman and we shared a smile, and I saw Arash, who was pushing and laughing with some other boys, getting his fur hat knocked on the floor. But I couldn't find Aziz in the crowd. I worried that he had been transferred.

Then I heard him: "Jonas, my friend!"

The relief washed over me. We shook hands and said our hellos. But then the nerves hit. I would have to go through with it.

*　　*　　*

The session was so busy that I couldn't find a moment to ask Torsten about Aziz until the end, when I saw Torsten herding a group of boys horsing around in the corner.

"*Tjena.* Good session today," Torsten said in Swedish, a little out of breath.

"Thanks! I thought it went well." I paused. "Hey, I don't know if you do this, but I was thinking that maybe I could be a mentor to Aziz while he's here. I mean, not a mentor, but maybe I could have him over for dinner or something?"

"I think he would like that." Torsten's eyes followed a couple boys engaged in a quickly escalating scarf-fight. "Have you asked him?"

"No, I didn't want to ask if it was against the rules."

"You can't come to the home, you know, because of security." I didn't even know where the home was. The location of refugee housing was secret, in fear of the anti-migrant firebombing attacks that had broken out in Germany. Torsten and the social workers would bring the boys to us, but we could not go to them. "But he could meet you somewhere else. He can come to your place if he wants to."

"Great!" I was a little amazed that it had been that easy.

I searched through the crowd of boys until I saw Aziz.

"Jonas, my friend!" Aziz said, zipping up his jacket. We performed our long handshake.

"Good job today," I said.

"Thank you. *Jag talar lite svenska nu.*"

"*Du talar jättebra svenska!*"

"*Inte så bra. Men jag blir bättre* . . . How do you say 'every day'?"

"Varje dag."

"Jag blir bättre varje dag."

"That's excellent," I said.

He smiled.

"But, hey, I have a question for you," I said.

"Yes?"

"And you don't have to say yes if you don't want to."

Aziz looked concerned. "Okay."

"Would you like to come to my house for dinner tomorrow?"

He was quiet. "What do you mean?"

I laughed nervously. I realized that Aziz might think I was making advances. "In Sweden, when you have friends, sometimes the friends go to each other's houses for dinner. And then they make dinner together and just eat dinner and drink soda and then go home, and nothing else. It's very simple. But it can be fun." I paused. "I thought that since you're my friend now, maybe you wanted to come over for dinner."

Aziz smiled. "Yes. I would like that. Thank you. I will come over for dinner."

My heart hiccuped in my throat. I typed out my address on Aziz's phone. He didn't have a Swedish phone number yet from which he could call me, and his Skype wouldn't work without a Wi-Fi connection, so I also wrote out my last name so that he would know which buzzer to ring.

"The buzzer only works one way. But ring it and I'll come down and let you in."

We agreed that he would come the following evening at seven.

He waved goodbye and walked off, apparently so surprised by the invitation that he forgot our handshake.

That night, I couldn't sleep. What if I couldn't think of anything to say to Aziz? What if Aziz didn't like the meatballs? What if I went to get something from the kitchen, and when I came back, he was gone?

What if everything went perfectly and we had a great time?

Then what?

My kitchen counter looked like the set of a cooking show. Red ground beef shining brightly in its plastic, bread crumbs in a little glass bowl, a cup of already measured cream, a stick of butter, no pork. The meatballs were better with a mix of beef and pork than with just beef, and I wasn't sure who followed what dietary rules—I had once seen Muhammad eat what looked like a pork hot dog—but I wanted to be safe. I was finishing cutting the onions when the buzzer announced Aziz's arrival. I charged out the door—shoes half-on, toes gripping tight while my heels flopped—and down the three flights of stairs to let Aziz in.

"Jonas, my friend!" He wore a rain jacket and jeans and rain boots.

"Aziz!" I answered, out of breath.

We performed our elaborate handshake. Then I didn't know what to say. It was like every other time I'd seen a student outside of school, only more acute.

"Shall we?" I opened the door to the tiny elevator for Aziz. I pushed the button for the fourth floor and pointed to the sign showing the stick figure having his neck broken by the trash can. "Don't bring garbage cans in here or you'll break your neck."

"I will not."

"Sorry, I was joking."

"Oh."

We were quiet. At the fourth floor, we exited the elevator and entered my apartment.

"This is where I live." I took off my shoes.

Aziz took his shoes off and placed them on the rack. I took Aziz's raincoat and hung it on the hook.

"This is the living room." I motioned to the small room with the fake-hardwood floors and the apartment owner's once-white IKEA couch, a little gray from lack of washing. "This is my room." I showed Aziz the narrow room with its narrow Swedish bed. But I didn't cross through the doorway into the bedroom. "And this is the kitchen, where we'll make dinner."

"Very nice."

I wanted to know what Aziz was thinking, but I couldn't gauge his reaction—couldn't tell if he thought this was good or uncomfortable or boring.

"Do you want something to drink?"

"No, thank you."

"Are you sure? I have all this soda." I opened the refrigerator to show a liter bottle of Coke, a liter of Fanta, a liter of Sprite, and a liter of the Swedish spiced Christmas soda, *julmust.*

Aziz laughed. "You really like soda, Jonas!"

"I do!" I said, though I did not like soda. "You have to drink some or I'll drink it all and my teeth will rot."

"Then I will have Fanta, thank you."

"Excellent choice." I cracked some ice from a tray and poured Fanta for Aziz in a giant plastic cup the apartment owner had left behind; I sometimes used it as a water pitcher. I poured myself a much smaller glass. "As they say in Swedish, *skål*."

"*Skål!*" Aziz said.

"This is a very Swedish dish that we're making." I unwrapped the beef. "This is beef—from a cow. In Swedish, it's called *nötkött*." I pointed to the word on the label.

Aziz nodded and repeated the word.

"Did you already learn that word?"

"No."

I went through all the ingredients, sounding out their Swedish names for Aziz.

"We put the cream and the bread crumbs in a little bowl. And then you let the cream and bread crumbs settle while you mix up beef, egg, onions, and spices."

"Why do you let the cream and the bread crumbs settle?"

I looked at the cream and bread crumbs muddying up their little bowl. "I have no idea."

Aziz laughed. "You are very good at this, Jonas."

Things were going well! Somehow, despite different languages and ethnicities and life experiences and ages, Aziz and I were on the same wavelength. He cracked the egg on the meat. He dumped the pepper and the chopped-up onions into the big metal mixing bowl.

"Torsten said that I may be transferred soon."

"That's fantastic!" A voice in my head screamed that Aziz couldn't leave yet, but I stamped it out.

"If I get transferred, then I can start school."

"You must be excited!"

"Yes, very."

"You'll do great in Swedish school."

He smiled.

I dumped the cream-and-bread-crumb mix into the bowl.

"Now's the fun part. You have to get in there with your hands and mix it all up." I dipped my hands into the sticky pile of meat, kneading it in with the other ingredients. "See? Just mix it all up. Now you try."

Aziz looked at me, then at the meat.

"It's okay!" I said. "It's actually kind of fun."

Aziz still looked skeptical, but he plunged his hands in and began kneading. "Like this?"

"Perfect."

He looked down at the bowl, concentrating hard, kneading the egg and the cream into the meat.

"You're a natural, Aziz."

We were quiet for a while. He kneaded, and I peeked over to see the yellow egg disappearing into the red of the meat, the onions dimpling the beef.

"Swedish cooking is hard work, isn't it?" I smiled.

Aziz didn't answer. His fist hit the bottom of the metal bowl and it clinked against the counter.

"Whoops, careful there. Let me know when you get tired and I can take over."

But the bowl clinked again, and then he pounded both his fists against the bottom, clanging it hard against the counter.

"Hey, take it easy there. Don't want to hurt yourself."

But he hit the bowl harder, and then the whole big glob of meat stuck to his hands, and he lifted the bowl up and slammed it down again and again.

"Hey!" I grabbed him by the shoulders. "Stop!"

Aziz threw the bowl down into the sink. The meat splattered. "I don't want to do this!"

"We don't have to do this."

"I don't want to do this!" His face was red.

"It's okay! We don't have to do anything—"

Aziz ran out of the kitchen and tried to open the front door. But the door automatically locked when you closed it. You had to pull up a little silver lid from the lock to open it, which Aziz didn't know, so he just pulled the handle down again and again, jerking more and more desperately.

"Stop it! Aziz, it's okay—"

He turned and rushed into the bathroom, locking the door behind him.

I waited for a minute. I listened for sounds but didn't hear any.

"Are you okay in there?"

No answer.

"I'll be here, whenever you're ready."

I looked at the bits of raw beef and onions covering the door handle and wondered how I had so thoroughly fucked everything up.

I waited on a chair outside the bathroom. I had decided to give Aziz fifteen minutes alone before I called Torsten. I looked at my phone. Thirteen minutes had passed. It had been too much. I had pushed too much on him—the Swedish words, the dishes, the apartment, the cooking. I should have just taken him to Burger King or something. I let my face fall into my hands. I heard the faucet in the bathroom turn on. Then off. The door opened and Aziz came out.

He didn't look like he'd been crying—more like he hadn't slept in days.

"Hey, buddy." I rose to my feet. "Are you okay?"

"Of course." He looked down.

"We don't have to make meatballs. We can go out to dinner. Or we can just hang out. We can do whatever you want."

"Of course we should make meatballs." He was speaking with measured concentration, looking down. "I behaved like a child."

I stood up. "You didn't behave like a child. You're—"

"I behaved like a child. I ruined everything."

"You didn't ruin anything. It was my fault. It was too much."

Aziz looked up at me, quickly, then looked back down again. He looked scared.

"Why don't you sit down in the kitchen and keep me company while I make dinner?" I put my hand on his shoulder, lightly. When he didn't shake it off, I led him to one of the seats at the two-person table in the kitchen.

"Have some more Fanta." I poured more soda into his giant cup. We were quiet.

"This is such a big glass," Aziz said.

"You know, it's the biggest glass I've ever seen." I smiled at him.

Aziz smiled back. It was a forced smile, the kind that made your cheeks ache—but it was something.

I pulled the bowl out of the sink. I put the meat that wasn't ruined on the cutting board and rolled it into little balls. I poured oil in the frying pan, then dumped the meatballs in. The kitchen filled with smoke and onion smell. We didn't say anything. The quiet was covered by the sound of popping grease.

Finally Aziz said, "How many meatballs are you making?"

I counted the raw ones on the cutting board where I'd stacked them and those in the frying pan where the meat was sizzling. "About twenty-five."

"Twenty-five." He nodded.

We were quiet again.

Once the food was ready, I served us both plates of meatballs and potatoes and set the jar of lingonberries on the table. "Swedish people like to eat their meatballs with these berries."

Aziz nodded.

I opened the fridge. "But you can eat yours with ketchup, if you prefer."

Aziz smiled and took the ketchup, popped the cap off, and squeezed a gob onto his plate.

"I'm going to eat mine with ketchup too." I took the bottle once he was done.

We ate without talking.

"Thank you," Aziz said, when I cleared the plates and put them in the sink. "I must get back to the home."

"Of course. Thank you for coming. It was nice having you over."

I walked him to the door and watched him put his jacket on.

"We could do this again. Or not exactly this. We could go to Burger King and have lunch one day. Would you like that?"

"Yes." Aziz pulled his shoes on.

When he finished knotting the laces, I lifted the silver lid off the lock and quickly put my hand on the door handle, so Aziz wouldn't see the raw meat still stuck to it.

"Do you know which bus to take back to the home? Do you want me to walk you to the stop? Do you want me to ride the elevator down with you?"

"No, it's okay," Aziz said. "I won't bring any garbage cans in with me."

I sat on my bed with the blinds open, staring out at the apartment building on the opposite side of the street. On the third floor of that building was a rooftop garden where tenants would have barbecues in the summer. Despite that each family spoke a different language and had different skin tones—one family being from Somalia and another from Palestine, one family from Kosovo and another from Kurdistan—they managed to laugh and talk and grill and have fun for hours at a time, without silence, without awkwardness, without hurting anyone. I lay down and replayed every one of the night's mistakes in my head, as if I could change the past by thinking about it.

THE NEXT DAY, I OPENED MY COMPUTER TO EMAIL STELLA. I wanted to tell someone about what had happened—to relieve the burden of carrying knowledge alone—but when I pulled up my email, I found that I didn't even know where to start. Instead I checked the American papers, where I read an editorial about Sweden's *migrant catastrophe*. The author, an American expert on Scandinavia, wrote about Sweden as if the country were in a state of lawless emergency after being overrun by refugees. He quoted the Danish foreign minister as saying that Sweden's disaster was a result of its irresponsible immigration policy. The author didn't mention that this was the same foreign minister who had, the week Alan Kurdi died, rolled out the Middle Eastern newspaper-ad campaign to keep refugees out of Denmark.

I was furious. The US was already quibbling over whether to accept just ten thousand Syrian refugees, and this was the type of bullshit that made Americans think it was okay not to care. I decided to write a rebuttal. All day, I researched numbers and read news stories about refugees. I forgot about my schoolwork, forgot about the Aziz disaster. Then I sat down to write. It was such a rush, such stress, almost like a race. Nothing mattered except getting the thoughts on the page before they disappeared, then wrestling them into coherence before I forgot what I'd wanted to say in the first place. By 10:00 p.m., I'd cut a rambling five thousand words into a lean six hundred. I logged on to the newspaper's website to find the email address for op-ed submissions.

The front page popped up. My stomach dropped.

DOZENS DEAD IN PARIS TERRORIST ATTACK

Loud days followed. The European far right screaming we told you so. American governors racing to be the first to say they would not allow Syrian refugees into their states. Presidential candidates suggesting America only grant asylum to Christian refugees. Donald Trump proclaiming that if elected he would deport all Syrian refugees.

I thought about the boys at the transit home—how much harder life would be for them now. I thought about Aziz sitting on a bench by the Burger King in the Central Station, scrolling through news sites on his phone, reading all the terrible things people were saying about him in comments sections.

I tried to imagine the innocent French civilians who had been killed. But I kept accidentally imagining myself in their place. Except in the fantasy I wouldn't die but would survive to write a moving piece of journalism on the attacks. Or would heroically kill the gunmen and save dozens. Or I would imagine that I'd lost someone in the attacks—that my old dorm neighbor Laurent had died—so that I could feel something. The way I saw it, there was self-serving empathy (I am you when it suits me), arrogant empathy (I know how you feel), and lazy empathy (I can't even imagine how you must feel). I wanted to feel the right kind of empathy, but it seemed like every kind of empathy was problematic.

I wrote Laurent a message asking if he was okay.

Yes, thank you, Jonas, Laurent wrote back. *I am okay. But I am tired of this shit.*

Laurent and I had sat in my dorm room the previous winter and watched coverage of the *Charlie Hebdo* attacks on my laptop.

I'm glad you're okay, I wrote back. *I miss you.*

The news announced that one of the terrorists in Paris had come through Greece posing as a Syrian refugee. Now anyone who needed an excuse to close their borders had it. The comments I read on social media asked if the bleeding hearts were happy now, inviting terrorists into their countries to kill them. Then someone would point out that the other terrorists, including the ringleader, had been French and Belgian nationals. Someone else would write that it was undeniable that Islam was a violent religion and that to say otherwise was naive political correctness. The boys driven from their countries, often by terrorists, would again be accused of terrorism. The onus was on them to prove they weren't terrorists.

In Sweden, a group on one side shouted that if *they* wanted to be here, they had to not just learn Swedish, but *become* Swedish, since Islam was a sexist, anti-Swedish religion. On the other side, a group shouted that no crime had ever been committed by an immigrant and that anyone who said otherwise was a racist. The center, where most of the country actually existed, appeared empty, and anyone who dared tread there would be shot down by both sides.

Masochistically, I logged on to Fox News and watched segment after segment in which the anchors and pundits took it as an accepted fact that most Muslims were terrorists. The opinions didn't have to be directly racist if the rules of the debate were. While the pundits felt sympathy for the suffering of those people, they had to consider the safety of American lives and couldn't support inviting in the ten thousand refugees who'd been granted asylum.

"It's ten thousand out of four million," said one pundit. "So it's a silly number, and it's all designed to make the Europeans take in more refugees, which we now know is probably a bad idea."

We now knew, from the action of one person who may have posed as a refugee, that 4 million people were probably a bad idea.

"The president's responsibility is to American safety first," the other pundit said. "You have to realize that now's not the time. You can't take in one hundred and seventy thousand from radicalized Syria."

That number, 170,000, was about how many refugees Sweden, not the US, was taking in from the Middle East and North Africa—but nobody corrected him.

"Why are no politicians talking about this?" said the pundit, though all the politicians were talking about this.

"Exactly! And where are they going to be settled? People should be asking their local leaders, 'Are you going to let Syrian refugees settle in my town?'"

"Let's hope the public doesn't remain passive."

I paced around my apartment, conducting arguments in my head, knowing I couldn't change anyone's mind, not only because I wasn't talking to another person, but because the time for changing minds was past. You believed what you believed. You googled the facts to support that belief. You surrounded yourself with people who echoed your belief.

I wanted to correct the world. But I was angry with myself for feeling the need to be right more strongly than I felt empathy for the victims of the attacks. I longed for drugs.

The next day, Torsten wrote to inform Katja, Ali, and me that the next Language Café would have to be canceled. *The security concerns are too great right now.* There were worries about retaliation. Facebook pages had sprung up offering instructions in Swedish on how to firebomb refugee homes.

I was sleepless and a little manic. Without my normal filter working, I wrote back, *Is Aziz okay?*

Torsten didn't respond for a full day. I felt idiotic for writing about Aziz as if I had some special connection to him when we barely knew each other.

All the boys are fine, Torsten finally wrote. *It's just a little tense.*

Can I come by and see him? I wrote, though I knew that Torsten wasn't even allowed to tell me the address of the home.

Torsten didn't reply.

I would lie in bed for hours, refreshing newspaper sites and social media and email over and over, looking for I didn't even know what.

When I saw the idiotic comments about how it would help if Muslims denounced terrorism and differentiated themselves from terrorists by fighting ISIS, oblivious of how the Kurdish and Iraqi armies had hundreds of thousands of troops on the ground fighting against ISIS, I'd get angry. But when I saw friends reposting articles about how Steve Jobs's father had been a Syrian immigrant or how the US had denied Anne Frank's request for asylum—posts that argued for my worldview—I'd also get angry, without even knowing why. Whatever I found angered me. So why, I wondered, did I keep looking?

The Swedish government finally capitulated. At a press conference on November 24, the prime minister announced that the rules had to change. The deputy prime minister stood to his side. When she spoke, her voice broke; she fought back tears. This was not an easy decision, she said. But she had become convinced that it was the right thing to do. The border would no longer be open.

When Bengt texted to invite me to Möllevången that night, I realized I hadn't left the apartment in three days. I was determined to get drunk and have fun and forget everything. I played loud music while I dressed and drank two tall cans of Carlsberg, trying to conjure some enthusiasm for the night ahead. Maybe I would meet a girl.

But as soon as I got on the bus to Möllevången, I wanted to go home. I took a seat near the back of the bus and watched the video of that day's press conference again on my phone. I wondered whether the deputy prime minister's voice break had been spontaneous or planned. If it had been planned, I wondered if it had been planned to give the illusion that the deputy prime minister was torn up about closing the border, or if it had been planned to communicate the real pain she was feeling about the decision, since that pain might not spontaneously manifest itself at the exact moment the camera panned over to her. But it didn't matter how the deputy prime minister, prime minister, or anyone else *felt* about it. I got off at Möllevångstorget and walked into a cramped and brightly lit curry place that sold cheap beers. I sat down with Bengt and a few of his friends, who were talking about a friend of theirs and his escapades during a study-abroad in Florence. Their conversation exhausted me. I didn't want to talk and wasn't interested in anything anyone had to say, regardless of what they had to say. I wanted to be alone to think, but there was nothing to think that I hadn't already thought.

One of Bengt's friends, a guy with round glasses and calculatedly messy blond hair, introduced himself to me, though we'd already met at a party where he was drunk and monologue-y. He said, "You're the American, right?"

"I am."

"What do you think about Donald Trump?"

I shrugged. "I'm not a fan."

"Your country is about to elect a fascist."

"He won't win."

"He might. Aren't you frightened?"

"I'm frightened of lots of things."

Bengt, sensing that I was in a conversation I wanted to escape, asked me about the Language Café. The guy with the round glasses started talking to someone else, so Bengt was the only one listening.

I tried to talk about the Language Café with the remove of a person who realizes he's doing little and isn't actually involved in the lives of the suffering. I tried to clinically describe what we were doing, while admitting that it obviously wasn't making a real difference. But soon I heard the born-again cadence in my voice.

"I don't understand why people think these boys are dangerous. All they want to do is learn! They line up with cell phones to take pictures of the Swedish alphabet we've hung on the wall so they can practice it at home! They don't want to break for *fika* because they want to keep studying!"

Bengt sighed and shook his head. "You're doing such good work."

"Do you want to come?" I leaned in. "We always need more Swedish speakers."

"Oh, yeah—okay," he said, suddenly shifty. "What day is it?"

"Wednesdays."

"Cool." He nodded. "Let me check my schedule."

I was surprised that he wasn't more excited. I drank quickly and tried to listen to everyone's stories and ask questions, but I was overwhelmed by headache, neckache, bodyache. I wanted drugs. I wanted to want to talk. I drank more. Eventually, we all walked over to Moriskan, and Bengt danced his way onto the stage. I tried to dance, but no matter how much I drank, my brain wouldn't submit. I left before midnight.

Lying in bed that night, I thought of my ex, Alexandra, back in Wilmington. Despite the mess we'd left each other, she had been a great listener. I'd never known somebody who so desperately wanted to know me. As it became clear that our relationship was collapsing and I began to worry that no one would ever want to know me like that again, I'd booked a romantic trip to Nashville. When I surprised her with the tickets, she was so happy, since my unwillingness to travel or try anything new had been a point of contention. But three days before the trip, she broke up with me, crying so hard that I felt worse for her than I did for myself.

I knew that the tickets were nonrefundable, but at $200 each, they accounted for most of the money I had at the time. I called the airline, and after twenty minutes on hold, I was patched through to a woman with a South Asian accent.

She asked the reason I was canceling my trip.

"I had planned the trip with my girlfriend. But she broke up with me." I heard myself sounding sad. I wasn't sure whether it was real sadness, an attempt to get sympathy and my money back, or a combination of the two.

"One moment." The woman was gone for a while. I heard clicking and voices in the background. I imagined a room full of over-educated Indians helping Americans with their airline tickets.

"Are you still there?" she said.

"Yes."

"This ticket is not refundable."

"Okay." I paused. "Is there anything you can do?"

"I can cancel the ticket for you. But you will not get a refund."

"Can I change it to a different ticket?"

"Yes, but you will have to pay the full price of the new ticket."

"Okay." This time I knew the despair was real. More than the money, I had to salvage something. "I realize I am not entitled to a refund. But is there anything you can do?"

"The ticket is not refundable," she said in the same tone, which wasn't unkind. She spoke as if I hadn't heard her the first time and she wanted to provide me with the information I needed.

"Okay." Even if she could type in an override to refund my ticket, doing so would break the rules. I could think of no reason why she should jeopardize her job for someone she'd never met just because his girlfriend had broken up with him.

I said goodbye and hung up. I sat down on the wood floor of my Wilmington living room, slanted by years of humidity. I put my face in my palms. At least I hadn't yelled at the woman or asked to speak to her manager. I took some pills and felt a little better. Or maybe not better. Just like someone had turned down the volume. I went to the airline's website and found a phone number with an Atlanta area code instead of an 800 number. I called and waited until a woman with a Southern accent answered. She sounded white.

I told her that I needed to cancel my ticket.

"Is there any particular reason? Or did your plans just change?"

"Well." I took a breath, again not sure whether I needed to gather my strength or just wanted to sound like I did. "This was supposed to be an anniversary trip with my girlfriend. But she broke up with me today. So I have to cancel the ticket."

The woman sighed. "I'm sorry to hear that."

"Thank you. I appreciate that." This time I knew it was real: I did appreciate it. I appreciated it a lot. What a nice thing for her to say.

"Can I put you on hold for a second?"

"Sure."

For a few minutes, there was no Muzak, no background noise, just a faint static.

Then she returned. "So, usually this ticket is totally nonrefundable. And I can't give you your money back. But given the circumstances, I'm going to give you a voucher that you can use for the full ticket price to buy a ticket in the future. I—"

"Thank you so much! You have no idea how much I appreciate it."

Her tone of voice didn't change when she said, "We do what we can, when we can."

"You have made a very shitty day much less shitty."

"I hope you get through this," she said.

For the rest of the afternoon, all I thought about was the ticket. I was so happy.

But that night I woke in despair. My girlfriend had left. I reached out to the nightstand, but the bottle was empty, so I hurried to the kitchen, where four backup pills were stored under the silverware. I chewed them down even though they tasted like paint and chewing them ruined the high. But soon everything calmed down. I thought about why the second customer-service rep had refunded my ticket when the first rep hadn't. Was it because the second woman shared my skin color and my nationality? Or had she, due to location, had more access to someone who could offer me a refund? Or had she just felt like helping me out when the first woman hadn't?

I couldn't say. But for weeks after that, whenever I was drowning in Percocet and Xanax and Dilaudid and heroin, I'd hear the woman's voice say, "I hope you get through this," and I'd pull my hand off my own head and give myself a second to breathe.

The following night, I went for a run into a swirling wind. I felt the wind pushing at my side, flapping my jacket into itself. When I turned left on Drottninggatan at the vegan Indian restaurant, the wind hit me straight on. I ran into the headwind for a block, two blocks, and watched the streetlights swinging back and forth on their lines, the whole street rocking and blinking. My legs burned with the effort of just going forward. Finally I gave up and turned back.

I needed to stop looking at the news. I needed to stop looking at social media and the stupid comments all these stupid people who didn't know a thing about anything were posting. I wanted to get high but not to feel a certain way—just like I wanted to stop feeling this way. Alcohol wasn't working. Running wasn't working. Reading wasn't working. Writing wasn't working. How stupid I had been to think that the fullness of my days had been the driving force behind my happiness. It must have been newness, not fullness, that had me feeling happy—the newness of living a life without drugs. Now that the newness had worn off, I found myself just the way I'd always been, scrolling through airline tickets and apartment listings in foreign cities, searching for a place where I could be someone else.

Two thirty a.m. and I couldn't sleep. It was twenty-two degrees and snowy outside. The cold breached the cheap insulation by my bed, yet I was sweating. I always sweated when I wanted something and couldn't have it—wanted to sleep but lay awake, wanted to leave a conversation but had to stay, wanted an answer but was left sitting in front of the computer clicking refresh. I wanted to teach the boys Swedish. I wanted to tell them that they were doing well, that it was impressive how quickly they were picking up the language. I wanted to shake their hands and pat them on their shoulders.

I got up, showered the sweat off, and dressed. I grabbed four pairs of wool socks and my second pair of boots—brown leather, a little over a year old, worn but not worn-out—and placed them in an IKEA bag. I walked into the quietly falling snow, out past the canals, past the constellations of lights over the railroad tracks, and down to the Central Station. Aziz probably wouldn't be there using the Wi-Fi at this hour. But maybe he would.

The station was occupied but quiet, in the way a basketball arena gets quiet when a player just broke his leg. It was not nearly as crowded as the night I had been coming back from Ulrika's, but there were still a few clusters of sleeping bags squeezed against the walls. Four teenagers sat at a Burger King table quietly checking their phones. I imagined that the station had more privacy at this hour than the transit home.

I sat down at the table next to the boys. "Hello," I said softly in English.

They all looked up, startled. I took out my phone like I was there waiting for a train—just using the Wi-Fi. The boys seemed to settle when they saw I wasn't there to evict them.

"English?" I said quietly.

"Yes," one of the boys said. He was young looking, short and skinny like I had been as a teen.

I held out the IKEA bag. "I have these extra socks—maybe you can give them to people who need them?"

The boy looked confused.

"These are for you." I handed him the bag.

The boy looked inside. "Yes, okay."

"There's also a pair of shoes in there. Size forty-five. Do you know anyone who has size forty-five shoes?"

The boy asked one of the other boys something in what sounded like Arabic.

The other boy nodded.

"His father."

"Then maybe he can give them to his father?"

"Yes, thank you."

I looked at my phone. "I have to catch a train. Good night."

"Yes, good night."

"Good night," the other boys repeated quietly. One of them waved.

A sign at the other end of the station told me that the Öresund train to Copenhagen was leaving at 3:25 a.m. But I didn't board any trains.

On the walk home, I decided that people should take turns caring about the world in four-month shifts. But under this system, my shift wouldn't even be over yet.

* * *

I woke up thinking of the boys. Then Anja. She was doing an internship semester on a Greek island, getting her diving certification and studying marine life. I would see her underwater pictures online sometimes, but we hadn't written in over a month. I missed her. But I couldn't say if I would have wanted her next to me if she'd been present as her real self, with the problems and difficulties that came with a real person, rather than as my memory of her warmth. I wondered what the boys were doing. I thought of how scared they must have been. Or if nothing else, how bored they must have been. I thought of the difficulty of waiting: how difficult it was to wake up to another day of nothing. They needed school. They needed stimulation and structure. They were so happy to have it for just a few hours a week.

I got out of bed, looked out at the white-gray morning, and wrote to Torsten to ask how things were going.

We're still pretty much on lockdown over here, he wrote. *There have been some threats, so we're asking the boys to stay in as much as possible, though they can leave if they want to. But the space isn't made to accommodate so many boys all day.*

I wrote back, *How about we try a Language Café tonight?*

Torsten said that he didn't know if they could bring that many boys on the walk to the university—they were short-staffed and there were still security concerns.

What if we come meet you at a location close to the home and walk the boys over? I wrote.

So that evening, Katja and I met Torsten and a dozen boys on a street corner that I assumed was near the transit home. It was a whole new group with nicer clothes—jeans with more fashionable fits and jackets that looked like they'd been bought for the people wearing them. The boys all wanted to talk to Katja; I walked behind them with Torsten. Aziz wasn't there. I didn't want Torsten to notice how anxious the absence of Aziz made me, so I asked about the new kids first.

"They're mostly from Syria. A couple are from Iraq. But the flow has slowed since the borders tightened. And because of the country's infrastructure, refugees from Afghanistan are the least likely to have a passport."

I had recently read a ranking of the world's "best passports." Sweden and Germany were tied for the top spot—a Swedish or German passport could get you into 158 countries. Afghanistan was dead last.

"There are still millions in Greece, Turkey, Jordan, Lebanon, Syria, Iraq, Iran, and Afghanistan," Torsten said. "But everyone here is giving up."

I had noticed the outrage at the border closing had died down. Outside of the far left, the growing feeling seemed to be that Sweden had done enough—that 160,000 or 170,000 refugees was all that could be expected of a country of 10 million to welcome in one year.

"Is Aziz here?" I asked as casually as I could.

"He was transferred. I'm afraid you'll have to find someone else to mentor."

"That's great news!" I said, trying to choke the quiver in my voice. "He was so excited to start school. Where did he get transferred to?"

"Outside Norrköping. It's a semi-independent living facility. The boys each have their own room, with a shared kitchen, and a social worker lives there with them. It's kind of like a dormitory. It will be good for someone as independent as Aziz."

"That'll be perfect! I'm so happy for him!"

I noticed that I was speaking too loudly and tried to tone it down. I hadn't even taken Aziz to Burger King. Who would teach him Swedish now? Who would know his sister's name? Who would tell him that he was doing well? He'd start his new life and have no use for another clumsy Samaritan whose sincerity he'd be forced to navigate. I'd never see him again. His last memory of me would be of my forcing him to make meatballs.

"I'm so happy for Aziz," I said to Torsten.

With only twelve boys at the Language Café, the volunteer-to-student ratio was almost one-to-one. All the volunteers that day were female, except for Ali and me. With Katja I sat down at a table next to a boy wearing an Oakland Raiders baseball cap. The boy looked at me, then at his classmates, clearly unhappy that he was stuck with a man when all these blond women were tutoring the other boys.

The boy sitting next to Katja smiled at me.

"Hello," I said to him. "My name is Jonas."

"Hassan," the boy next to Katja said, and reached over the table to shake my hand.

I also introduced myself to the boy in the Raiders hat, and he shook my hand lightly. He mumbled something I couldn't hear. Then he pulled out his phone and started scrolling.

Hassan snapped at him in what I assumed was Arabic, and the

boy with the Raiders hat put the phone away. We started going over a worksheet about colors, Katja and Hassan making great progress, while my student barely paid attention to my tutorial of yellow, red, black. He kept staring at Katja. The tops of her breasts were visible between scarf and shirt.

"Hey." I snapped to get the boy's attention. The boy turned to me with a sheepish grin.

"He is always looking at girls," Hassan said.

Katja laughed and the boy with the hat laughed.

"Is he disappointed that he's stuck with me when everyone else has a girl tutor?"

"Yes," Hassan said. "But he is always making trouble."

"The Oakland Raiders," I said to Hassan, pointing at the other boy's hat. "Tell him I know them. They're a football team where I'm from. I've been to their games."

Hassan translated. The boy looked at me as if to say, *And?*

I wanted to talk to Aziz. I wanted to make sure that the people taking care of him were good. I wanted to help him learn about Sweden. But, really, what did I know about Sweden? What could I do for him that he couldn't do for himself?

The next day, I read an article in the Malmö paper about a local college student who had traveled to Lesbos for a week to help the refugees stranded there.

It was an amazing experience, she said. *I don't want to do anything here now. I just want to go back there.*

She hadn't arranged her visit with any organization. She had just showed up and walked around until she found some Red Cross employees. Then she'd helped them make sandwiches.

It changed my life, she said.

I felt shitty. Here I was doing a few hours a week of basic language exercises, without inconveniencing myself in the slightest, and people were traveling to Greece to help. But then I scrolled down to the comments.

Congratulations, the first comment read. *You just spent thousands of kronor to do work that was already being done, just so you could say you'd been there. You made things harder for the Red Cross, who now had another person to worry about!*

While I didn't like their tone, I realized that the commenter was right. It was one thing when a doctor, a contractor, or a teacher trained in a relevant subject traveled to a crisis zone to offer expertise. It was something different when a tourist wasted money that could have been better used on aid so they could spread butter on sandwiches. If I traveled to Lesbos, with no medical training and no knowledge of Arabic, Dari, or Greek, I would have been even more useless than I was here. I fantasized about how pills could make this all go away. But then I reminded myself how I would feel even worse than I felt now—if that was possible—when I woke up from my high. I was running out of money, but I logged on to UNHCR's website and donated a few hundred kronor and felt not at all better.

I came home from a long day at the university—a nice ten-hour break from thinking about everything—to find a large brown envelope with American stamps on the floor by the mail slot. I ripped it open and pulled out two contributors' copies of the magazine with my story in it. On the cover was a glossy photograph of a woman standing in a field. It was a real magazine, with a magazine shape and magazine pages, rather than with the self-published-paperback feel of the previous journals that had published my stories. I turned to the table of contents and found my name. My stomach hiccuped.

I found my story and began to read, bracing for the shame and regret I felt whenever I read something I'd written months earlier.

My students turned in drawings of animals with extraordinary life spans.

I learned that there were species of tubeworm that lived for up to one hundred and seventy years.

Arctic whales more than two hundred years old.

Clams with a life expectancy of four hundred.

Sponges that had been alive for more than a millennium.

A kind of jellyfish—the immortal jellyfish—that, after reaching sexual maturity, could revert to infancy again and again, maybe forever.

I read the whole story in ten minutes and found, to my surprise, that I still liked it. It sounded like a real short story by a real writer. I ripped it out of the magazine, folded it in an envelope, and took it down the street to mail to Anja in Greece.

Later in the week, I met with Katja and Ali at Balthazar.

"I don't think we'll be doing this for much longer," Katja said.

"Torsten says that there are only twenty boys at the home now. Fewer and fewer are coming over the border. We may have to find a new group to work with."

We discussed other possibilities for groups we could work with—the Association for the Unaccompanied, the local community-college program in which some refugees with residence permits were enrolled, the Malmö local government. We had tried to reach out to groups in the past. A representative from the city had come to the university to meet with us. The man had talked a lot, mostly speaking to hear how he sounded in English, but he had left sounding enthusiastic, telling us to expect an email the next week.

We never heard from him again.

Katja said that she'd received a message from a group of students from Malmö University.

"They're in a class on global politics," she began, reading from her phone. "They would like to meet with the refugee boys."

"Why?" Ali said.

"Let's see." She scrolled down. "They want to discuss the boys' hopes, dreams, and experiences for a class project."

Everyone was quiet. I took a sip of my beer.

"Why don't you tell them," Ali said, "to go fuck themselves."

Back at my apartment, I found three messages from unfamiliar addresses in my inbox. The subject lines read, *You Really Have to Stop the Killing*, *your story*, and *Correspondence on your story*. I opened first the *Correspondence on your story*, which was from an intern at the magazine:

Hi Jonas,

We received this typewritten letter addressed to you. A photocopy is attached. Have a great day!

The photocopy read:

Dear Correspondence:

"You Really Have to Stop the Killing" is a glowing tribute to the art of the short story. It's a multi-layered tale about what it means to be a teacher, about substance abuse, recovery, about romance, fantasy, love and loss, about being young, and being not so young. All of this in the confines of a "simple" short story, which culminates with the prevailing of the human spirit through an act of kindness. I was infinitely delighted with this story.

I felt a rush of warmth, oxylike, surge through me. How praise from a stranger could make you glow. Then I saw that the letter writer's name was followed by a serial number and the name of a prison. I googled the name. The first result was an article from the late eighties, which detailed how the author of the letter complimenting my story had been sentenced to life in prison for stabbing a man to death and stealing his stereo. The second Google hit was an essay the convicted murderer had written for the magazine a few years earlier about life in prison. Which explained how he had access to an arts-and-culture magazine in a maximum-security prison. I was used to strangers commenting on the essays and articles that

I had published online. But online comments were from people either harping on their problem with two words from a five-thousand-word essay, or telling the world that you were a clueless liberal, a privileged white person, a self-hating white person, a racist, a sexist, or an idiot who didn't know the difference between *your* and *you're*. Worst of all were the people who found something legitimately wrong with your reasoning, then posted the fault right there, right beneath the thing you had spent so much time on, for everyone to see.

But print media. Correspondence sections! This was much better. If only all comments were from convicted murderers.

I clicked on the next email, which read:

> Jonas,
> Wow! Thank you for "You Have to Stop the Killing."
> Fantastic. It is propelling me out the door to a meeting.

I read the message again. Maybe my story was a distraction, however brief, from the man's suffering. The idea of that felt nice. He was an addict, which meant that his suffering, like my suffering, was self-inflicted. But self-inflicted suffering was still suffering. It was the only kind of suffering that I really knew.

Finally, I opened the last email.

> Dear Jonas,
> You hit the nail on the head with this one. As a professor,
> I could recognize how well you described the frustration, the
> loneliness, and the pain I felt in my early years of teaching.

I googled the name of the letter writer, curious where she taught. The first hit was from a college newspaper at a liberal arts school in Pennsylvania: "Cultural Studies Professor Arrested for Arson, Dismissed." I clicked and found that the author of the letter was awaiting trial for allegedly starting a fire in a Walgreens in suburban Philadelphia to distract the employees while she stole prescription painkillers. I clicked on a few more articles describing the same event. The woman was an assistant professor specializing in phenomenology in contemporary literature and film. I clicked on her academic profile, looked through her list of publications, and found that I had read an article of hers during the research for my thesis. This woman was desperate enough for oxy that she had brought a can of lighter fluid into a drugstore to set fire to a shelf of breakfast cereal. She had thought she would get away with it. A few years ago, I might have thought the same thing.

On an absurdly cold evening the week before Christmas, icy wind making everything miserable, Katja, Ali, and I held the last Language Café. Torsten brought only five boys, and they were all to be placed in more permanent homes by the end of the year. There were no other volunteers. Katja, Ali, and I had discussed petitioning the city to start a real Swedish-as-a-second-language class, but we were burned out. The thought of being relieved of our responsibilities was more exciting than the thought of helping, and emails now went unsent, proposals unwritten.

Hassan was there, but the boy with the Raiders hat was not. Today's worksheet was one I had designed about the weather. I sat at a table with Hassan and another Syrian boy. We went over the ö sound in *höst* and *snöar*. If you weren't Swedish, the sound was difficult to pronounce—a chesty moan. The boys kept trying to say it, and I would open my mouth wider and wider and yell, "Uuuuuuhhhhh!," until they were both laughing.

"Jonas, what are you doing?" Katja scolded.

"Sorry." I looked down guiltily and the boys followed my lead.

"Sorry," they said, giggling.

Later, Katja called me over, pointed to the young man sitting next to her in a V-neck sweater, and said, "He has a good question."

"Yes," he said. "In English, do they call it *fall* or *autumn*?"

"You can use either one."

The boy looked at me. "But doesn't *fall* also mean 'decline'? And why would they have two words that mean the same thing?"

"In Swedish, there's only one word for it." Katja pointed at the worksheet. *"Höst."*

"Huuuuuuhhhhhst!" I corrected.

"Uuuuuuhhhhh!" the boys back at my table yelled.

"Jonas, look what you've done!" Katja said.

The boys all laughed. They wouldn't leave the Language Café any better equipped to deal with Sweden than they had been when they arrived. But maybe they had learned a phrase or two they could use. Maybe they would feel a little more comfortable talking to Europeans. If nothing else, for a few hours a week, they'd been distracted. That was something—wasn't it?

At break, Hassan announced that he had baked an apple cake.

"He was hard at work on it in the kitchen," Torsten said in English.

Hassan began cutting it into slices, a crispy crust spilling out chunks of baked apple.

"It does not have milk or gluten, so you can all eat it," Hassan said.

"Why would we not be able to eat milk or gluten?" I said.

Hassan stopped cutting. "I was told that Europeans don't eat milk or gluten."

Katja, Torsten, and I laughed.

"I am lactose intolerant," Torsten said.

"And I don't eat gluten," Katja said.

"Good." Hassan shoveled a slice onto a paper plate for Katja. "You may take a picture of it, if you like."

On the bus ride home, I saw that I had an email from Anja.

> Jonas, how special to get an actual mail letter from you! I read your story! I really liked it, but I think mostly because some parts remind me of you. Your "character" likes immortal jellyfish too! Things are good here in Greece. I'm working a lot and it's very cold in the water but nice. My boyfriend (I started seeing a boy I go to school with in Germany) is coming to visit soon, which should be fun. But he's not a very good swimmer, so I don't know if I can take him diving. I hope you are well!

I shouldn't have been surprised. Anja was great and there was no reason for her to be single. In a way, I was relieved to learn that I had already blown it and wasn't still in the process of blowing it.

*   *   *

That night, I felt a pleasant exhaustion: an exhaustion that came from doing things rather than from an overactive mind. I fell into bed and opened my laptop to watch a Clippers game. There I saw that I had an email from Stella. She started by asking about Sweden, making a joke about ABBA, and then a joke about me fucking Swedish women that were out of my league. Then she wrote, *I know you said you can't make it to the wedding this summer. But Zach and I would really like it if you could come because . . . we want you to officiate! So now you pretty much have to come, right?*

To my surprise, I got choked up. She and Zach still cared about me, after all the time I'd spent away. I wrote back that of course I would officiate their wedding. I thanked them and wrote a long run-on sentence about how much I cared for them both. Then I booked a ticket with two layovers on my credit card, googled ministerial certification, and in five minutes had the right to wed couples in the state of California. I thought of Stella and Zach, whom I'd known since we were in the dorms together, eleven years earlier. I thought of how they were both deciding that this was the person, above all other people met and unmet, that they wanted to spend their life with. I longed, for the first time since I had come to Sweden, to go home.

Los Angeles, California

Summer 2016

I STOOD AT THE CURB OUTSIDE THE INTERNATIONAL TERMINAL at LAX, taking in the warm wind and waiting for the shuttle. Stella had offered to pick me up, but her driving was at once reckless and uncertain, and the thought of sending her on a three-hour trip from San Luis Obispo was enough to make me book a rideshare. On a nearby bench sat an elderly couple, bracketed by two large aluminum rolling suitcases that may have been the original model of rolling suitcase. The man got up groaningly every minute or so to walk over to the curb and peer down the highway-like road that led cabs and buses and shuttles and cars around the airport's perimeter.

"Are you waiting for the Coastal Shuttle?" the woman called out to me.

"I am."

"Why don't you come sit down?" She scooted over on the bench. "There's plenty of room."

"Thank you." I took a seat next to her. "I guess that shuttle is a hot ticket."

"It must be." The woman laughed. "Where are you flying in from?"

"Sweden."

"Oh, that's lovely. How long were you there for?"

"I live there."

"Really? But you don't have an accent."

"My dad's American."

"That explains it! You know, my grandparents were from Sweden. We've been to Stockholm and Uppsala. What beautiful cities."

"That's great. When were you there?" My jaw, I noticed, had unclenched. My whole body, which I hadn't realized had been tense, relaxed. It was so comfortable to be small-talked to and to be able to small-talk back in the same register.

"Oh, that was years ago. How many years ago was that, Bill?"

"How many years ago was what?" the man said, returning from his latest expedition to the curb.

"When we went to Sweden."

"Why?"

"He's from Sweden."

"Nineteen seventy-four."

"Forty-two years ago. Can you believe it? Before you were born!" She laughed and patted me on the leg with a grandmother's touch. "Long before you were born."

"Just a little bit." I smiled.

"What a beautiful city Stockholm is. All the water. And the light. People speak such good English there."

"I think it's partly because we don't dub anything. It's much harder for the Germans and the French and the Italians—they don't get to hear the language spoken by native speakers. Swedes hear English every time they turn on the TV."

"I had never thought of that! Isn't that interesting, Bill? They don't dub their TV so they speak better English."

"They speak great English in Sweden," he said.

"What do you do there?"

"I was going to school. But in the fall I'll be teaching Swedish courses."

"Oh, that's wonderful."

When the long winter had finally ended and the sun had come out again, Katja, Ali, and I had found new energy for the yearlong language class for refugees permanently settled in Malmö. We were finalizing a partnership with one of the community colleges in the city. This new course would give me a purpose. It would give me a reason, and the resources, to stay in Sweden now that my degree was done—for reasons I didn't totally understand, my professors had passed my thesis, though one had noted, *I am not sure that this is literary criticism*—instead of moving back to the US. Maybe I would visit Anja. It might be a little tricky with her boyfriend, but she might not have a boyfriend forever. I had been excited about teaching again, at first, but a few weeks earlier, I had run into Osman and Arash at Malmö Central, and they hadn't recognized me. After politely listening to my explanation of how we had met at the Language Café and learned Swedish together six months earlier, they had nodded in recognition, shaken my hand, said thank you, and hurried off before I could ask them about their lives.

In retrospect, I couldn't say why I'd thought they would remember me. The college students I saw almost every day for a whole semester began to forget me the day after finals ended. I knew that my effect on the lives of the boys at the Language Café had been minimal—a few hours a week designed to eat up some of the time they had to spend waiting. Yet on some level I had assumed that since they had taken up so much space in my mind, I must have taken up some space in theirs. If I had known the reality of the situation, I would never have asked Torsten for Aziz's contact info, forcing Torsten to awkwardly explain why that wasn't allowed. I wouldn't have spent so many evenings the previous winter scouring the internet for anyone named Aziz living in the Norrköping area.

"Is Swedish a hard language?" the old woman asked.

"It's not that hard if you know English. The verb conjugations are simple. There aren't that many words. The spelling is relatively consistent. But it's a difficult language if you're coming from Arabic, Dari, or any language with a completely different alphabet."

"Oh, dear. I've heard about that. Is it getting bad with all the Muslims there?"

I stared at the woman, whose expression had changed to one of slight concern. "No," I said.

"There aren't a lot of Muslims there?"

"There's probably a fair amount of Muslims in Sweden. But it's not bad."

The lady nodded. "Oh, yes, of course." It was as if she'd accidentally said that Oslo was such a beautiful city and, once I had told her that Oslo was in Norway, not Sweden, corrected her mistake.

The man leaned over. "Aren't you worried about all the Muslims over there?"

"Bill, he just said he wasn't worried about it."

I didn't want to beat down these old people for their ignorance. But I also didn't want to let it slide. Usually when someone said something surprisingly offensive, it took you a second to process the info, and by the time you thought of what you wanted to say, the moment was gone, and you were forced to replay it in your head for days, enraged that you didn't get to say what you'd thought of too late. But here someone had said something offensive, given me a second to think about it, and then her partner had leaned forward and said the offensive thing again.

"I don't see why I would be worried about Muslims. I think Islam is as good a religion as any other."

The man looked puzzled.

The woman said, "Yes, of course."

"And the birthrate among white Swedish couples is very low, while the birthrate among Muslim couples is much higher. It's lucky for us that Muslims are coming to Sweden. Without all the Muslim babies, in fifty years there'd be no taxes to fill the pension fund."

"Oh, yes, of course," the woman said.

"With any luck, it'll be a Muslim majority in Europe soon. I think business will go a lot smoother then. We'll all have to learn Arabic. But it shouldn't be too hard."

"Yes, of course," the woman said.

The man squinted at me, shook his head, and walked back over to the curb.

The woman hadn't been trying to provoke me. She hadn't been trying to indoctrinate me. To her, asking if I was worried about the Muslims was probably just as normal as asking if it wasn't difficult with those long Swedish winters. She and her husband were probably coming from an environment where being openly fearful of Muslims was normal enough to be acceptable small talk. They were living in a different reality—what were you supposed to do about that?

"Professor Anderson?"

At the sound of my name, I snapped out of my thoughts.

"I thought it was you!"

I turned and saw, looking taller than I remembered, in a blue skirt, blue blazer, and blue flight attendant's beret, with a sleek black rolling suitcase by her side, my old student Kayla.

Kayla's posture was still great. But she looked more tired than before—less prepared for a job interview to break out at any second. Her beret was perched neatly on her immaculately ponytailed hair, but her eyelids were heavy.

We hugged and shared our disbelief at running into each other like this.

"Look at you—a flight attendant."

"For two years now."

"That's great," I said. "Congratulations."

"It's fun. I get to see the world."

"I bet. And how's Hank?"

"Hank's gone."

"Oh, God. I'm so sorry."

"No, no! Not like that! We're in the process of getting a divorce."

"I thought you meant gone gone!" I was about to laugh but caught myself. "But still—I'm sorry."

"It's okay. It was for the best. We shouldn't have gotten married in the first place, but when you're that age, what do you know?"

"Are you still in Wilmington?"

"I live in Atlanta now, but I'm lucky if I spend ten days a month at home. I'm in a different city every day." She told me that she'd been to fourteen countries. "You know what's the worst place to fly?"

"What?"

She looked around, then whispered, "Marrakech."

"What's the best place to fly?"

"Everywhere that isn't Marrakech."

I laughed. "Do you like it?"

She didn't answer right away. It looked like she was staring at my shoes. I gave her a second to finish whatever thought she was lost in.

"Do you like it? Being a flight attendant?"

"I do!" she said, snapping back. "I like it now. But when I started, I was so bad at it."

"If you already knew how to do everything, there wouldn't be any point—"

"There wouldn't be any point to living. Yes, thank you, Professor, I remember."

I smiled.

"My problem was that I was so scared of being wrong. Every flight, a passenger would call me over and ask me a question I didn't know the answer to. They'd ask me what lake we were flying over or what mountain range, and I'd be so focused on doing my job right that I wouldn't even remember which flight I was on. Even when I knew the answer, I wouldn't know the answer. Once an old lady asked me if the laundry room was available. I said, 'Let me check on that for you.' The laundry room!"

I laughed.

"Every time someone asked me something, I just froze." Kayla laughed at herself. "And then, one day, I wasn't pretending to be a flight attendant anymore. I just was one."

"It's funny how that happens."

"But I'm not going to be a flight attendant forever. I like it, but I'm not going to do it forever. I was thinking of going back to school for an MBA. Or a master's in psychology or social work," she added, maybe thinking that I would disapprove of business school.

"It sounds like you're doing great."

"How are you? Still teaching?"

"Just a little bit right now. But I might start again soon."

"That was a crazy class."

"It wasn't my finest hour."

"You were great," she said, probably forgetting that she'd filed a complaint against me. But it wasn't like she'd been wrong—I *was* sending them to funerals. I was surprised that she remembered the class at all, three years later.

"Do you remember that story I wrote?" she said. "About the marine and the jellyfish?"

"Of course. The marine died, but then swam out to see his fiancée every day, until she found someone else. Then he saw that she was happy, and he swam away, happy for her."

"That's right! You have a good memory."

"It was a good story."

"I think I was trying to create the reality I wanted. Not with Hank dying, of course. I was in love with him. But I wanted to write something where the man would be happy for the woman if she found . . . I don't know. Not some*one* else. But some*thing* else. I think even then, I wanted to write a story where he got happy from just seeing me happy—even if he wasn't the one who made me happy."

"I think we all want that."

"When he was away, I was very devoted, you know. I would keep Facebook open all the time so we could chat as soon as he had a second to log on, even if it was in the middle of the night, and if he was going to be at the FOB, I'd get up early to do my makeup, and I'd wait by my computer to Skype before his shift."

She was talking fast, swerving far outside the lines of catching up, and I wondered if she was drunk. But I didn't smell any liquor on her.

"I never said anything when it turned out that he couldn't Skype after all. I didn't complain that I would be tired at school all day from getting up so early and hadn't even gotten to see him. That's what I signed up for. But then he came back, and he was just so angry all the time."

She adjusted her beret and looked away. Maybe it was just one of those days when you needed someone to listen.

"That must have been difficult," I said.

"He wanted me to have kids right away. And I want to have kids. But not right away. There are one hundred and ninety-five countries in the world! Back then, I'd only ever been to Mexico. Where has he been? Here and Afghanistan. We're supposed to settle down after that?"

"It sounds like you made the right decision."

She pulled a pack of cigarettes from her blazer pocket and lit one. The sight of her smoking was even more startling than the sight of her in a flight attendant's uniform. She held out the pack to me. I hadn't smoked in two months, but I took one. She handed me the lighter and we stood there, smoking on the curb, as hundreds of cars rolled by. The shuttle came and picked up the old couple, but I stayed. I'd cleared customs quicker than expected and there'd be another shuttle in an hour.

"Do you think I could've been a writer?" Kayla finally said.

"Did you want to be a writer?"

"I don't know. I liked writing that story." She took a drag. "Hank told me about this time a toy company donated a thousand Elmo dolls for marines to give to children in Afghanistan. For whatever reason, they sent all the toys to the village where Hank was stationed, but there were only fifty children in the village, so even after they handed out five dolls to each kid, there were still hundreds left over. They gave the extra Elmo dolls to the men in the village, who were confused, but they accepted them because they didn't want to be rude. One man's wife, maybe thinking the Elmo was a ceremonial gift, gave Hank a giant tote bag covered in shiny ribbons. Hank didn't know what to do with that, but he didn't want to be rude, so he said thank you and accepted it. In the end, everybody was stuck with these things they didn't want, just so a toy company could say they supported the troops or the children of Afghanistan or whatever." She walked over to the trash can, rubbed her cigarette out on the side, and dropped the butt in. "Do you think that could be a story?"

"If you write it, it could definitely be a story."

She smiled sadly. "I just haven't had the time."

"There's still plenty of time."

"But there's so much to do! I want to be a marriage counselor. I want to be a photographer. I want to start my own business. I want to have kids. I want to be a foster parent. I want to help Hank get his life straight and then never see him again. I want to go back to school. I want to fall in love again. I want to learn how to ride a horse." She laughed nervously and caught her breath. "But what I really want is to stop babbling! I'm so sorry. I must sound like a crazy person. It's the jet lag. I'm so jet-lagged. They say flight attendants don't get jet-lagged, but we do. We get jet-lagged too."

"Everyone gets jet lag." I smiled. "You don't sound like a crazy person, Kayla. You sound excited about life."

She was quiet.

I let the quiet sit.

"It was my birthday yesterday," she said.

"Happy birthday!"

"I'm already twenty-four," she said sadly.

I wanted to tell her that twenty-four was nothing. But I refrained, remembering every time that someone older than me had told me that my age was nothing, neglecting to consider that twenty-four, twenty-seven, and now thirty was significant to me. Twenty-four was significant to Kayla.

"Look at it this way," I said. "Most people don't get divorced until they're in their forties. You're already way ahead of the game."

For the first time, Kayla let out a real laugh.

"Thank you," she said, still giggling. "That's very comforting."

"It's what I'm here for."

"What are you doing in LA, anyway, Professor Anderson?"

"My best friends are getting married. I'll be officiating the wedding."

"Really?"

"Really."

"That's so *nice*." She looked like she might cry.

And it was nice. It was nice to be asked to stand on an altar with two people you cared about as they read their vows. It was nice to be standing here with an old student, seeing she'd grown into a person that I could never have predicted, with so much to do that she'd have to live forever to find time for it all.

"I have to get going," she said. "But I'm so happy we ran into each other."

We hugged goodbye. She pulled up the handle on her suitcase and started to leave. But instead of just standing there, I said, "If you ever want someone to read your stories, you can always send them to me."

She smiled. "That would be great." She handed me her phone and I typed in my email address.

I watched her walk away with her little suitcase rolling smoothly and silently behind her. Then I sat down on the bench and waited for the shuttle.

Acknowledgments

Thank you to my teachers, especially Mrs. Novak, Courtney Brogno, Paul Tenngart, and most of all, Amy Wiley and Robert Anthony Siegel.

Thank you to my agent, Chris Clemans, who is both very good at his job and very kind. To my all-star editing team, Marysue Rucci and Zack Knoll, who did wonders for this book. To the crew at Simon & Schuster for all their hard work copyediting, laying out, and promoting this book. To Alison Forner and Tyler Comrie for the brilliant cover. To Simon Toop for pulling my novel from the slush. To Rivka Galchen for generously championing this book. To Carol Ann Fitzgerald and Jill Meyers for investing in my writing long before it was worthy.

Thank you to Chris McCormick, Jessica Thummel, and Clyde Edgerton for reading early drafts of the novel and helping make it much better. To the faculty and students at UNC Wilmington for being generous with all the bad writing I made them read. To Wendy Brenner for giving me many great books when I was in need of them. To Ashley Hudson for being my workplace partner in crime. To Jeremy Hawkins for his writerly friendship. To Peter Baker for being the person I call with all my book problems.

For providing helpful information, anecdotes, and inspiration, thanks to Camilla Alin, Larry Inchausti, Max Mayo, and Sara Shepherd. Thank you to Annie Murphy and Molle Kanmert Sjölander for their advice on bridges and meatballs and other important points of Swedish culture. Thank you to Janine for always listening.

Thank you to I.B. and all the other young men at MUFR who so generously told me about their lives and asked me about mine. To the team at MUFR for creating a little light in the darkness.

Thank you to Antonia, Samuel, Lena, and Astrid & Christer for helping make Skåne home. To Jakob Nilsson for being my guide to Swedish.

Thank you to Kelly and Tony for their enduring friendship.

Thank you to Mike and Nina for being my second family.

Thank you to Per and Emile for all the laughter and love. To Gloria for making a house a home. To Stu for being such a supportive and enthusiastic fan. To Åsa for showing the way to love and art. To Lance for always being there, calm and caring, always ready for a good talk.

Finally, thank you to Sherilyn. You are the best to wake up to, the best to fall asleep to, and the best for every minute in between. How lucky I am to get to spend my days with you.

Text Acknowledgments

101: "Journalism is the art . . . I'll never learn that.": Quoted in Olof Lagercrantz, *Stig Dagerman* (Stockholm: Nordstedts, 1958), 128. (Translation mine.)

162–63: The article "about unaccompanied-minor refugees living in Germany": Katrin Bennhold, "Migrant Children, Arriving Alone and Frightened," *New York Times*, October 28, 2015.

180: "The sheer solipsism . . . implicated in the critique.": Sara Ahmed, "A Phenomenology of Whiteness," *Feminist Theory*, 8, no. 2 (2007): 164–65.

192: "Everyone staying at . . . one for the record.": Hassan Blasim, *The Corpse Exhibition and Other Stories of Iraq*, trans. Jonathan Wright (New York: Penguin, 2014), 157.

250: The Fox News segment is called "Do Syrian refugees pose a threat to national security?" and it aired November 15, 2015.

268: " 'You Really Have' . . . delighted with this story." Taken from a letter I received from John Purugganan (the letter was later published in slightly different form in the correspondence of the *Sun*).

About the Author

Johannes Lichtman was born in Stockholm and raised in California. He was named a 5 Under 35 recipient by the National Book Foundation in 2019. His work has appeared or is forthcoming in *Tin House, The Sun, Travel + Leisure*, the *Los Angeles Review of Books, Oxford American*, and elsewhere. He lives in Portland, Oregon. *Such Good Work* is his first novel.

Such Good Work

Johannes Lichtman

This reading group guide for **Such Good Work** *includes an intro-duction, discussion questions, ideas for enhancing your book club, and a Q&A with author* **Johannes Lichtman***. The suggested questions are intended to help your reading group find new and interesting angles and topics for your discussion. We hope that these ideas will enrich your conversation and increase your enjoyment of the book.*

INTRODUCTION

JONAS ANDERSON WANTS A FRESH START.

He's made plenty of bad decisions in his life, and at age twenty-eight he's been fired from yet another teaching position after assigning homework like *visit a stranger's funeral and write about it*. But he's sure a move to Sweden, the country of his mother's birth, will be just the thing to kick-start a new and improved—and newly sober—Jonas.

When he arrives in Malmö in 2015, the city is struggling with the influx of tens of thousands of Middle Eastern refugees. Driven by an existential need to "do good," Jonas begins volunteering with an organization that teaches Swedish to young immigrants. The connections he makes there, with one student in particular, might send him down the right path toward fulfillment—if he could just get out of his own way.

Such Good Work is a darkly comic novel, brought to life with funny, wry observations and searing questions about our modern world, told with equal measures of grace and wit.

Topics & Questions for Discussion

1. *Such Good Work* plays with the idea of things or behaviors that are good for you, or things that are good for others. Do you think those things are subjective? Or is there a list of "good" things that every person should be working toward?

2. Addiction is a prominent theme in *Such Good Work*, both explicitly and implicitly. Aside from Jonas's drug use, what are some other addictions, vices, or compulsions that you notice throughout the novel, on levels big and small?

3. Sweden is a country that is underexplored and underexposed in fiction as a setting. What did you know about Sweden when you came to *Such Good Work*, and what did you learn about it as you read? What was it like reading about an American living abroad?

4. How are the main female characters in the novel—Anja, Katja, and Stella—similar to and different from one another? What role does each character play in the larger story?

5. Jonas isn't necessarily an unlikeable character, but he is absolutely—and self-admittedly—flawed. Does that make him more accessible? More human? What did you like about Jonas as a protagonist and narrator?

6. At different points in the novel, Jonas questions whether addiction benefits creativity, citing Ernest Hemingway,

David Foster Wallace, and other writers who have battled demons in the midst of producing great work. Do you think there's validity to the theory that genius stems from dysfunction?

7. When Jonas is teaching in the US, one of his students is writing a paper on race relations, and throughout his time in Sweden, the people around him compare the responses both countries have to refugees, race, and the political implications of both. How are they similar and different? What does Jonas learn and how does he engage with each?

8. Jonas engages with some dark themes and topics throughout the novel, but there are also some moments of lightness and humor. What were some of your favorites? Do you think that incorporating them made for a better reading experience?

9. As he spends more time in Sweden, how does Jonas's view of the world and the ways his new and old home countries respond to crises change and evolve?

10. In the opening pages of *Such Good Work*, Jonas says, "When I used to get high, places were interchangeable. Everywhere was the best place ever—and then the worst. But now place mattered very much." What role does place play in this novel, in Jonas's life, and in your life?

11. Two characters who we hear a lot about but rarely see are Stella and Zach, Jonas's friends from home, but they are still really important to him. What role do they play in Jonas's life, and what do they represent in the larger story?

12. Throughout *Such Good Work*, Jonas thinks about the ways in which people—including himself—perform outrage at certain injustices but then do little to actually prevent them from happening again. Have you noticed a similar phenom-

enon in our world and daily lives? In the novel, Jonas "mentally rewrote each of these memories into scenes in which [he'd] done something." Have you ever done this?

13. What is a world or media event that has impacted you in the same way that Jonas is impacted by reading about Alan Kurdi and other refugees in crisis? In many ways, Jonas becomes much more affected by these issues when he meets Aziz and the other boys. Do you think we need a personal connection and human face to truly feel motivated to act and pitch in?

14. Toward the end of the novel, Jonas says he wants to correct the world. There is also another scene in which a person is criticized for doing more harm than good for dropping everything and going to volunteer with the Red Cross. After seeing the complexities of "such good work" in the novel, do you think that it's possible for one person—or a group of people—to solve the world's problems?

15. Thinking about the title of the novel, the story, the characters, and the themes, what does it mean to do "such good work" or be a good person? Has your definition or perspective changed as you've read and discussed Lichtman's novel? Do we do "such good work" for others, or for ourselves?

Enhance Your Book Club

1. As a group, choose a cause you all believe in and find organizations that support that cause. Discuss how your group can fundraise for the cause in your community.

2. Find a recipe for Swedish meatballs or other Swedish foods and serve them at your next book club meeting!

A Conversation with Johannes Lichtman

Okay, so, first question. What initially inspired you to write *Such Good Work*?

Well, I started writing what eventually became the first chapter of *Such Good Work* as a short story called "You Really Have to Stop the Killing" in 2013. The short story I wrote was very different from what ended up being the first chapter. There was a teacher who was trying to hold it together and there were facts about animals that lived a really long time, and that was about it.

But there was something about the narrator, about the voice, that I liked, so I worked on that story for maybe two years. I also wrote two other short stories from the narrator's perspective, so by the time I published "You Really Have to Stop the Killing," I had a good chunk of material from this narrator's perspective.

I thought about doing a collection of linked stories, but eventually I decided to try to write between the stories and build it as a novel instead, partly because there's something really freeing about writing a work in which the chapters don't have to be able to stand on their own and can just function as parts of the whole (in short story collections, each story, of course, has to work on its own). There were a bunch of other reasons that I chose to swerve into writing it as a novel, too, and now I'm realizing, about two minutes into my answer, that I'm answering the question "How did you write the novel?" rather than the question you asked, which was: "Why did you write the novel?" I think the *how* is easier to explain. It took me about three hundred pages to answer the *why* when I was writing the book, so who knows how long it would've taken me to answer it here.

On the surface, it seems like you and Jonas have a couple of things in common. Your names are similar, you both have familial ties to Sweden, hold dual citizenship, have lived in California, and you've both been teachers. That leads us to wonder: How much of the novel is autobiographical, or taken from life?

How dare you ask me that?

Just kidding. This is, understandably, a question that comes up a lot. Which I get. When I read books by Jenny Offill or Ben Lerner or Rachel Cusk or whoever, I wonder how much is autobiographical. I don't think it affects my understanding or experience of the texts much—but I'm still curious.

The short answer to how much of the novel is autobiographical is: maybe fifty percent? When I was sending the novel out, I was asked by a number of people if I had considered publishing it as memoir, since I think there was an assumption that it was pretty much nonfiction. But there was way too much made up, and the stuff that is taken from my life is so exaggerated, condensed, combined, or altered that even the autobiographical portions couldn't be published as nonfiction.

That said, by giving the character a similar name as me and giving us similar biographies—not trying to make him a fifty-something Danish history teacher or whatever—it was a nod to the reader to sort of say, "Yes, this is based on my life. It's also a novel. Do with that what you will."

Both Jonas and I are Swedish-American (though I was born in Sweden and he was born in the States) and both of us went to grad school in North Carolina and Sweden and are writers who teach or have taught. So there are parts of me in Jonas, and we definitely share some headspace; but I think I tend to make better decisions than he does. He also has longer hair.

Often in novels about addiction, there is a plot point incorporated to "explain" why the lead character struggles with their particular vice, but in Jonas's case it just seems to be a fact of his life. We have an idea of why he uses, but there's no singular traumatic event, really, that leads him down that path. Was that a specific choice, to focus a novel on a character whose problems can't necessarily be traced back to one defining thing?

Definitely. It was a very specific choice and one that matters a lot to me.

There's often a lot of narrative psychology at work when we talk about addiction—both from addicts and from people trying to understand addicts—and while I get why that is, at times I find it a little aggravating. I really wanted to go in the opposite direction. Sure, people often start using a substance at least partly because of pain, trauma, or a lack of ability to cope with whatever they're trying to cope with. But eventually most addicts get to a point where they are using drugs solely because they're addicted to drugs. Their bodies have started needing the substance the way it needs food or water. There's very little narrative about it anymore—it's biological. And while it's easier and sexier to go with the tragic-past narrative—certainly much easier for addicts, who often tell themselves they have a tragic past, whether or not that's true—I think that's a very incomplete way of talking about it.

With Jonas, there are of course personal reasons that make drugs tempting to him. But I wanted to get away from the "this event caused my addiction" narrative.

Such Good Work is set in the very recent present and features ripped-from-the-headlines names and events instead of recognizable fictionalizations—which ultimately makes the novel seem that much more real and urgent, and also brings the story of this Swedish city back into the larger world. How did you choose which real-life moments and people to bring in, and the parts of the novel in which you would do so?

The one event that I had to bring in if I was going to write about the refugee surge was the picture of Alan Kurdi. The reaction to the photo exposed the best and worst sides of Western charitable impulses: the intense desire to do something but also the intensely temporary and conditional nature of that desire. Lidia Yuknavitch writes about this in really interesting fashion in *The Small Backs of Children* (or, not "this," since I believe she wrote her book before the photograph, but about the phenomenon more generally).

The Paris terrorist attack also kind of had to be there, because that marked a turning point in the attitudes of centrists in Western Europe, many of who had been unusually pro–open borders up until that point.

Such Good Work is a book about a lot of things, but one theme that continues to pop up, however implicitly or explicitly, is writing and storytelling—more specifically, who has the right to tell a story. Was that inner conflict Jonas feels over whether he can properly convey a story about other people something you experienced while writing?

Yes! It's something I still feel intensely conflicted about! But I don't think it's something I can really explain better here than I tried to do in the book.

Adding to the question above: How much research did you do about the refugee crises around the world for the novel, and

how much did you already know? Was there something that surprised or shocked you that you ended up including?

In the beginning, I wasn't thinking of it as research—I just kind of got wrapped up on a personal level. Like Jonas, I volunteered to help out a little, and though our experiences were different on that front, I also spent a lot of time thinking about and reading about the situation. (In ways that I suspect were not particularly helpful to anyone.)

When you start reading about it and talking to people, the whole thing is shocking. Maybe not to refugees, the children of refugees, or people who grew up close to refugees. But I was born in Sweden and grew up in the US, which means I possess passports to two of the richest countries in the world, and if one of them were to find itself in a dangerous conflict on its soil, I could just go to the other. So I was lucky enough to be born about as far from being a refugee as possible. This was one of the many reasons that I never wanted to try to write from the perspective of a refugee. I am not arrogant enough to believe that my imagination is that powerful.

I think the parts of the refugee stories that stuck with me most—and I am a little frightened to think what this says about me—were the parts that I had at least some modicum of frame of reference from which to consider. So, for example, I don't have that type of frame of reference from which to consider murder, rape, and torture. For which I'm very thankful. When I read about those types of horrific experiences, they made me very sad. And then they disappeared from my consciousness. Again, that's a little frightening to notice.

But the thing that never disappeared from my consciousness was the thought of all the waiting the asylum seeker must do. I obviously don't know what it's like to wait to be granted asylum or to be released from a refugee camp. I do know what it's like to wait, generally, though, and that shared experience, however different and comparatively luxurious my waiting has been, made the things I read and heard about the experiences of waiting stick with me.

The average time for a refugee spent in migration before returning to their home country is seventeen years. That part was shocking to me. You don't arrive in a refugee camp and get a ticket that says "In two years you will be allowed to move to Germany." You're often waiting with no idea how long the wait will be and no one who can tell you. So the length of waiting and the level of uncertainty stayed with me.

Jonas also refers to a bunch of different writers and books throughout the novel. Are those writers some of your favorites? Which books or authors have influenced you as a reader and as a writer?

Sure, many of the books I mentioned are ones that were at least important to me at some point in my life. Denis Johnson's *Jesus' Son* in particular is a book that's had a profound influence on me (not always good—though it's a remarkable work).

As for which books or authors have influenced me—how much time do you have?

In no particular order: *Dept. of Speculation* by Jenny Offill, pretty much all of Milan Kundera, Ben Lerner's novels, Sarah Manguso's essays, James Baldwin's essays, Janet Malcolm (who I think is America's greatest living nonfiction writer), Stig Dagerman, Kurt Vonnegut, Orwell's nonfiction, Geoff Dyer (particularly *Out of Sheer Rage* and the essays), Rachel Cusk's Outline triology, Omar El Akkad (journalism and fiction but also this great talk I saw him give on migration).

Karl Ove Knausgård, Zadie Smith, *The Corpse Exhibition* by Hassan Blasim, Aleksandar Hemon, Percival Everett, W. G. Sebald (especially *The Emigrants* and *On the Natural History of Destruction*), *Where I'm Reading From* by Tim Parks, Teju Cole, *The Wallcreeper* by Nell Zink, *Ablutions* by Patrick deWitt, *Tell Me How*

It Ends by Valeria Luiselli, *Americanah* by Chimamanda Ngozi Adichie, *A Visit from the Goon Squad* by Jennifer Egan, *Karate Chop* by Dorthe Nors.

The essays of Leslie Jamison, essays of Eula Biss, essays of Natalia Ginzburg, *Journal of an Ordinary Grief* by Mahmoud Darwish, *Regarding the Pain of Others* by Susan Sontag, *Little Labors* by Rivka Galchen, *HHhH* by Laurent Binet, Elif Batuman, J. M. Coetzee, *Season of Migration to the North* by Tayeb Salih, Faulkner, Hemingway, Michael Chabon, Viet Thanh Nguyen, and, for this book in particular, a Swedish work called *Andrum* by Viktor Banke. Lots of other people, too.

The writer who first inspired me to write was David Sedaris. I had loved other writers before him, but I had never read a book and thought, "I could do this." Then when I was eighteen I had a composition class with a great teacher named Courtney Brogno who introduced me to David Sedaris, and I thought to myself, "This guy is just writing funny stories about his family—I could do that!" Of course I was both wrong and stupid (conditions I have struggled with for much of my life). The great thing about David Sedaris is that he creates the illusion that what he's doing is easy. But it was enough to lure me in.

There are, of course, some dark themes and topics that you cover in this novel. Yet Jonas tells them with a surprising edge of subtle humor. How did you know when to incorporate that without making it seem like you were joking about such serious issues?

I have always liked reading things that are both sad and funny. I like texture in a book. Whenever you have too much of something—whether it's suffering or laughs—I feel like the reader becomes numb to that. Balancing both brings out the flavor in each. In my experience, people often respond to pain with humor. I do think that a natural reaction to tragedy is to laugh. Your own tragedy, that is—it's probably not too good to laugh at others' tragedies.

Which brings up a kind of difficult point: I felt much more comfortable mixing the funny with the dark in the sections that were almost solely about Jonas's life than I did in the sections about the young men coming to Sweden. But hopefully I found a good balance in both. I don't know, though. It's tricky.

This is a question featured in the Topics & Questions for Discussion section, but it would be interesting to hear your thoughts on it as well: Do you think we do "such good work" for others, or primarily for ourselves? Did you have the same answer before writing this book?

That is a very difficult question, which may be impossible to answer in such a general way. The answer is almost always: It depends. Often a bit of both. It's complicated, I guess.

Hopefully the reading groups handle it better than I did.

Such Good Work **is your first novel. What did you learn from writing it about yourself, or about the kind of work you want to do in the future? Are you working on anything else?**

Such Good Work is, in fact, my first published novel. It's not the first novel I wrote, though—it's the fifth. The first four remain unpublished due to an enduring bias against publishing bad writing.

As for what I learned from writing it, the answer to that is pretty long and boring. But it was a great experience and I'm happy with how it turned out. Or at least as happy as I can be with anything that's shipped into the world with my name on it.

As for what I'm working on now, I'm just finishing up a nonfiction book about the great enigma of twentieth-century Swedish literature, Stig Dagerman, and about the ethics of literature. Who gets to tell what story? How does the writer use their life to build their fiction and what are the consequences? I was over in Sweden this past fall doing research and I've been really enjoying the project. I think it's funny and sad and deals with issues that I'm fascinated by—but who knows.

I am about to start work on another novel, which I can see in my head, vaguely, like a picture of the future that isn't in focus but is happy. But I will say no more than that, as I firmly believe that the literary gods punish writers who discuss unwritten works.